Closer Apart

Closer Apart

The Ardara Variations

Gayla Reid

Published in Canada in 2002 by
Stoddart Publishing Co. Limited
895 Don Mills Road, 400-2 Park Centre, Toronto, Canada M3C 1W3

Published in the United States in 2003 by
Stoddart Publishing Co. Limited
PMB 128, 4500 Witmer Estates, Niagara Falls, New York 14305-1386

10 9 8 7 6 5 4 3 2 1

To order Stoddart books please contact General Distribution Services
In Canada Tel. (416) 213-1919   Fax (416) 213-1917
Email cservice@genpub.com
In the United States Toll-free tel. 1-800-805-1083 Toll-free fax 1-800-481-6207
Email gdsinc@genpub.com

www.stoddartpub.com

National Library of Canada Cataloguing in Publication Data
Reid, Gayla
Closer apart: the Ardara variations
ISBN 0-7737-3337-X
I. Title

PS8585.E5C58 2002   C813'.54   C2002-900749-6
PR9199.4.E45C58 2002

U.S. Cataloging-in-Publication Data Available from Publisher

Cover design: Angel Guerra
Text design: Tannice Goddard

THE CANADA COUNCIL | LE CONSEIL DES ARTS
FOR THE ARTS | DU CANADA
SINCE 1957 | DEPUIS 1957

*We acknowledge for their financial support of our
publishing program the Canada Council, the Ontario Arts
Council, and the Government of Canada through the
Book Publishing Industry Development Program (BPIDP).*

Printed and bound in Canada

For my family
&
for Eleanor

You cannot build bridges between the wandering islands;
The mind has no neighbours, and the unteachable heart
Announces its armistice time after time, but spends
Its love to draw them closer and closer apart.
— A.D. HOPE, *THE WANDERING ISLANDS*

CONTENTS

$\mathscr{A}$LMOST $\mathscr{T}$OUCHING

First light. Rose is sitting in one of the swings beneath the enormous Moreton Bay fig. The doves have begun their mild *roo cou cou,* domestic and assenting. Sydney doves, her father calls them. The fig tree starts on the street but reaches into the front garden, right up to the house.

It's early summer, and a burning bright day is on its way. But for now, in the garden, it's cool. At least a whole hour before the twins will stir. Worth getting up early. The swings are side by side: sturdy affairs of rope, with seats made out of packing cases, covered with cushions that have to be taken in when it rains.

Rose pushes herself into the air. The branches of the fig arch and make a tunnel. At the end of the tunnel is the sky and up behind the sky is Frank, who is famous and in heaven.

What surprised her most about his death was that, within days, everything that had been murky and ambiguous about their marriage had fallen away. There it was, rinsed and clean: *Frank, beloved husband of.*

Quite quickly the tree is losing its simple blue-night colour. Branches, trunk, and buttress roots are emerging in the day, thick and complex and layered. Swinging, her daughters say, is like swimming in the air. Rose can't swim herself, has never learned.

She stops pushing with her feet. Lets the swing slow, then idle. She looks up at the pale sky, listens to the doves, and wonders if anyone can know the truth about the people they love. Is it possible?

The sky is never really blue, her father says. That's just the distance.

AFTER THE FUNERAL, Rose brought the twins back here, to her father's place on Ocean Street. For their eighth birthday she had their picture taken beneath the fig. Rose and her father dragged an armchair out to the lawn while the photographer hid his head under a black cape and fiddled with his equipment.

In this picture, her father, Gus Hampton, sits carefully upright in the chair, with his granddaughters perched on either side. The twin girls, Ellen and Veronica, although not identical, have matching sets of black hair, hazel eyes, and keen, narrow faces. (They take after their father's side of the family.) Gus has his arms stretched out around them. On Gus's lap, Jones-the-Scottie sits with one front leg resting on Ellen's side of the chair. Rose is behind the chair, looking down at her father and her children. Her face, partly hidden, is uncertain. Behind them is the brick house, two storeys, both with verandahs. French doors, abundant iron lacework, a substantial mid-Victorian achievement.

"Now for another one," said the photographer, growing bossy. "Let's have the little girls lying on the roots." The fig's buttress roots, wide and thick, could almost accommodate them. The figs of Ocean Street had been planted fifty-odd years before, in the 1860s, the same time they were planted in Centennial Park.

The twins obliged. Pretended to be lounging on the uncomfortable roots to please the photographer.

2

Up the coast, figs flourish wild. "Figs," Gus told the girls, "spread out and out, like families."

THE TWINS' FAVOURITE TRICK is to swing at exactly the same pace, so they can reach out and join hands. They lean back, let their heads drop as far as they can, and together they examine the deep world upside down.

Rose stands on the verandah. She's warned the twins to be careful when they hold hands on the swing. "If one of you gets out of rhythm you'll both fly off."

"It's a trapeze act," calls out Ellen. Grandpa Gus is pushing.

"Back into the past," says Grandpa Gus, pulling the swings back in unison, letting them go. "Then up, way up, into the future."

"Look at this, Mother, look!" Ronnie shouts.

"Careful," Rose cries. "Father, do be careful."

"They're fine," he says, siding with them, complicit.

Rose has overheard her girls talking about the funeral. Ronnie remembers the lush, dusty smell of the taffeta. It rustled like a small animal when she knelt to pray, startling her. Ellen recalls the people at the steps of the church. Or perhaps she has heard others speak of them, and it is not memory but story.

What they are both certain about is sitting together at the front of the church, their legs touching. When Ronnie swung her legs, Ellen did, too.

The funeral will never be over.

Rose watches her daughters swinging back and forth in the air. *I am a widow now.*

AS THE CORTÈGE PREPARES TO LEAVE Holy Cross for the journey to the Catholic section of Waverley Cemetery, one of the bystanders remarks that Dr. Frank McGinty, for all his bag of tricks, has been able to produce for himself only girls, and even those in no great abundance: two in thirteen years.

Trailing out behind their mother, here they come, the McGinty twins: Veronica and Ellen, aged seven. In black taffeta, heads bowed, carefully subdued.

A light rain has begun to fall, thinning the crowd.

Another onlooker says that there are two sides to every blanket. His words fall away as the crowd turns to watch a woman who comes running along the footpath in awkward, ill-fitting shoes. Rushing from the tram, red hair wild beneath her hat.

"Am I too late?" she cries.

Her clothes are good quality, but worn. Beneath the open coat she wears a mourning brooch on a green silk blouse. The brooch is an oval of black enamel surrounded by seed pearls, framed in gold. She pushes her way forward and stands there, breathing heavily. She looks up at the steps.

The crowd quickly loses interest because the new widow has just emerged from the church, leaning heavily on her father. The widow is all she should be, in the dignity of full mourning: wide skirt; hat with a thick veil over her face and down her back.

The sight of the widow assures you that here is a funeral worth watching: the shining four-wheeled hearse is led by two black geldings — their impressive muscles shine, they shake their plumed heads like the professionals they are. The hearse has plate-glass windows with small, decorative edges that do not hinder a proper view of the coffin or the piles of late-season gold and white chrysanthemums.

Even in this modern era — it is the Sydney winter of 1914 — the mark of a decent send-off remains the slow *clop-clop* of horses. This funeral offers no fewer than eight horse-drawn carriages, followed by the motors (Standards, Argyles), followed in turn by sulkies. And you can bet there'll be a few people on foot bringing up the rear. The cortège will proceed at a walking pace. All along Bronte Road men will be removing their hats, and boys their caps. They will stand silently, out of respect, and get in a nice long look.

Motor hearses are available, and unfortunately more and more in use, but you can't see the coffin nearly as well. And the motor gives

4

the dead a final form of indigestion, inducing odious, virulent gases. One man in the crowd knows a gravedigger who died of the gases.

Lit up his pipe, he did, and *pouf.* Just like that.

Another attractive piece of news is the way the doctor died. Came out from a house call onto a dark street: fell down a manhole, broke his neck.

Hearing this, the woman, the one who ran from the tram, lets out a quick, jagged cry. The crowd falters for a moment, then carries on:

A house down in the Glebe. The hole in the footpath was there because — for poor and rich alike — the city is putting in the sewer.

In perfect health, the doctor was.

Fit as the proverbial.

Could happen to anyone.

Hasn't happened to any of them.

Almost as satisfying a spectacle are the members of the congregation itself, who are now emerging and hanging about at the top of the steps: men in frock coats and top hats, grand and serious and possibly quite well known.

THROUGHOUT SYDNEY'S EASTERN SUBURBS, from Taylor Square to Campbell Parade, Dr. Francis X. McGinty had been a man to recognize. Black Gladstone bag in hand, Frank McGinty went from house to house and did not call only upon the wealthy, the silvertails. In many houses he was paid on the spot by mothers who had to place his account ahead of those of the butcher, the grocer, the gasman. He'd sit down with you after, have a cup of tea, whatever was going. A ladies' man, the soft, deliberate pressure of his fingers a dead giveaway.

He didn't live ostentatiously, didn't big-note himself. Frank McGinty had a gaunt, narrow terrace on the Paddington edge of Woollahra. The back windows overlooked houses in which people routinely layered newspapers between blankets in winter — should they be fortunate enough to have blankets. These were houses in which people lived on bread and dripping, and expected to cure their own ills with prayer, castor oil, lemon, and honey.

If you broke a leg or something drastic, you'd end up at the casualty ward of St. Vincent's Hospital (didn't have to be RC to get in). In the deep dark-green of the windowless waiting room, sitting on a wooden bench under close guard of the nun at the door, you heard your name called. You were admitted to a cubicle drowning in light from a large window.

Dr. McGinty, his face closely and smartly shaven, his mouth smelling cleanly of aniseed, would turn to look at you and, with a smile in those clear brown eyes, offer you his hand.

Dr. McGinty, one of the finest physicians in New South Wales. You had reached your goal. He was all yours.

THE WAKE IS HELD at the house on Ocean Street, Gus Hampton's place. Gus Hampton is another one of Sydney's leading medical men, and his daughter, Rose, is the widow.

Rose sits on a prominent chair to accept condolences. She does not remove her veil.

Frank, my darling, forgive me. Whatever did I think I was doing, dressing you up like that?

Frank, in his best suit, freshly pressed. His grave clothes. It was an occasion, Frank claimed, on which a man would want to wear something comfortable. You're a long time looking at the lid, he'd say.

Frank, Frank, you mustn't speak of such things, mustn't even think them.

Frank said he pictured heaven as a big glacierium — a skating rink — at night, under lights, everyone skating about, excited and singing. Angels in the middle, standing on the ladder going up to the throne of thrones. Frank was afraid he wouldn't like it; he wasn't the least interested in skating. The meek shall inherit the earth, Frank said, because everyone else will have elbowed his way into heaven.

Cheer up, Frank, she said — she'd wanted so much to help him, to be of use — why shouldn't heaven be a fresh field full of flowers, with exactly the right number of shade trees? Of heaven we have been told to expect the very best. But Frank was not to be comforted. What could be more useless than a doctor in heaven?

Looking out the window he was, with no clothes on. Restless. Lovely.

Hang on a minute, darling, she said, how about the general resurrection? All those bodies needing to be reassembled. Parts lost and found. There would be a call for a doctor in the house that day, he could bet on it.

You are mine own true love.

And you said, True?

BRIDIE, GUS HAMPTON'S COOK, has got some girls in to pass around the claret cup.

Rose will have to endure for hours yet. As her reward, she'll pay a visit to Holy Cross Church on the way home. The intimate red lamp burning up front, just her and God and Frank (none of that skating-rink crowd, going round and round forever). Until then, she has one task: *don't think.*

Frank used to play cards with God every day. He acknowledged the inadequacy of this image but was attached to it nonetheless. Frank was puzzled by people who did not feel God's immanence in this world, who did not in fact feel anything at all about Him with the capital "H." It was Frank's job to stare at the cards and see if he could work out a stratagem for life, betting on his own hand against God's, bluffing when he had to.

God liked the opposition, Frank said. Liked physicians to make their claims, to see them try their hand. The game could change at any time, which was what was so engaging about it. The sly old coot owned the game, the cards, the card players, the lot. He could begin to play for different stakes. He could pretend to lose interest, leaving things in the balance. He could let the doctor win. For now.

Frank knew of nothing more worth his while. It was what he had been born for, he said.

What had she been born for? Two children, just the twins, in thirteen years.

Frank's daughters will have to be told, and she will tell them. About Frank's famous work. About Frank's credo: It was a privilege to be at the card table. But what will they know of him? They are so young.

WHEN EVERYONE HAS ARRIVED for the wake, when the gathering has established itself — much of it positioned near the whisky — Gus Hampton crosses the room to stand behind his daughter.

He watches the priest from St. Mary's looking over at Rose. Sees the priest decide that this is the right time to approach the widow. Here he comes, Gus thinks, suave in his black togs, smoothly threading his way among the crowd, moving in to make his claim upon my family. Not impressed with me, the Protestant father. He knows I'm some kind of mild Presbyterian. That ought to be an oxymoron, but out here in New South Wales it certainly isn't. In the strong antipodean sunlight, all but the sturdiest of faiths wither, no match for the ancient melancholy of the scrub. During sermons Gus sometimes daydreams of standing up and shouting, What do you think you're playing at? Forget the stained-glass windows, take a look out the doors, we're *here*.

The priest doesn't even glance at Gus. Keeps his eyes on Rose, who remains hidden away under her veil. That's all you're getting, Gus Hampton says to himself. But the priest is in fine humour, full of his own little story. On a weeknight less than two months ago, Frank McGinty came to him with a request for a special mass to be offered in his name, a *missa cantata*, with some Bach. McGinty was quite specific as to which. But, the priest told him, the cathedral boys' choir already has its plate full with the Latin; they don't run to German. Just the music will do, McGinty said. You can forget the words.

"Frank McGinty," enthuses the priest. "Who'd have thought he'd be the first one to go?"

Rose, mute beneath her veil, moves her head from side to side.

Assent or disagreement? (Hard to tell.) The priest places a proprietary hand on her shoulder, leans closer.

Gus scowls. And catches the girl's eye for more claret cup. One of Bridie's lot, fetched from the vast, disreputable Holy Roman network that runs like a rabbit warren throughout the sandy soils of Sydney. Bridie Ahearne has connections Gus is happy to know little about.

Save us from anything passing itself off as "cup," he thinks, holding out his glass for more. Save us from anything not safely enclosed in its bottle. Had Frank smelled it coming? Does a man know? When his time is up, does he have some presentiment?

Gus had met McGinty as a hungry young pup, had watched him expand and grow outwardly self-assured, in nervy Celtic fashion. He'd watched Frank court and marry his daughter. After they were married, Frank had often come to the house with excellent bottles of claret (better than this stuff) and they'd polished them off together.

McGinty had that typical Irish look to him: big eyes, blue-black hair, face alleging total innocence. After he'd drunk half a bottle, McGinty looked at you in that butter-wouldn't way that said Yes, he knew the world found him attractive, and this information, far from being a lightning bolt, sat rather easily within him. It was a look, Gus realized, that must have thrown women into confusion, at first discouraging them, then later — not much later — goading them on. Gus Hampton usually liked some degree of physical arrogance in a man. That it flirted with foolishness made it all the more vibrant. It was the way life slithered along, hissing and sparkling and daring you to falter. But when it came to Rose, his own daughter — well, he'd wanted to reach out and clout the bugger.

The priest assures Rose that he will remember Frank and the family in his prayers. Then he straightens himself up and begins to speak with Gus.

IN GUS'S OPINION, there is far too much chitchat in the room about the war that is brewing in Europe, about the Serbs, about Bosnia and Herzogovina. (Are you meant to be on the side of the distressed family with their dead prince, or on the side of the rebel Serbs? The gathering is not quite sure.) Frank McGinty's twerp of a brother has just declared — quoting some ratbag politician — that if they are going to be in it, they'll be in it to the last man and the last shilling.

Plenty are down to their last shilling already, Gus says, without having to go galloping off to the Balkans.

The priest, less than enamoured of British trade wars himself, is willing to take over the conversation, to expatiate.

Gus Hampton, who's had more than enough of the Roman clergy for one day, is relieved when he notices that the solicitor is trying to catch his eye. The will, thank goodness for the will.

Gus excuses himself and takes the solicitor into the study, shutting the door. After the nonsense in the front parlour, the legalities, with their scrupulous insistence on detail, will be reassuring. Daily life reduced to the solidity of words and phrases: *per stirpes*, residue, for her own use absolutely. So much cleaner than medicine.

But when the will is read to him, Gus is left without words.

A CONSIDERABLE SUM of Frank's modest estate is to go to one Violet Bibbs of the Glebe. Gus calculates rapidly. McGinty's house will have to be sold. This home here on Ocean Street will one day be Rose's and is twice the size. Rose and the girls can move in as soon as everything is settled.

Who is this woman, this Violet Bibbs of the Glebe?

Violet Bibbs is a widow who has a son, sixteen years old.

To give himself time, to steady himself, Gus studies the details on the document — she lives down near Blackwattle Bay. Not a promising address. By the place and date of his death, Gus sees that the husband of this Violet Bibbs was a soldier, killed in the Boer War.

The solicitor waits. And waits.

"What am I to tell my daughter, Rose?" Gus blurts out at last, hating himself. The solicitor is ready for this, Gus knows. The blighter has the upper hand.

"A stranger," suggests the solicitor. He spreads his arms, just a little. (His shoulders are thin. A childhood illness. Which one?) "A needy patient, an indigent."

A damnable lie.

"Yes," says Gus, so quietly that the solicitor has to lean forward to hear. "A stranger."

AS A YOUNG MAN, in the last years of the nineteenth century, Frank McGinty had been the first doctor in the colony of New South Wales to read the works of the French epidemiologist who described the path of bubonic plague, from rat to flea to man. Frank spoke with approval of this theory to Dr. Augustus Hampton, who at that time ran the Board of Health, where Frank was a new employee, supervising reportable diseases.

Shortly after their conversation, Dr. Hampton invited Frank to dinner at his club.

The roast beef bled a little onto the plate, precisely the way Gus liked it. The wine in its crystal decanter shone dark as a night ocean. Tasted halfway decent, too.

Hampton, looking over at the young Frank, was predisposed to like the earnest young fellow. Frank, growing relaxed with food and drink, clarified his views of the plague pathway, the isolation of the plague bacillus, the role of the commensal rat. Commensal: eating together.

"Like us," put in Hampton.

Frank laughed eagerly.

Rattus rattus, the black rat, was sociable and sedentary. Enjoyed nothing better than lounging about the granary with its mates. Its cousin, *Rattus norvegicus*, the grey or brown rat, enjoyed the more solitary life of the sewer. Both were capable of making the long journey by boat.

That was how they would come, Frank predicted, sweat blooming on his face.

It was a humid December. The city steamed.

Before God told Frank he was meant for medicine, Frank had spent a year in the seminary. As a relic of his days in a priestly soutane, Frank always carried a clean white handkerchief up his sleeve. He took that out now and mopped his forehead.

Frank was aware he was making a good impression. If only he wouldn't sweat so much.

The rats would make their way ashore at the docks at Darling Harbour, he told Hampton. Only a matter of time.

"A temporary disease in the rat, an epidemic in man," Hampton said thoughtfully. Poured himself more wine, offered the decanter to Frank.

"Hong Kong, Mauritius, Honolulu, Noumea," Frank recited. The names made him feel almost faint. (It could have been the heat and the heavy food.)

Gus Hampton leaned forward and said, "When the rats rain from sky to earth; Leave, oh leave the hearth."

Frank looked inquiring, as he knew he should.

"Sanskrit," confided Gus Hampton. "Sanskrit, my good friend, and we're just now puzzling the damn thing out." He sat back in his chair and let out a hooting laugh.

Later, on Pitt Street, in the thick night, Gus Hampton took Frank's arm in a brief, solid gesture. At that moment Frank knew that a door was about to swing open and his life take shape.

LESS THAN A MONTH LATER, Dr. Frank McGinty was called to a loft in Sussex Street, to the bedside of a sailmaker.

Commanding the top of the stairs was an enormous black marsupial cat, the size of a small tiger. With confident, golden eyes, the marsupial cat appraised Frank.

"Don't think for one moment I haven't seen the likes of *you* before," said McGinty, walking up the stairs without hesitation and pushing his way past. He, Frank McGinty, was the doctor here; he was the one holding the cards.

But not for long, he realized. The flaxen-haired sailmaker was pallid, bloated, listless. In his groin the man had a swelling the size of a pigeon's egg: a brown, purplish, hard lump. It could be worse, Frank admitted. At least the man was headed for stupor rather than restless delusions.

The man's fair hair was thick, still silky with health. Odd how these things happened, how your eyes kept coming back to that hair.

Gently, Frank placed his fingers on the lump. Hiding his excitement, he searched the rest of the man's body to see if he could find what he wanted.

Found it!

Flea puncture on the back of the left leg.

Frank let his hand drop. Then brought it up to the man's hair, to stroke it, murmuring as he did so.

Frank's hand moved, and the dying man knew himself to be seated in the grass; it was a long, pale northern evening, midsummer; beside him were white shoes joined to skirts that went on all the way up to Mother. Her arms reached down, her fingers stroked his head, admiring him, exulting in him. (It was Frank's gift, his talent; he scarcely dared think about it.)

Upon questioning the man's wife, Frank learned that he had, a few days before falling ill, removed a number of dead rats from the WC.

Proud of the WC, she was. A step up from the cesspit.

"How many?" Frank pressed. The woman looked startled.

"Just the one WC, sir." Strong Dublin accent. She lifted her face to him: a round platter spattered with dark freckles. Her own clutch, this man's children, hid behind her skirts. (For the rest of their lives they would be beguiled by cheap, soft cotton fabric, its mysterious power to comfort.) Each of the children had fair-white hair and wide-set blue eyes, heads domed like small eggs. No ambiguity as to their paternity, Frank noted.

"How many rats?"

She wasn't sure. Half a dozen. Seven.

It added up. This one, the case at Brown's wharf. The two at the Haymarket. And the dead rats. There had been a report of rats dying down at Brown's; Frank had taken the news to Dr. Hampton immediately.

There could be no doubt about it.

It was on.

FRANK MCGINTY WAS INVITED to Sunday dinner at Gus Hampton's house. Rose, nineteen years old, sat at the dining table and watched Frank's face, the way it caught fire.

They would go to the council, Frank told Father. They would mount a campaign such as the city had never seen. "We have to make them realize," Frank said. "We have to make them realize that the only thing to do, the only thing worth doing, is to *kill the rats.*"

As the epidemic spread, Frank was at the house more and more often. He ate Sunday dinner with them, then adjourned with Father to the study to take a little port.

Rose carried in the tray herself; Bridie had the afternoon off.

From where she sat in the back parlour (reading), Rose could hear Frank talking with Father. She could see his shadow on the hallway wall.

Like a lantern slide, exactly.

Father agreed that the way to encourage people to kill rats was to institute a capitation fee. The mayor, however, believed it would result in rat trade from Melbourne.

"Go higher," urged Frank. His arms waved long on the wall.

Gus Hampton talked to members of Parliament, got them to petition the premier. Government acted: twopence for every rat delivered to the rat furnace in Bathurst Street, free rat poison for councils, more jobs for rat-catchers.

"Twopence is insufficient encouragement," Frank insisted. "The fee has to be raised to sixpence."

"Rats are being brought down from the bush," Gus Hampton pointed out. "They've found the sacks at Central."

"That has nothing to do with anything," declared Frank.

How large Frank looked in the shadows. How determined the upward thrust of his chin.

His fingers stroked the air.

Back went Gus to the premier. Sixpence it was. The furnace was relocated to superior premises on Darling Island.

Frank had won.

WHOLE AREAS OF THE CITY had to be cordoned off, fumigated. Daily, Frank went about in a white coat, hat, and mask. Exhorting and tireless. And came, every night now, to talk with Father and to let his shadow dance on the hallway wall.

Up in her bedroom after Frank had gone home, Rose lifted the jug and poured the water into her basin. She took the washcloth and cleaned herself. In a whisper she said the word, in Frank's voice: "furnace."

She understood — her hand was beneath the washcloth, lifting her breast — that he was a doctor. Nothing was hidden from him, and it was right and proper, it was his vocation. As a doctor, he had seen women. He *knew.*

During prayers at the side of her bed, Rose acknowledged that God had called upon her to love Frank McGinty, to stand by his side and console him. (She did not ask herself what she was meant to console him about.) Although she was in her own room, in the safe comfort of her dressing gown and slippers, these thoughts made her want to hide. She pushed her fingers through her abundant fair hair. Surely he must have noticed her hair, her crowning glory. With her eyes closed, Rose began to explore her face. The curve of her upper lip, the little pleat beneath the nose — they felt unfamiliar, secret, and quite delicious.

There were difficulties with quarantine, mix-ups, absurd decisions. "There was no need," said Frank, "no need to send off whole families to be incarcerated at North Head. Only the victim and his direct contacts."

Incarcerated. Direct contacts. When Frank felt particularly strongly about something, as he did about quarantine, he would stride up and down on the carpet beside Father's desk. His entire body was spread out against the hallway wallpaper, as if he were a shadow walking through a valley.

Rose stared and could not look away.

It was a courtship, of sorts.

FRANK, GUS, AND ROSE WENT TOGETHER to Centennial Park to see the continent become a nation. It was January 1, 1901, a day of memorable humidity. Starting at the Domain, an ambitious, eclectic procession made its way to the park through triumphal arches: schoolchildren, fire engines, decorated carriages, bands, troops of the NSW South Africa contingent and old lags from Lucknow. Some sly bugger had put the brewery contingent right in front of the teetotallers.

All the major pollies were out: Andrew Barton from New South Wales, Alfred Deakin from Victoria, and the rest.

Rose wore her best dress: stripes of beige, dove grey, and white. White gloves. A white hat, with a heap of grey and beige ribbons rearing up at the back. (She was well aware that her hair escaped in fine little tendrils down her neck.) Her mother-of-pearl hatpin.

Frank, Gus noted, was in something of a wild mood, cheering everything in sight. Mighty cheers for the railway band in their black-and-silver uniforms, even mightier cheers for the bushmen on their horses. Strong, healthy fellows they were, too.

Gus sucked on his pipe and considered Frank. He could tell, by the way Rose echoed Frank's every cheer, that it was high time to consider Frank. He had felt it his duty to make inquiries about Frank's family, and he was not pleased with the results.

Frank's mother was clearly on the debit side. Now an ancient brown lizard hiding from the heat up in Katoomba, Frank's mother had once been Elsie Madden, from the bogs of Donegal. It was Elsie Madden who, on a vacant piece of land at the corner of Kent and Liverpool streets, had set up a tent and claimed to be able to cure all ills. To build interest she'd extracted teeth — no pain, no charge. At a table near the tent flap, she'd set up a large glass bowl, filled with water, into which she dropped the teeth. By each afternoon's end, the glass bowl would be full.

Gus had interviewed some of her customers, intercepting them before they went off. As their tongues darted about their mouths, inspecting the gaps Elsie had made, they could remember the events only vaguely — entering the tent, lining up. Of the extractions themselves they could say little. With a strong sense of their own advantage, they insisted they had felt no pain. They still felt no pain.

Gus reminded Elsie Madden that such goings-on were against the law. She had no licence to operate as a dentist, no training.

Elsie placed a hand on his jacket and claimed that he misunderstood.

Gus was not mollified.

At the back of her tent, he countered, he'd uncovered a bag of bloody teeth, some with the ribbons of abscesses still attached. The teeth in the glass bowl, clean and white, were, he charged, a parcel of deception. Those were his words. A parcel of deception.

"It is a gift," Elsie said. "And the bowl, why, the bowl is to make people feel unafraid."

Gus grunted.

"You have perhaps not heard," Elsie continued, "of the parable of the talents?"

She knew — and this was what galled him the most — that as long as she didn't hang out a sign saying "Dentist," there was not a single thing he could do.

Definitely also on the debit side was Frank's brother, who had made his fortune on Great Cape York Herbal Remedy, the most potent blood purifier on earth, guaranteed to prevent and cure bubonic plague, cancer, Bright's disease, hydatids, and all other ills known to afflict the human body.

Cheap gin.

Of Frank's father, old McGinty, nothing was known. He seemed not to have existed. Somebody Elsie had met, no doubt, in her younger days on the goldfields. It was restful, at least, to be dealing with a man who had no father.

What else was Frank hiding up his sleeve?

Frank belonged to the Roman Church, and while that was a definite liability, Frank had the good sense not to drag it into things. Didn't go around embarrassing himself.

Frank knew little of how public life worked, he had no instinct for it. During the epidemic, Frank had turned to Gus. Tell them to do this, he'd said; make them do that. Frank did not understand. It was not a matter of the good doctor explaining, and everyone accepting right away what was best. Gus had had to trade and wheedle across green baize tables, had been obliged to meet later at the club, privately, to advance and retreat some more. He had been forced to call his favours in.

Today Frank was applauding the fathers of federation mindlessly. Giving the same approval to Deakin, who was sound, as to "Toss-Pot" Barton, who definitely was not. Yelping praises for that overfed idiot Reid, who never would discover which way was up.

But Gus had seen Frank with plague victims and knew him to be a doctor in the intimate way that was invaluable. The way in which he, Gus, had always felt a fraud, a failure. When a man's eyes followed you, asking for the hope he dared not put into words, when a woman fumbled, a stranger to her own folded body, that's when Frank flourished. His mind and hands were busy, and his attention absolute. What the patient wanted, Frank most sincerely desired, too, and with everything he had. With a patient it was a matter of particulars, and Frank's gift was for particulars. What a patient said to Frank did not disappear into his head, to be considered abstractly. Frank listened, he heard, he answered, with all his heart.

Let him leave public health and go back into private practice, Gus thought. A surgery of his own, and he may go far.

ON THE MORNING OF THE FEDERATION celebrations, Frank had been at the home of Violet Bibbs, whose husband was off fighting the Boer.

He had arrived moments before a summer downpour. Let himself in and stood at the window, watching the rain. Young Michael, not quite two and a half, was with a neighbour. He was disappointed not to see the child.

Frank had been looking forward to taking the boy on his lap. He loved to feel the small boy's thighs, his legs, his feet, his toes. He would smell the boy's ears, pretend to gnaw at them, and listen — conscious, suddenly, of his own intricate ears — for the child's snort of pleasure.

They were the same, all bodies: the same bones and tendons, pumping blood, everything the same. *We are all the same!* It was so obvious, and not just with your own children. You looked in a man's face and your own face stared back. This boy would have a child of his own one day, and at two and a half that future child would be this one over again. Frank imagined that other little one sitting there, too, and in turn yet another. He opened his arms to encompass those children. His, as well.

But today the boy wasn't home, and he had to go without.

Violet hurried in from next door, wiping the rain from her face with the back of her hand. The sight of the tiny raindrops in her auburn hair made Frank want her — it was reassuring to want her.

Violet was in a fairly good mood, leading him to bed right away, allowing him smiles and whispers. At times she was capable of much more passion: face crumpled up, breathing rapid, belly hardening. Or she could grow chilly, drawing her skirts around her. Then a remote, businesslike Violet would emerge, wanting to complain about how her family had lost their money in the depression of the 1890s. You could not predict what you were going to get with Violet.

When he was with her, Frank felt as if he were falling down a mineshaft and noticing, as he fell, the different layers of earth. Down he went, as the air rushed past him.

Violet had astonished him at first and continued to do so. Used to circumspect professional rituals for exposing flesh, Frank had been shocked by the way Violet took off all her clothes and walked around unashamed. She acted like an artist's model, he thought. At least that was how he imagined an artist's model would act. After the class was over and the students had gone home.

Frank had met Violet when he was attending her dying mother. This was years before he became an officer of public health, before he knew Gus Hampton and Hampton's only child, Rose.

A month after her mother's death, Violet had sent Frank an invitation to afternoon tea. It was a courteous way of thanking him, he supposed. A month later she'd invited him again, and soon after that, another invitation arrived. By the third time, he understood that she was no longer in mourning.

He played while she sang. She stood by the side of the piano, facing him. "Fair lie the fields of Athenry," she sang. He was made aware of the lift of her green shimmery blouse, held in place with a black enamel brooch. As she sang, she moved her neck, to show the whiteness of her throat. "For she lived to hope and pray for her love in Botany Bay." He was puzzled as to why no others had come. Hadn't they been invited?

When, on the fourth invitation, she made it plain that no others had been meant to come, that he had been trying her patience, he was utterly confounded. He moved to seize his hat and coat and make a run for it.

Violet was a worldly woman, a married woman. In pretty little shoes, moving smartly over the hall rug, she beat him to the front door.

He continued to be amazed by her, by how soft and determined she was. What had he done to deserve her?

Today she told him that she was taking Michael to Centennial Park in the afternoon. "It's something Michael shouldn't miss," she said.

The boy was his; he had only to touch him to know it. Not the soldier husband's. Soldiers, Frank thought, had only basic arithmetic and could not afford to let their imaginations run riot. Even so, the husband's placid assumption of paternity, and Violet's connivance, gave rise in Frank to a series of fierce, contradictory emotions, from indignant possessiveness to equally intense relief.

"I don't know how much the boy will remember," Frank said.

"He'll be able to tell his grandchildren."

They both laughed at that.

She went down the hall to make them a pot of tea. It was a small house, this place in the Glebe. No piano. (The money had melted away.) Two bedrooms at the front, hers and the boy's. The only other room was the kitchen, with a table and chairs, a wood stove, a dresser and meatsafe. In the apron of a backyard behind, a timber prop held up a clothesline. Behind that, the outhouse had passionfruit vine climbing all over it.

Frank wandered around the front bedroom, thinking about nothing in particular. He looked at the wardrobe and at the screen, behind which, when she was feeling cross, Violet would dress herself with no help from him, thank you very much.

But when she was sweet, she was very, very sweet. She'd sit propped up against the brass railings at the head of the bed. He'd sit at the other end, feeling the bones in her small feet. She'd sing to him, "It's so lonely round the fields of Athenry," and he'd join in, and as the simple melody built from one of the end of the bed to the other, they'd be sailing down to the harbour, out between the heads and away. Talus, he'd whisper, as the song died. Navicular. Metatarsals, phalanges.

Ah, Frankie, she'd sigh, all kitten-limp, content.

He'd stroke her feet and move on to her legs, working his way slowly upwards, naming her bones as he went. He'd bend to kiss her, breathing into her a new warm wave, his face in her body.

Odd, after they surfaced, to find the room exactly the same. When he left the house on those evenings, Frank had the feeling that everything up until then had been unreal, invented. He could not believe how light he felt. (Or how late it was.)

Standing in the bedroom now, Frank heard the kettle whistle, the clattering. She'd be getting out the best cups and saucers because he was here. Frank paused in front of the dresser. Reached out and picked up the picture of the husband. Held it in his hand. (Afterwards he would wonder why he had done this.)

Violet's husband, in uniform, sat on a buttoned sofa looking resolutely ill at ease. In an effort to appear dignified, he'd tightened up his face. Violet said he'd rather ride a horse than go to bed with a woman. She might have been telling less than the truth, Frank realized. (You don't rush to inform your lover of your husband's finer points.) And surely this soldier would love a woman as soft-skinned as Violet, unless someone had scared all the possibilities out of him. God knows, that happened. Too often when he examined a man's body he would come across a nest of knotted growths, deeply embedded and steel-hard: fear, highly sensitive to the touch. How long have you had that? he'd ask. The man would have grown so accustomed to its presence that he'd say, Oh, that; I've always had *that*.

As he ran his hand over the soldier's portrait, Frank knew that the man was wounded and would soon be dead.

Frank put his hand to the image again. *Shot in the throat.* He returned the picture to the dresser and stood well back.

A man who had been shot in the throat would look up at a doctor with pleading amazement; it made Frank heavy to think of it.

He was a long way away, this husband of Violet's, and there was nothing he could do.

If Violet came back into the room she'd sense the change in him. She had the ability to pick up on secret things in him, to drag them out. Then who knew what she'd say?

In a very fleeting way, Frank supposed he must feel some superiority over this man he'd cuckolded. Mostly he didn't think of him at all. He was simply away.

The husband would be dead, and the boy, the boy was young.

Frank began to sweat. He lay back down in Violet's clean bed. She'd made it nice for him, put on fresh sheets.

Frank lay in Violet's bed and realized he was waiting for something. A stone had been cast into a well. If there was water in the well, he told himself, he would be all right.

He thought of his medical work and of Gus Hampton, their friendship, the older man's respect. Testing himself, he shut his eyes and thought of Rose. He knew how she sat eavesdropping as he spoke with her father in the study. How she handed him his coat and hat, shy but needy. It made him plunge out into the night and gulp down great mouthfuls of air. Before he walked away, he would turn and look at the lights shining in Gus Hampton's fine house.

In Violet's bed, Frank was waiting, listening intently.

The stone fell into the water with a ripe, plump sound.

With that, he began to feel a tipsy happiness that stayed with him all afternoon in Centennial Park and afterwards, when he went to Gus Hampton's house for the celebrations on the verandah, on the lawn.

ROSE HAD CHANGED into her daffodil muslin, with long amber beads. The beads made her feel quite grown-up.

Father's friends sat on the verandah and talked about federation politics. One people; one destiny. On the lawn, Frank and two other young medical fellows got up a lively conversation about *X. cheopsis*, which Rose took to be an Egyptian pharaoh. Turned out to be a flea. When the other fellows announced that they had to push off, Rose was able to sit beside Frank, just the two of them.

Frank leaned back in his chair, relaxed. "It's been a great day," he said. "The first day of federation. A new century, a new country."

Rose could hear people from the house next door dancing the cakewalk. The people next door were in business.

"It's something to be in on, eh?" Frank offered.

She agreed that it was.

"In a new country," he said, moving forward in his chair, "we have a chance. A chance for everyone in a clean home, well lit, well drained." As he spoke, he saw in his mind the flaxen hair of the sailmaker. "Fresh air, clean water, blue skies," he added. "In the years to come, we will tackle them all: scarlet fever, typhoid, diphtheria. All of them will be wiped out."

If only we could be dancing, too, Rose thought.

"Just give me fifty years. Give me one hundred!"

The perky, syncopated rhythms of the cakewalk floated over the fence like an invitation to — what? Why, to a flask of wine, a book of verse, "before we too into the dust descend." *Ah*, thought Rose — who certainly was a great reader — *Ah, fill the cup: / what boots it to repeat / how time is slipping underneath our feet.*

At that moment, Frank gripped her hand. He had never touched her before. "I promise you," Frank said, "I promise you. Every home on the sewer, all the pipes with fresh air inlets; no damp, no dirt, no defective ventilation!"

Rose had to wonder about Bridie's punch.

He was thinking of the sailmaker's pale hair, of the fine whiteness of sails. "What do you say?" he asked her. The sails were filling with sweet blue air.

And Rose, leaning into his mood, said, "Yes, Frank," her voice rising, "oh, yes."

VIOLET, STANDING AT HER KITCHEN TABLE, shifted the boy, heavy with sleep, onto her left hip. In the tram on their way home from Centennial Park, she'd felt his head droop, jerk up; she'd watched his eyes attempting to resist, then fluttering in surrender. Worn out with the excitement of marching bands, even though he was mad about tram rides and determined not to miss a single minute.

Violet was peeling peaches. She'd started them earlier in the day, after Frank had left. A little water, sugar, just to the boil, let them cool, and the skins simply slip away. Peaches, softened like this, then mashed with the back of a fork, were the boy's favourite. They'd have them for tea tomorrow night. She'd turn to take them out of the cupboard, and he'd smell them before he saw them. He'd start kicking his legs and flailing his arms, ablaze with anticipation.

Did he smell them now, in his sleep, perhaps?

On her hip, the boy was beginning to give off what she thought of as his animal smell. That's what away-in-a-manger was all about — the slumbering infant's breath, soft and deep as the donkey's brown eyes.

She could put the boy down, but she liked working in this way, with his weight upon her. There was an awkward pleasure in holding him with one arm and doing something with the other — peeling the peaches, moving quietly to the cupboard, taking down a bowl. Their boy. One look at Frank and you knew what the boy meant to him. She'd seen it this morning, when she'd come in from next door. A swift glance, and he'd said to himself, *The boy's not with her.*

As long as she had the boy, she had Frank, she knew that. The neighbours could tut-tut about Frank's visits until they tripped over their tongues (the sooner, the better), but this boy was her ace in the hole. When you loved a man and you had his son, the rest didn't matter. Didn't matter that you spent your time waiting, that you had to save up most of your living for a few hours here and there. (Although it was brief, so very brief, over before it had begun; sometimes she wondered if it had happened at all.)

The boy stirred but did not waken. She sank her face into the round warmth of his head. "See, baby," she whispered. "See what Mummy's made for you? *Peaches.*"

"I WILL DO EVERYTHING I CAN for you and the boy."

Frank was standing in Violet's kitchen and turning his hat in his hand, turning and turning it.

He was going to get married, Frank announced, but he would continue. To care, to provide. "I want everything to stay the way it is," he said quietly. "It's just that we'll both be married," he added, to remind her.

Violet still had not received the news of her soldier husband's death. It would come slowly, by boat. This very day she had received a letter from him. One of those bright, stout letters that can be read aloud to neighbours who lean against the back fence, their hair tied up in coloured scarves.

Frank claimed he was glad the fellow was doing well. (There were times when Frank surprised even himself.) "I'll still see you regularly," he said, to reassure.

At this, Violet laughed, a cynical, relieved laugh, full of bitter power. "I'm sure you will, Frank McGinty, I'm sure you will."

Marry Frank did, that Easter Monday, 1901. At the boarding house in Sans Souci on the first night of their honeymoon, Frank lay down beside Rose in her new nightdress (terrified, excited, rigid) and did his best not to think of Violet's relaxed, confident thighs.

ROSE WOULD TELL HER GIRLS, "Father proposed in the middle of the cakewalk." To Rose, this sounded lighthearted and stylish, quite unlike the married woman she had become.

Veronica and Ellen thought about cake and were happy.

Rose looked at herself in the dressing-table mirror. "Mrs. McGinty," she said aloud.

She'd warned herself not to ask for too much. She'd welcomed the momentous, messy arrival of babies. Twins, no less; such success. Only girls, but they were off to a good start. A very good start.

Nobody had prepared her for the babies' round heads, or for the way in which their glistening eyes, their incomparable eyelashes, made her weak with anxiety. It was amazing how children pushed you into life, into danger. Gentle Jesus, keep them safe. If the twins were safe, what more could she ask for? Surely that should be sufficient, more than enough?

As for Frank, nobody had prepared her for him, either. How you could want someone with a longing that robbed you of breath, but when the moment came, the man himself became insubstantial and slipped away? She would drop her head onto Frank's shoulder, hoping and nervous and trying to please. And he would respond with an affable, abstracted assent.

Gus Hampton judged his daughter's marriage to be a success — a reasonable success — in the complicated, shifting, resilient way of marriages. But he was not surprised that Rose occasionally suffered a mild form of nervous prostration.

Frank came home early and sat by Rose's bed for a long time. He slid his left hand behind her head. With his right hand, he soothed her face. Didn't she realize, didn't she remember? She was his Rose of Sharon, forever blooming in his heart.

Rose put on her bed jacket and announced that she was feeling much better, really, there was no need to fuss.

"Father is very devoted to medicine," Rose said to Ronnie and Ellen. "Father believes in service to others above all else."

GUS HAMPTON HAS TO DISCUSS the will with Rose.

He decides to tell her after Sunday dinner. First, he will assure her that she has nothing to fret about. She can move into the home on Ocean Street; the girls can go to the nuns at Star of the Sea for as long as they like. A small sum, he will say — as an afterthought — has gone to a stranger, a patient, no doubt. An indigent. Gus searches his mind for a part of the Gospels he might call upon, should the need arise. Surely this kind of thing had come up?

Since Frank's death, Rose has not shrunk. Rather, her shoulders seem to be expanding, she is being competent and brave. It has already occurred to Gus that his daughter might make a first-rate widow; so many did.

The baked custard and stewed fruit have been cleared away, the children excused, and there is nothing else for it.

He tumbles the story out, aware of his clumsiness. A doctor, he knows, should be an expert in delivering bad news.

Rose looks at him and tightens her lips.

I must not let her ferret everything out of me, he warns himself. (How much does she suspect; what does she already know?)

It is only for a few moments, sitting at the table cleared of its dishes, the white linen tablecloth stretched out between them, that Rose slumps in her chair and lets herself go. "We will be down on our knees, down on the ground, grubbing out potatoes," she cries, in a thrill of self-abasement.

"Get a hold of yourself, Rose," her father implores.

Ronnie and Ellen, standing in the hallway, hear.

SPRING, AND THE GARDEN of the house on Ocean Street is full of fluttery brown moths. Rose has spread a blanket on the grass under the fig near the swings. Gus is above them, in a cushioned wooden garden chair.

Ronnie bats at the moths with her hand.

"Good enough to eat," Grandpa Gus says, to make Ronnie shudder. "Highly nutritious, quite delicious."

"Cook-you-bugger sits on an old gum tree," Ellen sings, being daring and wicked on the swing.

Bridie laughs.

"You shouldn't teach her such things," says Rose, to Bridie.

They are having a picnic tea on the lawn. A nitpick tea, Grandpa Gus says, for a joke.

Rose speaks to the girls of their father. "Father said: It was a privilege to be at the card table."

Ronnie and Ellen discuss what would be on the table — besides cards, of course.

"Chocolate cake," says Veronica.

"With pink icing," adds Ellen. "And hundreds-and-thousands sprinkled on top."

Grandpa Gus tells Ellen and Ronnie the story about the rats and the fleas and the people: The rats came in on the ships. They were down in the hold, eating grain and sleeping. They woke up and looked out the porthole, and there were the heads of Sydney harbour. When the rats decided to go ashore and investigate, the fleas went along for the ride.

Grandpa says that Father realized what the connection was between the rats and people. He was an important doctor, Grandpa says, who saved Sydney from the plague.

Grandpa Gus strokes Veronica's hair, then Ellen's. They have to let him; it is polite. Besides, there is something attractive about it, *letting* him.

Their father had been a doctor, like Grandpa Gus himself and St. Luke, the doctor who wrote one of the Gospels. A beggar named Lazarus was full of sores and lay at the gate of the rich man. And you know what? The beggar got into heaven ahead of the rich man. A woman was troubled with an issue of blood for twelve years, but she touched the hem of Jesus's garment. (Unmentionable, but there it is, right in the Gospel.) "Physician, heal thyself." What exactly does that mean?

At tea the next evening Ronnie announces that to serve others as Father did is more valuable than anything.

Rose smiles and lets the girls each have a third piece of treacle tart.

Ellen says nothing. She is thinking about fleas, the hidden connections of things.

AS THE GREAT WAR DRAGS ON, the girls learn how to knit khaki socks. Bridie is kept busy making cream sponges for the Cake and Fancy Fair. It is to help the troops overseas, now fighting Johnny Turk.

Our troops are fine, big-limbed athletes. In England they walk down the cold, narrow streets and are so healthy and tall and sunny-handsome they remind everyone of Greek gods in the old poems.

After the war, Grandpa Gus promises, the girls will have a tennis court.

Rose is out of the house at all hours. She's begun to go about in a grey dress with a marvellous crisp white apron. The girls were hoping the apron would have a scarlet cross on it, but it doesn't because their mother isn't really a nurse. Rose is in the volunteer auxiliary. She organizes things; it is highly important work.

"I look like something the cat dragged in," says Rose, not meaning it. She is smart and sharp and almost in uniform. "There is so much to attend to," she says with satisfaction. "So much."

At war's end there is even more to attend to, with the Spanish flu. Rose wears a mask and laughs like a schoolgirl. She runs to catch the Mosman ferry to Ellamatta, the war veterans' hospital on the harbour's north shore. With newfound confidence, Rose tells her father that some messages are best not delivered by doctors. Who, she asks her father, wants to see the doctor staring at his pricey polished shoes, polite and finally useless? At the moment when the breathing stops, when the equipment — whatever it is — might as well be pulled away, Rose is the one to take the message into the other room, to see the shoulders drop.

He is gone. He is gone and this is how it feels. (But how does it feel? And why is there something almost promising about the news?)

AT ELLAMATTA, ROSE KNOWS the nicknames of all the soldiers, the diggers: Bob Bronte, the Rock Lizard, Wobbly Wilf, Dublin Mike, and the Saviour. She knows their enthusiasms, for toffee, for the rugger scores. Some even have hobbies of a sort — in the spring, the Rock Lizard keeps a colony of silk worms in a shoebox beside his bed. When the twins come to the ward he produces the worms and holds court.

What Rose discovers is that such men do not live in compliant despair. "Outsiders," Rose says to Bridie, "think of them huddled in their beds like lumps of damp bread, uttering the occasional moan. It isn't like that at all. Not at all. Men who are hanging on for dear life will give you a run for your money."

Take the Saviour. He emerged from the fog of Villiers-Bretonneux in the certain understanding that he was His Only Begotten Son. But last week the Saviour announced he was giving up performing miracles.

"A mug's game," he confided to Rose. "Decided to give it away."

"Good on yer," Rose replied, in a soldier's voice, and they both laughed.

THE DAY AT ELLAMATTA begins innocently enough.

Early morning: the probationary nurse is sweeping the ward for the first of six times that day, sprinkling tea leaves in front of the wide broom. (It is the old-fashioned way to pick up every trace of dust.)

The diggers on the ward are already awake, looking forward to their first cup of tea. Glad to put the night behind them, they are sitting up with woollen caps on their heads — they feel the cold, even into October, the end of the fickle Sydney spring. Outside, the jacarandas are coming into bloom, a sea of purple flowers.

Rose has been rubbing the Saviour's legs, which in the night have turned a painful mottled colour.

He weeps, "I didn't do it. It wasn't my fault."

"Of course it wasn't your fault," Rose says. "Everyone knows you didn't do it." She pulls the curtains around his bed. (The men in the adjoining beds, aware of how pain degenerates into humiliation, have already politely turned away.)

Rose sits on a chair, close to the head of the bed. The Saviour turns, lets his face brush her blouse. Outside, the bottle-o is making the first of his day's journeys along the street with his horse and dray. "*Hibuy beny kind bottles,*" the bottle-o cries, from leathery lungs. Between the cries, Rose hears the slow sounds of the horse and dray.

The Saviour has stopped weeping. Together, they listen to the horse's gait, strong and calm and certain, with the dray rolling along behind.

Rose moves her chair closer. When the Saviour reaches out, Rose knows his hands have become his feelings. Deliberately, without hesitation or haste, she begins to unbutton her blouse. Guides his fingers. "Not your fault," she whispers. "God knows, it's not your fault."

Afterwards, Rose walks down the corridor as if on crumpling legs and makes her way out onto the verandah. An ambulatory patient is sitting there with a blanket over his knees, his eyes upon some difficult landscape in his head. She's noticed him before; he often sits like that, away from the group.

To calm herself, Rose invites him home for Sunday afternoon tea. It isn't guilt, she tells herself. It's goodwill, pure goodwill.

ON FRIDAY AFTERNOON, at Holy Cross for her weekly confession, Rose remains on speaking terms with God, although there are some things she would rather not discuss.

God and her husband Frank sit somewhere behind the priest in the confessional, back there in the shadows. God's face is unfathomable, but Frank's has a loopy grin, the one he wore when he came home extra late.

"Bless me, father, for I have sinned," Rose whispers, then launches into the usual litany of sins, skipping over the charitable gestures she offers the Saviour. The priest's head is so close she can feel her breath rubbing his cheek.

She leaves the confessional and kneels in a dark corner of the church. The small red lamp burns beside the altar. If Frank hadn't died, if that terrible war hadn't happened, she'd never have discovered what kind of men the diggers are. Would never have realized how she, Rose, can keep track of everything from distant relatives to the delivery of the best chump chops on the north shore. (Bridie knows the butcher.)

Surely there is something perverse and sinful in that? For so many women, the war has ended everything. Husbands, sons: lost, gone. And the world, forgetting. You can always pick out such a woman: walking along any Sydney street, stopping at the barrow to buy fruit and veggies, putting them in her string-bag. What gives her away is her utter indifference — picking and buying without a single gesture of triumph or scorn. In her presence, the other buyers at the barrow stop talking. (If all is dross, what do you think you're up to, nattering about fruit and veg?) For as long as she stands there, you can feel the silence surge. Sometimes the barrow-man keeps talking, his voice becoming higher and ever more chirpy. Then trailing off.

And the worst thing is, one day, months later, you see the same woman, all dressed up, stepping out with a man, trying to appear carefree, her face taut.

Rose puts her hands together, not in prayer but just being there with *the layers*: first the stone floor, then the polished pews, and above that, the wax from the candles. Higher than the candles, way up with the hanging lamps, drifts the residue of incense. The twins in the Christmas play at Star of the Sea, wearing tea towels. Bringing Frank incense and more. "No," she told them. "Myrrh. My yachts ride right home." That was the way you remembered the spelling.

In a hurry to get back to Ellamatta, Rose runs to the quay. She is vaguely aware of the cries of birds, the minor clamour of setting out, the wooden gangplanks being pulled away, then her own panting. *Made it!*

She sits out on the wooden seat on the deck, smelling the salt and tar and watching the green of the harbour and the ferry's dark cream wake. The Saviour will ask, Did you have to run to catch the ferret?

A breeze picks up. Rose turns her face into it, lifts her arms.

It is a brief trip, with the flash of orange-tile roofs ahead and the khaki bush of Taronga Zoo coming up on the right. The lions, deep in their pits, denounce their boredom, especially by night; the Ellamatta diggers wait and listen. They understand them, roar for roar.

Amazing what the diggers talk about. They know about Jessie the elephant and her single dawn ferry ride across from Moore Park to her new zoo quarters. Apart from some wary tiptoeing over the pontoon to the wharf, she'd treated the trip with the bored nonchalance of a daily traveller. All the diggers speak of Jessie's ferry ride with the fond authority of eyewitnesses. But it happened in 1916, when they were on the other side of the world, in the mud of Europe.

Looking over at the approaching shore, Rose sees the bottle-o and his horse. They are making their way past a vacant lot where broken-down boats sail the heavy seas of paspalum.

"Oh, breathe on me, ye breath of God," Rose sings to herself. The Ellamatta diggers won't be leaving to go home. They will be hers for the rest of their lives. "So shall I never die."

WHEN THEY SEE MRS. BIBBS, people say, "Ah, the ship's come in." Some of them add, "If wishes were horses." Leaving children to wonder.

Out for his constitutional with Jones-the-Scottie, old Gus Hampton sees Mrs. Violet Bibbs.

After she'd got her hands on Frank's money in 1914, she'd moved from the Glebe to a better house in Bondi Junction. In the last year of the Great War, Violet had come to see him. With news. The boy had been killed at the Somme. The son of Violet Bibbs and Frank McGinty would have been all of eighteen years old when he died. And there was — said Violet Bibbs, her lips a-tremble, resentful at having such a story to tell — a young mother, a child.

Don't tell me, Gus thought, not another one.

A baby girl this time.

Gus was obliged to cough up, so that Frank's bastard's bastard (that was the fact of the matter) could be sent away to the country.

Violet assured nice old Doctor Hampton that she'd never meant to be a nuisance. Or a grandparent, she added, for the huge relief of a joke. When she opened her mouth and laughed, he could see the moist, sweet pinkness inside.

She had him then; she knew it.

"Funny how life turns out," she ventured. "You never expect."

Once again, Gus had been forced to call his favours in: the Imperial Hotel in Murwillumbah, on the far north coast of New South Wales. Work for the mother in the dining room. In time, the daughter could lend a hand with the housework.

Another young mother! God, how tangled it was, and how swiftly it all took place, the leap from one generation to the next, and the next.

Gus imagined her in a crowd of others. Simply dressed, in pale pink, with that exposed, daunted look youthful widows have. On deck in the summer glare, holding the child on her hip, one free arm grasping the railing. Watching as the steamer nosed its way into the last of those wide, brown northern rivers, which one by one had put distance between the time before and the time to come. She would be taking the child all the way to Murwillumbah because she had nowhere else to go.

WHEN GUS HAMPTON had first been forced to think of Violet Bibbs, he'd imagined tubs of powder, silk shawls discarded, frivolous shoes: all of this spread in disarray around the parlour.

Well, he'd been right.

He, Gus Hampton, knew about women, could pick which ones would be lovely trouble. Such a one was Violet Bibbs.

Entertaining Gus in her front parlour, Violet lounged in the middle of a mess, smoking a cigarette in a holder. She was planning her costume for a fancy-dress ball. (Being at her house was one thing, but going out in public with her? Gus wasn't sure.) She was determined to go, and as something ridiculous — a whirling dervish, or queen of the harem.

Beneath her absurd costume, her small, assured body was not yet old, by any means. When you kissed her in full bloom beneath you, she tasted of salted nuts, of plum pudding. And also of loss.

Their brief liaison didn't amount to anything, a few desperate little kisses. Hollow and tinkly, like the music everyone was demanding to dance to.

You couldn't go on like that. Couldn't expect to, wouldn't want to. Violet had known that perfectly well. She'd come to him with her eyes open. And her hand out.

Then the war was over, it was another decade. Women went flat, chopped off their hair, developed opinions — Rose among them. "I'm a thoroughly modern woman," Rose announced. Gus, hearing these words, felt too tired to be puzzled. Rose was learning to drive a motor car. A terrifying thought.

Half a dozen years later, here's Violet Bibbs, coming up Oxford Street in a long, old-fashioned skirt, her hair pinned up. In Jones-the-Scottie, recognition stirs. He goes rigid, tail straight up in salute. Begins to bark in earnest recognition, short front legs lifting right off the ground.

Worn out with memory, old Gus is forced to lean his head against a shop's plate-glass window while the street shifts and the morning whirls around him.

ROSE, SETTING OUT EARLY for another satisfying day at Ellamatta, sees Mrs. Bibbs passing by. Rose knows where Mrs. Bibbs is going. She's off to the wharf, to meet the boat.

In Sydney's eastern suburbs, Mrs. Bibbs has become what the newspapers call "a local identity." Everyone has found out that Mrs. Bibbs reads the shipping news to check when the boat is due to dock, then hurries down to greet it. Mrs. Bibbs, the story goes, had been the victim of an irresponsible man. The child had grown up and gone to the war, and this was the boat that took him away. Some say this woman's son died at Gallipoli, storming those cliffs in the Dardanelles near where Helen had stirred up such grief. Others say he died in France towards the end. It doesn't matter which.

Mrs. Bibbs is one of those women who carry their silence with them. Today, once again, she is on her way to the wharf to welcome a child who will never come ashore, either whole or damaged.

Rose recognizes a mother's heart: its unalloyed, foolhardy intensity. The child may have been illegitimate, but he was still his mother's son. As a sign of respect, mother to mother, Rose stands still and watches until Mrs. Bibbs has turned the corner and is out of sight. She doesn't know the name of this woman's son. She can, however, remember the names of the places; she lets them toll inside her like a gloomy bell. (It is not an unpleasant sensation.) Suvla Bay, the heights of Sari Bair, Ypres, Flanders, the Messines Ridge, Montdidier, Amiens, Bullecourt.

I will remember, Rose silently promises Mrs. Bibbs, feeling a surge of virtuous energy. I will *never* forget. My children will remember, too. I can promise you that. My children's children; they will remember.

She'll tell the diggers at the hospital she did this, she decides. To remind them how she loves them, how she will love them forever.

ABOUT TO PLAY A TENNIS MATCH before school, Ronnie and Ellen see Violet Bibbs going to meet the boat. Bridie, in the garden cutting roses, sees her, too. "Mrs. Bibbs was quite the beauty once," says Bridie. "Hard as that may be for you youngsters to appreciate."

Funny old thing looks like a candidate for the rathouse. The bin.

"What do you think she does," asks Ronnie, "down at the wharf?"

Ellen plans to discover the name of the boat Mrs. Bibbs goes to greet. She's begun to read the shipping news in the *Herald*.

It's Ellen's serve. She holds one ball in her hand and throws the other up into the blue, exactly the right height, and *bam*. (This is the Davis Cup, and she's playing for Australia.)

Ronnie is across the court with her rather weak backhand, managing to return serve. Ellen, in at the nets, cannot resist the temptation to sneak over a half volley. It isn't fair, but who could resist the satisfying force of the ball, right in the middle of the racket. At the end of the match, Ellen's the champ again. (Wimbledon roars; the Aussies have shown them.)

"We could follow her," Ellen says. "See what she does." She throws her racquet onto the grass beneath the canopy of figs and sits on it, courting death by spiders.

"You'll have grass stains all over your skirt," says Ronnie, sitting down beside her.

They take off their sandshoes. They look at the sky, where their famous father is. Father is distant and never changes. Down here, Mrs. Bibbs hastens along the street, ragged with longing.

ROSE IS LATE GETTING HOME from Ellamatta. She's just got in, but it's so humid and stuffy she's come out again for a cigarette. Bridie's joined her. The two of them are puffing discreetly in the dark. The night pulses with crickets and other small things that sing in the grass.

Mrs. Bibbs is coming up Ocean Street beneath the Moreton Bay figs. She's going to pass right by the house, by the garden. The thick branches of the fig obscure the streetlights, so Mrs. Bibbs walks in shadows.

Before, they've always seen Mrs. Bibbs in daylight, on her way down to the boat. This is the first time they've caught her making her way home. This is different.

Mrs. Bibbs weaves a little. Stops. Gathers and holds her ridiculous, outmoded, ankle-length skirt. With deliberate, unsteady care, she begins to step her way over the roots of the fig tree.

In the garden, Rose and Bridie crouch in the darkness of leaves.

"Do you think she's been drinking?" whispers Rose.

"What would you do, after the boat comes in?"

Mrs. Bibbs is on the footpath right outside the fence. They can hear her breathing.

She's so close. If Rose reached out, they would be almost touching.

The Bright Blue Air

One of the most embarrassing things about Grandpa Gus being old and ill is that he tells them stories meant for little kids. But the twins, Ellen and Ronnie, are in their fourth year of high school at Our Lady Star of the Sea. Next year, 1924, they'll be sitting for the leaving certificate.

"Listen," Gus tells the twins, "you walk to the farthest end of the last street at the end of the world and there it is, a well by a garden wall. Climb into the well and find a ladder, an iron ladder. Go down and down to the top step of a flight of stairs. You have to feel your way with your feet. If you're strong enough, you take the stairs out over the edge of the world. Are you? Strong enough?"

Ronnie and Ellen nod, to humour the old boy.

"The stairs," Gus says, "are lit only by the faint blue light in which the whole world spins."

Ronnie and Ellen know about blue. Down at the beach, huge gusts of blue come plummeting, crashing straight into your face.

Of the two, Ellen is the better swimmer.

Ellen runs into the surf, yelping at her body's surprise at suddenly being wet. She turns sideways, putting her right arm up to break the impact of the crashing wave. She pushes farther out, selects another wave to dive under, then turns, leaps forward, kicking madly. Misses, falls back, dives under another wave, tries again to catch one.

Ellen and Ronnie swim all year round, but summer is best.

In the strong light of morning, already *zum-zumming* with cicadas, they are immediately fully awake and in a hurry. They want to be among the first to walk upon the untouched sand. Quickly, they put on their bathing suits, then their clothes. Their togs, made of some nasty woolly stuff, are scratchy when dry, but they don't mind, it's worth it. Bolt down breakfast, run for the tram, and take the loop to the beach. Everyone on the tram is looking out for the diamond flash of ocean.

"Wasn't it crazy," says Ellen, "when Mother was a girl? You had to bathe after dark or before eight in the morning. Just before eight someone would sound a gong and you'd have to get out of the surf."

"Ridiculous," agrees Ronnie, with the easy contempt of the young.

"Not that Mother swam," says Ellen. Swimming is what *they* do, not old people. Old people huddle beneath umbrellas and try to keep the sun away from their skin. They believe it will hurt them.

Ellen and Ronnie like to think they know about surf, can spot rollers and dumpers. They stand on Bondi Beach with their hands on their hips, pointing out waves to each other. Surf can be deceptive. Waves breaking evenly can hide a sneaky rip coming in from the south. Especially in the summer, the season of king tides.

After they've had their first dip of the day, they lie in the sand, eat broken biscuits from a brown paper bag (that's how you get them cheap), and discuss Gabriel Oak. In Hardy's *Far from the Madding Crowd*, which they're doing this year at school, Gabriel Oak's entire flock of sheep went over a cliff somewhere back in freezing England. He's in love with a woman who's giving him the bum's rush because, without his flock, he has to work as a hired hand.

"It is a marvellous book," Ellen declares. Hardy, she tells Ronnie, knew his rural world was slipping away. He wanted someone to remember. The sheep-washing pool. Horses tramping in the night. Hiving the bees. Then, just when you think he's gone all sentimental, he throws in a nasty accident. And his accidents never simplify things.

"Why would someone like Gabriel want that snob Bathsheba for his wife?" Ronnie asks Ellen. "He could see right from the start she was vain."

"Of course he did," Ellen replies. "Yet he loved her; she was his first sweetheart." But it wasn't quite that simple. When Gabriel finally gets Bathsheba there's something grey and exhausted about them both.

"Can you imagine?" asks Ronnie. "Having a sweetheart?"

They tilt their heads to the sky, to imagine.

It's mid-afternoon on a weekday, and only a few people are paying visits in St. Mary's Cathedral. A stranger walks up the aisle, genuflects, moves into the pew in front of her. Ronnie tries to pray but all she can see is his broad male back, his neck, his dazzling head.

Ellen is standing in a tram, hanging onto one of the straps. The bell has rung and the tram is jerking to life when a young man, sprinting along behind, makes a stunning leap onto the running board. He's trying to haul himself up, and Ellen's reaching down to help him.

"It won't be like that," says Ronnie. "Life never turns out like what you imagine."

"All the more reason to imagine, then."

Heat is building on the sand. The relief of the southerly breeze is hours away.

"What do you say we don't take the tram all the way home. Let's walk as far as the Junction," suggests Ellen. "That way we'll have enough for a ginger beer now."

They won't mind dawdling home. They'll stop to look at the sea, late-afternoon navy blue. Take their time going up the back way, up through lanes that smell of lantana and sewage mixed with sea spray. Today the spray is heavy in the air, making the light bounce about. By the time they get home, their skin and clothes will be stiff.

Having bought and drunk the ginger beer, they go in the surf again, then lie face down in the sand, letting the water dry on their skin. Ronnie falls asleep. Ellen, beside her, lazily licks her sister's arm, to taste the salt.

BECAUSE GRANDPA GUS is no longer able to handle the stairs, they've moved his bed into the front room. When he's feeling strong enough, he gets up and sits in an armchair. Jones-the-Scottie follows him from bed to chair, from chair to bed. Grandpa Gus calls him the faithful hound.

The front room is furnished in heavy Edwardian style: mantel drape with bobbles, ottoman, velvet cushions, crocheted runners, a wicker table covered in a heavy dark-green fabric with more bobbles.

To make space for the bed, the piano has been moved into the adjoining dining room. Ellen, who has finished eighth grade, is completing her morning practice of the *Pathetique Sonata*. Ronnie is turning the pages, listening.

Ellen sets out bravely enough, taking the home key up and up, left hand keeping the tremolo rumbling. (The trouble is, if you are to play this at all, you have to pretend you are far more self-assured than you feel.) From the bright idea of the opening, she moves on to the second theme, which is more hidden, reticent. She clears the hurdle of the melody leaping from the bass register to the treble. (The rhythm is all right. Not brilliant, but all right.)

It's in the next movement that she really runs into trouble. The lyric melody eludes her. It demands to move inwards, but she can't muster the necessary strength, the dignity. "I can't get it," she admits to Ronnie, who nods. "I hear in my head," Ellen complains. "I just can't get it out. It won't *come.*"

Their mother, Rose, has made no attempt to bring either front room or dining room up to date. Far too busy over at Mosman, running a hospital for soldiers messed up in the Great War. "My diggers," Mother calls them.

"Dunno what Rose'd do without her diggers," says Bridie Ahearne, cleaning the room with an air of injury. "Dust-catchers!" she exclaims, poking at the bobbles.

In between bouts of housework, Bridie is teaching the girls how to foxtrot, to the tune "It Had to Be You." "Nuns don't know everything," claims Bridie. "They're unable to equip you for the finer things in life."

When Bridie suggests a dance practice, Ellen and Ronnie abandon the piano and begin to hum the tune. They are learning in the hall.

"You're getting the hang of it," Bridie says. "Remember, quick quick slow, quick quick slow."

While the twins practise together ("I wandered around and finally found/the somebody who"), Bridie does the steps by herself, stopping to rap out the rhythm on the plaster. In between dances, Bridie stands back, measures the wall with her hands. "This place could easily be divided up," she announces. "You could get four or five flats in here, no trouble at all."

After the dancing, there's morning tea in the kitchen: Gus and the twins and Bridie, who has one of her vast tribe of rellies in for a feed and a gossip. Bridie holds forth about some nun up at Sacred Heart who went nuts and ran through the streets in her nightdress. "A crying shame," decrees Bridie, pouring water into the teapot. "They bring those young girls out here and keep them locked up. On Sunday afternoons they gather on the convent verandah, face towards Ireland, and weep."

The young nun received a letter from home, Bridie explains. In his farmhouse back in Cork, her father had died alone. "What can God be thinking of?" asks Bridie. "It's beyond me."

Bridie settles in to enjoy herself. "You know how they take baths, don't you? They get dressed up in a long white shift and they slip into a tub covered with sailcloth, with a just a hole for their head to stick out. So they won't get a glimpse."

Ellen and Ronnie eat their biscuits, fresh from the oven and yummy. Bridie's made what everyone calls Anzacs. Anzac biscuits are the current rage — rolled oats, golden syrup, bicarb that fizzes, and other stuff. (Neither of the girls has learned to cook.) Bridie fills a brown paper bag full of Anzacs for the silent visitor, who swiftly tucks it into a large, cheap purse.

"When a nun enters, all intercourse with the world" — says Bridie, using the shocking word deliberately — "ends. Full stop. She does not go out to the doctor. If she falls seriously ill, a doctor might be summoned, and that rarely. Even if she lives in the same city, just down the road, she can't go home to help her dying parents. Can't even attend their funerals. She can never leave the convent walls.

"It'll be a relief when you two are done with Star of the Sea and safely out of their clutches."

After the biscuits, Bridie gets out the Christmas boiled fruitcake to top up with whisky. (She made it weeks ago.) "You have to check on how it's doing," she says, "you have to keep it good and moist."

Bridie and her visitor slosh whisky into their tea. "Want some?" Bridie offers Grandpa Gus, who's installed by the back door to keep cool. He's got his head in the *Sydney Mail*, studying the cricket scores. The English are here, looking for victory. "They're going to go home empty-handed," Grandpa Gus predicts happily.

On the floor beside the door, Jones-the-Scottie is stretched asleep on his stomach. Jones's back legs stick straight out, black pads turned upwards like little flippers.

SCHOOL'S BROKEN UP for the long holidays and the twins take the tram to town. It's a heavy, humid summer morning and they racket past gardens full of creamy Christmas bush and agapanthus blue and white. Jump off at Foy's for the Christmas windows. Hike down for morning tea in Griffith Bros. tea room, where Madame Josephine stares into the cups and reads the leaves.

Madame Josephine sees a sea voyage for Ronnie. "Where to?" asks Ronnie, trying for her money's worth.

"All I'm getting is clouds," says Madame Josephine.

They really shouldn't be doing this; the Church doesn't approve. But Bridie reckons it doesn't do any harm, and anyway, who's going to know? On her afternoons off, Bridie goes down to Darlinghurst and consults with shuddering tables. This tea leaves business is just a bit of sport for amateurs.

"I see the colour burgundy," Madame Josephine announces with authority, looking into Ellen's teacup. "The colour burgundy, billowing across the sky."

Amazing, thinks Ellen, leaning forward to stare into the straggle of sodden leaves. Burgundy is the colour of the notes when she plays the sonata's final movement. Not really a rondo at all, but something darker, rich and spacious.

"Hang on a minute," says Madame Josephine, inspecting the cup more carefully. "Drab. Some heavy, ugly material, serge."

Ellen draws back, dissatisfied. "Serge?"

"I'd go for the remnants if I were you," snaps Madame Josephine, in brisk dismissal.

Silly old chook. Shouldn't have wasted their money. It was Bridie's fault.

Next stop Elbow Arcade, to sniff the fruits in De Luca's: twelve-inch bananas down from Queensland, red currants over from New Zealand, fresh oranges rolling down a chute and being squeezed.

Under the domed glass ceiling of the Strand, the cloche hats in André's Millinery are embellished with tiny sprigs of lily of the valley. Everyone over the age of ten looks like a stunned mullet in those silly helmets, Bridie says. Why ever do we get sucked in?

Umbrellas, nuts cooking in oil, fur collars (real and imitation), silver teapots, the deeply honest smell of stationery.

Lunch at Sargent's dining room, where the tablecloths are always spotless. Lamb and mint sauce, three veg, fruit salad and cream, and tea, all for only one shilling.

Off to the Sydney municipal library in the Queen Victoria Market building, with its smells of glue and the canvas they use for binding covers. (Ellen is borrowing *Jude the Obscure*, to reread.)

In mid-afternoon they reach their final destination: the posh Town Hall concert room, shining with polished wood. Arriving early, they bag good seats at the side, with a view of the immense organ. They pretend they are somewhere in Europe. On the continent.

All stand for the Alleluia and sing along. With Ronnie's clear, clean voice beside her and the organ thumping away, Ellen is filled with grand, Christmasy excitement. *King* of Kings, and *Lord* of Lords.

ON CHRISTMAS EVE, the family has a picnic tea at Neilsen Park, on the harbour. Everyone goes — the twins, their mother Rose, Bridie, and Grandpa Gus.

The girls swim behind the new shark-proof fence. (In the morning, before dawn, sharks come and nibble human-sized holes in it.) Grandpa Gus gazes out in silence at the heads, at the quarantine station, at wind-worn honey myrtles and tea trees.

He stares at the water.

"It's as if he wants to get in," Ellen says.

"Everything happens in his mind," says Bridie. "After a certain age that's where you live; you'll see."

Jones-the-Scottie barks at gulls, then finds something stinky to roll in.

It's almost dark, but their mother lets the twins go rowing, out in a borrowed boat. Ellen fits the oars in the rowlocks, pushes off from shore. The water is smooth; the oars dip softly, they break the water: light then dark, light then dark.

Ronnie skims her hand in the water. "I see a voyage by sea," she says in a silly voice.

"We could row anywhere, you and I," says Ellen. "Where to? Up the Amazon? The Nile? White or Blue?"

Tonight the harbour is still and sleek. The warm air from the land drifts out like smoke.

"The water's purring," says Ronnie.

"Don't you love it?"

"Couldn't you stay out here forever?"

Farther along the beach, some other families — they must be rich, they have brought their phonograph — are entertaining themselves with trite, good-natured music.

Ellen feathers the oars.

Tea for two and two for tea
Me for you and you for me

"Spare us," says Ellen

"The pair of us," says Ronnie.

ON CHRISTMAS DAY, after the hectic dazzle of the morning and church, after the procession of heavy food, Gus, bony and white-blue, sits in the armchair and talks, as if to himself. On the wicker table beside him is a glass and a large brown bottle of dinner ale with a blue flag on its label. Jones snores at his feet.

Ellen is sitting at the piano. The others have gone upstairs for a lie down.

Gus speaks in a voice that in recent weeks has become watery. Today it is filled with a furtive urgency that compels attention but does not invite response. "No trouble with the blackfellas," he says. "Never any reason to investigate. No reason whatsoever. The blacks were humanely treated, nobody meant any harm. Father even knew a few words in blackfella language."

At this point Gus stops. He looks around, baffled. What is he doing here if he is really back there? "Father," he repeats, trying again.

He has come back to a complex passage, Ellen realizes, and is trying to get it right. She is not surprised when he falls silent.

Ellen's been playing the second movement again. Maybe if I don't push so hard, she tells herself, it will get better. She's opened the French doors from the dining room to the verandah. The corrugated iron of the verandah roof cracks in the heat.

"Thought it was a bird at first," confides Gus. He's at it again. But slowly this time, more relaxed, wanting her to ask. "Turkey gobbler. In the tree."

"What was it, Grandpa?"

"In his Sunday suit."

"Who was in his suit?"

"Turkey gobbler up the tree. That's what I thought. He was wearing his suit."

"Who was wearing a suit?"

"It'd rained in the night, but the sun was climbing up; it was a summer's day. His suit was beginning to steam."

"Where was this, Grandpa? What are you talking about?"

"In the yellow box gum. Big tree, brownish trunk, grey-blue leaves. Only bit that's yellow is the timber. His freshly polished shoes. That's what I noticed. How shiny his shoes looked. Hanging there."

"Who was hanging there?"

"Our house on south hill. Nice place, one of the first, local blue brick. Big verandah."

The house on south hill. On the tablelands, in Armidale, where Grandpa Gus grew up. But surely not. Grandpa Gus is raving, he must be.

"Father," he says, in a baffled voice. "When I came closer I saw it was Father."

AT THE BEACH A WEEK LATER, Ronnie and Ellen are taken in a rip.

The moment before it happened, they were ducking under waves then rearing up, pretending to be monsters. Fooling around.

The surprise of being lifted and sucked into the current, the beach receding and the rip not stopping — surely it will run out of strength, but no, the rip ploughs straight out and out, carrying Ronnie, helpless. Ellen, in the rip's tug, is battling and kicking to escape it, and watching Ronnie being carried away, going under. Ellen is plunging again, pushing, pushing against the weight of the surge, trying to get to Ronnie, grabbing her, holding her, down into the heavy darkness, breath swallowed up in the wildness of kicking.

Ellen hits the air, unbelieving. One arm holding Ronnie, the other arm straight up, the distress signal. Way back on the beach, tiny figures of lifesavers are running with the reel; two of them are hurtling into the waves, diving under and beginning to swim. The rest stand on the wet sand, reeling out rope, one to the other, arms above their heads.

Ellen keeps hanging onto Ronnie, whose eyes are clamped shut in panic. The sounds are distant yellow ribbons, flashing. Ronnie is dragging at her, the sinking weight of Ronnie is taking her back under, to blank, bursting seconds beyond recall.

The lifesavers have reached them, secured Ronnie, and are guiding Ellen out of the rip. Ronnie is carried up the beach. The life-savers are concentrating on her, shouting to one another.

Ellen finds the sandy bottom with her feet, totters through the ankle-deep surf, collapses into the shallows, and is helped out onto dry sand. She puts her head down between her knees. Somebody has retrieved her towel, draped it over her shoulders. Beside her, Ronnie lies on the sand, curled up, heaving. (Back at the clubhouse, arrangements are being made to take them home in a car.)

Already the lifesavers have drawn back, putting distance between now and what happened out there in the surf. They've dropped their aroused, hard-voiced commands. They're speaking politely, like men who know they've discharged a duty and are now busy being modest.

The crowd, taking its cue, has begun to look away, to ignore the girls.

The life of the beach resumes.

AT HOME ON OCEAN STREET, in the dim afternoon light (the blinds are down), terse words come and go, come and go, quick quick slow, quick quick slow.

A heat wave is upon the city. Bridie has made great batches of lemonade with extra-strong lemon essence.

Ronnie sits on the verandah steps, which are deep in shade. She's fresh from a bath. Her thin cotton summer dressing gown is sticking to her back.

Ellen's just come out from practising.

Bridie is also sitting on the verandah steps. (Too stinking hot in the kitchen.) She's scooping out passionfruit for jam, putting the orange-yellow pulp and its dense black seeds in a white kitchen bowl. Bridie picks the passionfruit from the vine along the back fence by the abandoned outhouse, where it grows with the aplomb of weeds. The smell of the fruit in the bowl is sharp, flowery-rotten.

Ronnie explains that it was the hand of God that reached down into the blackness. Immediately, Ronnie claims, she knew He was bringing her back because He had chosen her for Himself.

"That was me," points out Ellen. "That wasn't God, that was me. *I'm* the one who grabbed you." (But why should she have been the one strong enough to hold her own in the rip?)

Ronnie smiles, unconcerned. "Of course it was you," she says. Her face has taken on a remote, closed-off look.

"Give it time," says Bridie cautiously. "You never know. Things may look different in a little while."

Small brown ants are gathering at the bowl of passionfruit. Bridie goes to the kitchen for a tea towel to cover it.

In the silence, currawongs slide down the corrugated iron of the verandah roof. Their toes make a disturbing scritching noise.

THE SCHOOL YEAR BEGINS. By Easter, Ellen tells herself, Ronnie will admit it was just the shock of being carried out to sea, of nearly drowning. But already there have been conversations at the convent from which Ellen is excluded. Solemn sentences are spoken, filling

Ronnie's face with power and uncertainty.

Easter comes, the May holidays, the winter retreat. The nuns rejoice. Veronica McGinty has received a vocation.

"Don't mind the nuns," Bridie comforts Ellen. "Nothing but a bunch of toothless tabbies."

"Raging lions is more like it. Going about seeking whom they may devour."

The two of them are having toast in the kitchen. Ronnie's off at early Mass.

"It's Ronnie I mind," says Ellen.

"Just bide your time. Young girls often get carried away with these things," Bridie says. "She'll come round."

"Do you think so?"

"Fingers crossed she doesn't end up a lily on the dustbin."

And yet, almost right away, it has all been arranged. The twins will finish the year, sit for the leaving certificate. As soon as that's done, even before the summer holidays, Ronnie will enter the convent.

ONE SATURDAY MORNING, Ronnie is sitting at the dressing table brushing her hair, holding it up to the window's light, studying it in the mirror.

She suggests they go to the beach.

Ellen's surprised, although she's been waiting for this. Biding her time. Wanting to go to the beach is a good sign, surely. "Your hair's just going to get all wet in a swimming cap," she says, acting calm and neutral.

"I wonder what it's like," asks Ronnie, speaking to Ellen's reflection in the mirror, "to have all your hair chopped off."

Ellen looks back at Ronnie's image, then at her own. There have been times when she's looked in the mirror and mistaken herself for Ronnie. Even though they're not identical, they are very much alike.

If only something would happen to shift the momentum. Not a shooting, like in *Far from the Madding Crowd*; that would be too much to hope for — this was Sydney. But something.

Because Ronnie hadn't really meant it; she'd just said it out loud, and that seemed to make it true. Now she's having to go along with it, repeating the nuns' words about having a vocation.

Ellen recognizes Ronnie's face in the mirror — half afraid, half eager. She's trying to fit herself into the idea. Not sure, not sure at all.

They catch the tram and Ronnie says it's all right, she isn't afraid of the surf any more. But instead of running into the waves, they stand in the shallows. The tide hisses at their ankles, sucks away the sand they're standing on.

"I'll always be with you," Ronnie says to Ellen. "We'll never be apart, not in any essential way."

Ellen won't answer. (What's essential? Passionfruit in the kitchen bowl? Grandpa Gus rabbiting on?)

"For a long time," says Ronnie, "it's been there, just beneath the surface, waiting to explode."

"You *won't* always be with me," Ellen says. "You'll *never* be with me. That's the whole point."

Ronnie stares at the horizon. Ocean all the way to heaven.

"You'll never once come out. We won't talk except on a rare visiting Sunday. And you'll be hidden away in a ghastly habit. I won't be able to see your face properly. How will I even know it's you?"

Ellen is gathering steam now, unable to stop, although she knows she should. "What I don't get, is how you can be born on the same day, sleep in the same room, share everything, even your looks. Then up and leave."

"The nuns say it's like falling in love," says Ronnie softly, embarrassed. "Only infinitely more so."

Ronnie's first sweetheart turns out to be none other than Jesus Christ. *Wham.* That's just great, that is.

"And what might you know about falling in love?"

"I've no choice," says Ronnie. "I've been given a vocation. God's taken over now."

"Taken is right," says Ellen, plunging into the waves, refusing to look back.

Ronnie stays in the shallows, mild and defiant.

"I should have left you out there," Ellen turns and shouts above the breakers. "Should have left you to drown."

ELLEN'S MUSIC EXAM IS COMING. If she is to have any hope of getting to the Con — the Conservatorium of Music — the nuns say she has to come through with flying colours.

Not that it will matter. Ronnie will be locked up by then, for the term of her natural life. A high brick wall, an iron gate closing, *clank*. Go ahead then. Go bury yourself alive. *Clank clank clank.*

Ellen knows what will happen. Ronnie will go through with it. As for her, she'll never get this music to work. Not if Grandpa Gus keeps interrupting.

Gus is in what Bridie calls his garrulous phase. Demanding, full of words. Ellen is forced to stop practising and listen.

"That business at Ramornie Run," Gus says, lower lip beginning to tremble. "The blacks were in a camp with the river behind them; their bodies floated in the river to the settlement near the coast.

"It wasn't in Father's district," he insists. "Not his district. Just there to investigate."

"It was a such a long time ago. You shouldn't upset yourself so."

"Father," Gus whispers, with slow emphasis. "Father hanged himself in the yellow box gum." He sits back, exhausted, relieved. There. He's done it now.

Ellen begins to play.

His father hanged himself from a tree in the front yard. Gus, a child, walked over, looked up into the tree. The Aboriginals were in a camp somewhere up the coast. Caught in front of the river when the men came for them. Was Gus's father a member of the group, or the leader of the group? (And does that make a difference?) Everyone in the camp knew they were caught, cornered.

What did they do to them? Drown them? How many? Men, women,

children? All? She does not ask because she knows he cannot answer. *Why?*

This time she almost finds what she's after, in the twice-repeated melody, in the broken chords, in the short, quiet ending.

THE DAY BEFORE RONNIE ENTERS the convent, the whole family goes by ferry for a picnic at Balmoral, on the other side of the harbour. Bridie is up early, making sandwiches — one half roast beef, the other curried egg. Batches of Anzac biscuits are cooling on the table. Her fruitcake tins are full and ready to go.

"Oceans of food," says Ellen. "Are you planning on feeding an army?"

"As a matter of fact, my girl, I am. What do you bet your mother is planning on taking along some of her hard cases."

Bridie's right, of course. Once they're on the north shore, Mother will be thinking of nothing but her hard cases, her wounded diggers.

And sure enough, the arrangements turn out to include a separate car for men from the hospital.

"Wouldn't be a proper outing," mutters Ellen to Bridie, "without Mother's lot hawking their guts out."

"Mustard gas," replies Bridie, changing sides, "was nothing to sneeze at. An entire division gassed at the Western Front, lots of Sydney boys."

At the picnic spot, Ronnie and Ellen walk up into the bush. What seems at first to be uniform olive isn't drab at all, close up. Pink sprengelia, pale boronias, small myrtle wattles, orange pea flowers. "Easy to miss," says Ronnie. She's pleased with them, these little plants, pleased with them for hiding away in the bush, for being complicated and intricate and lovely without anyone's knowing they even exist.

The family sets up their tablecloth and blanket at the Edwards Beach end. This is a harbour beach, a swimming beach, no surf in sight. At its far tip are makeshift camps — tents with blackened billies out front, a few upturned rowboats. Behind the tents are scrappy shelters of corrugated iron and chaff bags. Jones-the-Scottie rushes over, stiff with excitement.

Men come out of the shelters, sit on their haunches, and invite Jones to shake a paw. The hard cases begin to drift across to join them.

Bridie, heaving with vindication, piles plates high with sandwiches, biscuits, and fruitcake. She carries them over to the camp. Ronnie insists on helping.

Ellen lies on the sand, wriggles her toes, brings them up, watches the grains scatter. Closes her eyes.

What happened, that day on Bondi Beach, was this: the rip carried them out; Ronnie went under. She swam over, grabbed Ronnie, put her across her shoulder. Carrying her like that, she kicked out of the rip. It happened so quickly. One moment she was fighting the current with the dead weight of Ronnie on her; next moment they were in calm water. The two of them, bobbing up and down, out far beyond the breakers. That's where they are now. Everything has gone completely calm and clear. They aren't afraid of sharks, don't even think of them. The ocean holds them up, effortless. All they have to do is move their feet in simple accompaniment, treading water. The land is way back there somewhere. Doesn't matter any more. Nothing to worry about, out in the sweet, deep Pacific.

Jones barks.

"Ellen," her mother says, "Ellen, lend a hand. Make yourself useful."

The music exams are coming; she'll get her letters but not with flying colours. (She'll never make it to the Con.)

When she practises, Grandpa Gus continues to worry away at his story. What was she supposed to do with *that*? Why should you feel guilty about something just because you heard about it, years later? When they ate of the tree of knowledge, what they tasted was guilt. There has to be something wrong about that. There has to be. She'll talk to Ronnie about it.

But this time tomorrow Ronnie will be in the convent. *Clang.*

Ellen stands up. Ignores the picnic preparations. "I'm going for a swim." She wades into the water, feeling its push against her thighs. Dives, surfaces, lies on her back and begins to kick as hard as she can. Tossing the water up into the bright blue air.

$\mathcal{B}$ARE $\mathcal{W}$ET $\mathcal{F}$EET

On the boat from Italy, Sister Tarcisius is travelling with a nun she does not know; some young thing fresh from the mother house. At night, squeals of merriment from the other passengers float down to the cabin. The band plays the latest tunes of the mid-'30s, especially "Begin the Beguine." They amount to no distraction whatsoever. (Although Tarcisius does puzzle, briefly, over what a beguine might be, when begun.)

Her two years incomplete, Sister Tarcisius is being sent home to Sydney in disgrace.

During the day, they walk back and forth on the deck, carefully keeping custody of the eyes. This is how nuns exercise: one of them is always walking backwards. It reminds Tarcisius of a small machine on a pulley, capable of only this one, repetitive movement.

Keeping custody of the eyes means she does not look up at the billowing mountains of clouds amassed on the horizon.

She sees them, nonetheless.

IN HER ORDER, two of the nuns are sent each year to Italy: one to Rome, the other to Florence. In Italy they are to imbibe "the odour of sanctity." When they get back to Sydney, what they have received is supposed to rub off on the convent girls, graziers' children down from the bush, where the country still rides on the sheep's back.

The sheep pay for all of this; it doesn't come cheap.

At the convent in Rome, Sister Tarcisius is assigned to Sister Damasus. Sister Damasus accompanies her whenever she goes out to visit churches and pray. Sister Damasus comes from England, but her father's brother is a solicitor in Sydney. She'd been Gwen MacIlwaine in the world. The only child of a C of E vicar, but she'd converted.

"Caused one hell of a stink," Damasus says, risking blasphemy.

When they enter, nuns are supposed to forget about their families in the world. None of them does.

"My sister's name is Ellen," Tarcisius plans to tell Damasus. In the brief time allowed for personal conversation, Tarcisius will tell Damasus about her family back home:

I am the younger by ten minutes. We are twins, but not identical. Ellen married, quite suddenly, the year I entered. We'd barely finished school; I was still a postulant. An older man; he'd been wounded in the Great War, in France. Mother wrote, "Your sister Ellen, in an entirely successful effort to annoy, has insisted upon an engagement." When Ellen married, she moved to the country. In Australia we call the country "the bush." Ellen lives in the bush. She has one daughter, Alice.

Damasus will repeat these things carefully, *en français*. While she is soaking things up in Rome, Tarcisius is also to improve her French by speaking it with an Englishwoman.

SISTER TARCISIUS FEELS right away as though she belongs; in Rome, a nun is never a tourist.

Here on the other side of the world, the life of prayer is triumphantly the same. From the time the bell rings at five to five in the morning, breaking Great Silence, all the way through to the final peace of compline, identical prayers unfold the day.

The daily chant of the office is for her a core of tenderness. The community gathers in the chapel. Individually they breathe in prayer, but when they breathe out, it becomes a single song. "My spirit is sweet above honey," the song says. "Thou art the God of my heart." Every day, these words float up through the roof, into the sky, heading straight for heaven.

Sister Tarcisius does not often think about her body. She knows her breasts are warm in a way that is quite different from the warmth of her belly or her arms or legs. As for the rest, it is a country she does not visit. The comings and goings of her own blood do not arouse much interest. They simply do not compare.

Ubi caritas et amor, Deus ibi est. Caritas and amor. Who wouldn't want that? The whole shooting match. Sister Tarcisius wants it. She wants it with her heart and her flesh, *caro mea et cor meum.*

She would do anything for that.

SISTER DAMASUS AND SISTER TARCISIUS are making their way through the streets of the Holy City. With her long rosary beads sliding about in the folds of her habit, her crucifix stuck neatly into her cincture, Sister Tarcisius understands, as if for the first time, that "catholic" means universal, and that Rome is another word for home.

Two days a week, they take lessons in violin from the Benedictine nuns. While Sister Damasus is having her lesson, Sister Tarcisius slips into the oratory next door and prays. When it's her turn for the lesson, Sister Damasus has time for her own prayers. The oratory is small and private, with a sparse, dignified Romanesque chancel.

Today, after their lessons, they're off to the catacombs of Saint Callistus.

"The dead were laid out on shelves," Sister Damasus says. "No coffins. They were wrapped in two shrouds, with a coating of lime in between."

Sister Damasus is edified by these ancient deaths, the continuity of faith. The dark, the smell of dust, the candles: all of these are the outward and visible signs of the greater truth. Sister Damasus speaks of assignations in the catacombs, covert alliances between rulers and ruled, the swift, dangerous exchange of passwords, the constant risk of discovery, the marvellously awful deaths.

"On the Feast of All Souls, at matins," Sister Damasus says, "we go down into the catacombs with candles and sing a Te Deum in their praise."

By the fourth century, Damasus explains, when St. Jerome was a boy, the catacombs of Saint Callistus had already become a place of pilgrimage. The catacombs are sacred to St. Jerome, who quoted Virgil: "The very silence fills the soul with dread."

Sister Tarcisius doesn't like the catacombs either, finds them grim and claustrophobic. "They give me the creeps," she admits. If a saint could say he was frightened, she can, too. She's relieved when they are in the fresh air again, up among the cypresses and weary flowers.

"The blood of the martyrs is the seed of the Church," Sister Damasus reminds her.

"Yes, Sister."

Sister Damasus has that kind of cheery English vigour people think of as horsy. (It seems very C of E to Sister Tarcisius.) She also has the convert's zeal, a vast enthusiasm for all things Roman, both spiritual and secular.

The long and tangled building history of the many churches is one of Damasus's specialties. In Santo Stefano Retondo, Sister Damasus points proudly to the instructive martyrs' frescoes numbered alphabetically. Exhibit A is *S. Margarita virgo*, a sturdy woman being stretched on the rack. At the same time she is being lacerated *in toto corpore* by a nasty device like a pitchfork but with only one prong.

"Most edifying," says Sister Tarcisius.

For a moment Damasus looks taken aback.

She introduces Sister Tarcisius to the details — all for the greater glory of God — that one could so easily miss. She points out the carved bees swarming over the high altar in St. Peter's. She's familiar with dark chapels in obscure places; knows where to find, behind an altar, a door or dusty curtain, a particular tomb crowded with classical garlands and lizards. And knows, in the gloom, exactly where to locate the light switch.

Damasus recites the English poem that likens God to a hound. "I fled Him, down the nights and down the days," Damasus proclaims in her best elocution voice. "I fled Him, down the arches of the years."

Sister Tarcisius can see pink-cheeked Damasus running along a tree-lined English lane, fleeing him down the days, fully immersed in the healthy pleasure of exercise, while looking forward to the certainty of the outcome: the happy, puffed-out surrender.

Sister Tarcisius does not find the hound an apposite image. On the contrary, God, she believes, is the elusive one. Sometimes in her prayers she feels as though she has entered a street He has just left. Saw her coming and slipped away. He's just around the next corner, she can tell.

On she goes, turns the bend.

Gone again.

SISTER DAMASUS SPEAKS of the real Tarcisius. Tarcisius was a young man killed on the streets of Rome, back in the third or fourth century. (In the life of Holy Mother Church, what's a century more or less?) He was carrying a consecrated host, sneaking it to some fellow Christians in prison. Intercepted by bystanders.

"He did his best to protect the host, but they killed him, right there in the street."

"I wonder if Saint Tarcisius is tucked away in the catacombs somewhere?"

"It isn't known," Sister Damasus says.

Sister Damasus has written a monograph on the early Roman martyrs. There's a copy in the Vatican library. Even though Sister

Damasus's vicar father was Low Church, she herself seems a bit of a toff. Quoting Virgil, for Pete's sake.

Sister Tarcisius has to quash uncharitable thoughts.

"They would have beaten Saint Tarcisius to a bloody pulp," Sister Damasus says, decisively.

But pulp could be stored in a catacomb, surely. For relics, later.

What had he done, the young Tarcisius, to arouse the suspicion of the hostile men on the street? Was it his nervousness that gave him away? At what point did he realize that they were on to him, that he was in real trouble?

There are times when Sister Tarcisius prays for her saint as well as to him.

She didn't choose his name of course; it was given to her. You haven't a clue what your name's going to be until you're in the middle of the ceremony in the chapel, making your vows. She'd heard the name, Tarcisius, and immediately found *young, a martyr, from Rome.* A sharp, brief image of a frightened face. I will come to know you, she'd thought.

Sister Tarcisius's name in the world was Veronica, who shows up at the sixth station of the cross. When Christ was carrying the cross along the Via Dolorosa on his way up to Calvary, Veronica pushed through the crowd and, with a towel the size of a nappy, wiped his face. Christ, who even then was busy thinking of others, left the imprint of his face on the towel as a thank-you.

Tarcisius and Veronica: two acts of courage, probably both impulsive.

SISTER DAMASUS AND SISTER TARCISIUS are at a church off the Via di S. Teodoro. They're going up the steps on their knees, praying on each one.

"Body of Christ, save me," says Sister Damasus.

"Blood of Christ, inebriate me," Sister Tarcisius replies.

Up they go — it's a long flight of steps. In Rome, one is always going up steps.

They're at the top, finally. But instead of standing, Damasus turns to Tarcisius and tells her this: in the middle of the last century, a friar at this church found he had the gift of being able to predict lottery winners. Word got round and pretty soon the church was packed every Sunday. The Pope put his foot down and the friar was dispatched to the countryside. Before he went, however, he managed to give one last sermon that included the numbers for the next week's draw.

Both nuns have their heads bowed; they're still on their knees. Sister Tarcisius whispers to Sister Damasus that she has described the perfect patron saint for Australia. Then she can't help it; neither can Damasus.

To an outsider they'd appear to be overcome by prayer.

They are laughing the silent laughter of nuns.

THE ENGLISH VICAR COMES TO VISIT his daughter, Damasus. He looks uneasily about the parlour, as if he's found himself in a house of infectious diseases. Possibly worse.

Sister Tarcisius sits discreetly off to one side. Nuns are not allowed to be alone with visitors, including — in this case, especially — members of their family.

The vicar tucks into the sweet wine. Dunks in the little cakes and after a while cheers up. Looking over towards Sister Tarcisius, he mentions his brother out in Sydney, in Watson's Bay. "Don't happen to know the MacIlwaine family, do you?" he asks. "Henry MacIlwaine's my brother. Four children: Matthew, Mark, Luke, and Dora. Had been hoping for the set but the girl messed it up."

The vicar laughs a polite hand-shaking laugh, not all that interested in what he's saying.

Sister Tarcisius keeps her head lowered (custody of the eyes) but quickly shakes her head to signal no, she's never met the MacIlwaine family, Watson's Bay branch. (What were Proddies doing with an Irish name like that?) She remembers Watson's Bay houses riding above the ocean, federation-style houses that are all orange-tiled roof. The vicar probably thinks that going to Sydney is coming down in the world. And now this. His daughter, a nun. Whatever has he done to deserve *this*?

His daughter does not eat with him. Nuns do not eat with seculars; that would be breaking cloister.

Sister Tarcisius is surprised that he drinks the wine, because Sister Damasus has said he's Low Church, very low. This means he understands nothing of candles, incense, flowers, music, saints, miracles. Sister Tarcisius allows herself to wonder what a Low-Churchman would make of the best wine at Cana, right at the end when the guests would have been soused, or of the sudden provision of loaves and fishes, bog in, don't wait.

Forty days in the desert, now that would be more like it.

While father and daughter talk, Sister Tarcisius is reading St. Augustine. Augustine's out in the desert on a retreat with his mother; they've both converted. "The flame of love burned in us," Augustine wrote, "and raised us towards the eternal. We spoke of the eternal, longing for it and straining for it with all our hearts. And once, for one fleeting instant, we reached out and touched it. After we'd reached out, we sank back, with a sigh. We returned to the sound of our own speech, where each word has a beginning and an end."

Sister Tarcisius is reading this and the voice inside her, the one that distracts her, says she'd love to have that happen to her, with her sister Ellen.

With Sister Damasus? Maybe.

Very occasionally during the singing of the office, Sister Tarcisius feels that she is plucked up, set aloft over the Holy City, looking down at the cold, wet streets. (People don't tell you how it rains in Rome once summer has gone.) She can identify some of the places: the dome of St. Peter's, of course, the Spanish Steps, the Appian Way. For the most part, though, she travels above streets she does not recognize at all: holy streets, all of them, of that she has no doubt. What is less clear to her is why she should be seeing them so precisely — the wet slick on the roads — and why these streets should be so consistently deserted.

She prays to understand through His mercy, through His loving-kindness. These are the exact same streets the martyrs walked, old St. Peter at the tail end of his days, and the young Tarcisius.

She's sifting her way through these thoughts when the father of Sister Damasus leans towards his daughter and says emphatically, "That bounder in the Palazzo di Venezia, he'll get his comeuppance one day, you mark my words." He taps the table with his right middle finger, to make sure his daughter is paying attention.

Sister Damasus says nothing.

Sister Tarcisius can see his finger tensed against the table. He turns, looks at her again. "The Vatican has a lot to answer for," he says in an even louder voice. His hostility at this moment is directed entirely towards her, Sister Tarcisius. She's startled. And amused at his equation of her with the Holy See.

The conversation between Sister Damasus and the vicar moves to the vicarage vegetable garden, its prize marrows. "They're growing so much bigger now Mother has passed on," the vicar says.

THEY'RE OUT ON THE STREET AGAIN, this time in the wide Lateran Square. It's raining, and Sister Damasus has a big green umbrella to cover them both. As Tarcisius lifts her eyes up to the coloured wet canvas, she experiences a frisson of secular excitement. Surely here, of all places, you'd think they'd have nothing but a steady supply of black.

They are on their way to the Basilica of San Giovanni. As they walk along, they're praying together. The Litany of Loreto.

"Virgin most prudent," Damasus says.

"Pray for us," they both respond.

"Virgin most venerable," Tarcisius says.

"Virgin most renowned."

On it goes, soothing, predictable, assured.

Tarcisius reaches the basilica and enters it with Sister Damasus. She can see the burning lamp at the sacrament altar, its familiar red throb in the gloom.

Almost as soon as they kneel down, they are made aware that today is unlike other days. Outside there is marching and shouting. They are forced to raise their voices to avoid being distracted from their prayers. "O Precious Blood, stream across my heart and wash away from it every stain of sin," they pray.

"DOOCHAY, DOOCHAY," the crowd shouts.

They have to stay inside the church for a long time, until the shouting has died away.

Going home, they encounter more crowds: young men, students by the look of them, roaming about in groups, exuberant and wild. These young men begin to sing something. A bold, loud song to urge themselves on. The two nuns are forced to turn into an alley and stand in a doorway as the men march by. Neither looks, but each can hear, at the end of the alley, a scuffle underway.

A crowd of men has gathered around something on the ground.

Sister Tarcisius reaches automatically for her beads. Blood is pounding through her head; she feels a trapped, animal fear.

It's a man. She knows because he cries out something. The other men are kicking him. His cry is something defiant, she can tell by the tone. She hears the grunts the man on the ground makes, then stops making.

The two nuns speed to the convent gate. The moment they're inside, they shut it and fall to their knees. They begin a special prayer — for the man on the ground, for those who were above him, for the noisy, eager students, for all the day's disturbing cacophony.

"Jesus, strength of martyrs," says Sister Damasus, gasping for breath.

"Have mercy on us," Sister Tarcisius replies. Her thighs are shaking; her knees barely hold her up.

"Through Thy cross and dereliction."

"Jesus deliver us," Sister Tarcisius answers, gathering strength.

"Through Thy faintness and weariness."

"Jesus deliver us."

In such a situation, others might embrace.

IN HER CELL AT NIGHT, in Great Silence, Sister Tarcisius finds that she is replaying her visit to the basilica: the rain, sharing the green umbrella, Damasus's white hand on the umbrella's wooden handle, the shouting outside the church, the students going by singing, their having to wait until things died down before they set out; then, on their way back to the convent, the men at the end of the street, the kicking.

A few days later, when they are off to their music lesson, she brings this up with Sister Damasus: "What were they singing, those young men on the street?"

"They were singing about making a brush of the emperor's beard. To polish the Duce's shoes."

"The man who was down, he called out something." He was grunting in pain as they kicked him, and then he cried out in defiance. That is how it would have been with Saint Tarcisius, surely.

"I heard it," replies Sister Damasus. "But I couldn't catch it."

All the while, the boots had been making a thick, blunt, solid sound on his body. The men who were kicking also grunted. She heard that as well.

At chapter of faults, Sister Tarcisius confesses that too often she has allowed herself to be distracted by curiosity. She asks Reverend Mother for a penance.

TRUCKS WITH LOUDSPEAKERS PROWL the streets, playing stirring music. "Giovinezza" and "Marcia Reale." Sister Damasus knows the names.

One evening, early in October, pealing church bells and sirens mix with the music. As she listens, Sister Tarcisius smells the change in the season. It's easy at this particular moment to imagine a stepping forth of vigorous young men. Now Italian families will have more land; they will be as fruitful as the vines around their table. Caught up in the fervour, Sister Tarcisius prays, "This is the day that the Lord has made, let us rejoice and be glad in it." A morning prayer, but exactly right for the occasion.

Sister Tarcisius has seen Italian families: bringing noise and easy laughter, they come to the convent on occasional feast day afternoons, to visit daughters who have entered. Huge mobs of families they are, the big boys helping with the youngest, the babies.

The vicar arrives for another visit. "You know what they've gone and done, don't you?" he promptly accuses Damasus. "They" turns out to be the Italians, who have marched into Ethiopia. "Sneaked across the muddy Mareb River," says the vicar, who must know that Damasus wouldn't have looked at an atlas or a newspaper in years. "Despite the Ethiopian emperor's eloquent appeal to the League of Nations" — the vicar says, gathering steam — "despite the League embargo, the sordid slaughter continues."

The vicar's face has grown red with conviction. In the convent parlour it seems wildly misplaced. "Butchery," he spits. "Them and their *mare nostrum*, their pathetic Mediterranean empire. Bunch of jumped-up thugs yelling, To us, to us! The League has got to show them what's what, once and for all."

"We must pray for them, Father," says Damasus, in a small voice.

"You go ahead and pray," says the vicar, who is winding down into bitterness. "Pray for those who have only stones to throw at airplanes. Pray for the wounded eaten alive by carrion birds."

Damasus says nothing.

"They have pretty big birds in Africa," adds the vicar, in a more conversational voice. "Ten-foot wing spans. An ornithologist's paradise."

ON THEIR MUSIC DAY, when Sister Damasus has her lesson first, Sister Tarcisius goes into the oratory. The streets seethe with military traffic. In recent weeks this has come to seem normal.

Near the Lady altar, a man is lying under a pew. He is bleeding badly from his head, and moaning. His leg, too, is bleeding. The blood has soaked his trousers. He looks up, and although he is dazed, Sister Tarcisius notices that he keeps trying to look beyond her, to see who might be coming.

He shudders.

Even in this quiet place, she can hear marching in the streets, lorries going by, shouts.

He has crawled into the church for sanctuary. He is a man in trouble, in hiding.

YEARS LATER, WHEN SHE SPEAKS of this day to her twin sister, Ellen, this is what she says she did:

I took the holy water font out of its stone holder by the door. Then I reached up under my skirts and began to tear at my shift — a long plain garment we wear beneath our habit. You couldn't call it a petticoat; the word is far too decorative.

When I saw him huddled and hurt, how could I not think of Christ stumbling along the Via Dolorosa? Of Saint Tarcisius beaten in the street?

I soaked strips of the shift in the holy water. With that, I washed his head. Thick brown hair. Then I tore off more of my shift and bound his head. Although I had never done anything like this before, I found that I knew perfectly how to clean a deep head wound, how to bandage it. I knew how to take care of him; I had no training, but God assisted me; I understood what to do, completely.

I think he must have been barely conscious by this time.

Then I had to remove his trousers and clean and bandage his leg.

All this time I was praying to the Sacred Heart: *O immense passion, O profound wounds. O profusion of blood. O sweetness above all sweetness, I open my soul to you.*

The man was breathing, "Orte, Orte." A small mouth, very pale, startlingly delicate lips.

69

Although I did not know the word, I understood what he was saying. He had to get there, to Orte, wherever it was. *It is his home,* I thought. He needs to make his way home, to hide among family, to be sheltered by friends. If somebody comes asking, Do you know where he is? they will say, He is not here. He went away. Years ago. We have not heard from him.

When I'd finished, and both his head and leg were bound, he became really much better than anyone could have expected. The grace of God had worked through me, you see.

There were sirens, the sound of heavy boots, running. Militiamen, policemen, soldiers. That was when I realized that in order to get him out of there I was going to have to give him my clothes.

I took off my habit and showed him how to put it on. He looked horrified — not at my emerging body, but at the notion of putting on these garments himself. He was tall, and when we had finished, his boots stuck out, male and ridiculous. (I had just replaced the boot on his wounded leg with such care, and him being so brave, biting his lip and sweating and trying not to swear.)

Using motions with my hand, I told him that he'd have to take his boots off, go barefoot. Discalced he was, with big hairy toes.

I saw him leave the church, awkward, but in some ways a passable nun. Waiting for Sister Damasus, I hid behind the altar, with his boots and clothing at my feet. It was not surprising that my torn under-garment, my shift, was drenched with blood.

I had little time to prepare myself for what was coming.

AN AGED DOCTOR VISITS THE CONVENT infirmary to examine Sister Tarcisius, her body. He pushes open her legs. Shines a light down there.

O blood of my saviour, she prays, *I bathe myself in Thy crimson streams. I sink deep down in Thy depths; wash me, wash me; O sacred chalice, strengthen me, save me, pardon me the sins of the past, wash away the sins of the present, the sins I know and those I have forgotten.*

The light is from a black, goose-necked lamp.

The doctor puts something cold in there, pushes it up.

Then the doctor speaks with Reverend Mother. Behind the screen there is tense whispering, in Italian.

SISTER TARCISIUS IS RETURNED to her cell and left there. She is not permitted to leave, not even to chant the office.

When at last she is summoned to Reverend Mother, she explains what happened. "I believe I have been blessed," she says, humbly. "Through His most precious blood."

Reverend Mother warns her to guard against the sins of the flesh, against the sin of deceit, and most of all against the terrible sin of pride. She gives Sister Tarcisius her penance: mortification of the flesh, fasting, and daily use of the "discipline" — a whip made out of small chains about nine inches long; each nun has one.

It is the daily office that Sister Tarcisius misses most: praise, in the mouths around her, in her own mouth, rising whole and rosy and moist.

One week later, she is sent for again. "Blessed with the grace of healing," she again explains to Reverend Mother. "Through His infinite mercy."

"We will speak of this no more," Reverend Mother says sharply.

Sister Tarcisius wonders what Reverend Mother has written to the head of the order back home. Knows better than to ask.

She is to have no contact with any of the other nuns; she is to continue her penance. Once a day, food is placed at her door.

The English-speaking chaplain arrives, the spiritual director. Sister Tarcisius lays bare her soul to him, as she has to Reverend Mother. "Every best gift, every perfect gift," she reminds him, "comes from above."

For a few seconds there it looks as if he might fall off his chair. Recovering himself, he speaks of the sins of the flesh, then of the sin of pride. Of all the seven deadly sins, pride is the most deadly.

"The Samaritan interrupted his journey," she persists. She can see him quite clearly, this Samaritan. He's climbing down off his donkey, cranky; this is going to make him late, people will be down his neck.

The priest promises, in a puzzled and suddenly weary voice, that he will pray for her.

"Thank you, father," she replies.

He gives no blessing.

She is returned to her cell.

At prayer during Great Silence, Sister Tarcisius feels her soul plucked up, taken out of her body and set adrift above the convent. Clearly, she can hear Christ's injunction, "Watch and pray." Obediently, she looks down at the wet streets of the Eternal City. The huge, shadowy lumps of stone that are the churches. The thin strip of solid dark that is the Tiber. The wide, deserted squares.

Something is happening down there: in the silence of a rainy winter night, military lorries are moving in slow, close convoy.

SHORTLY BEFORE SHE IS DUE TO LEAVE on the boat home, Sister Damasus comes to her. During Great Silence.

It is against the order's rule to leave your own cell during Great Silence, against the rule to visit another nun's cell, against the rule to speak. No nun is cynical or casual about the rule; the rule is at the heart of what she desires above all else: her spiritual formation. So when Sister Tarcisius hears a quiet, rapid knocking on the door of her cell, she knows she is opening the door to something dissonant and momentous.

Sister Damasus enters with breathless, pink determination. *I fled Him, down the nights* . . . Sister Tarcisius thinks, briefly. *I fled Him, down the nights and down the days* . . . *I fled him down the labyrinthine ways / Of my own mind.*

"They found him," Damasus whispers, coming straight to the point. "The man at the oratory."

"What?" says Sister Tarcisius, feeling stupid.

"He blew himself up."

72

A man who has been healed by God's grace does not blow himself up. Sister Tarcisius is sure of that.

"An explosion in the Via Panisperna," Sister Damasus says. "They found your habit in his room."

Sister Tarcisius shakes her head.

"The papers were told not to mention this," Sister Damasus says. "But it was in the middle of the city, and of course everyone found out about it right away."

A man who has been healed would have work to do in this world, Sister Tarcisius knows.

"It appears he had been planning to blow up a church. Santa Maria degli Angeli. Something went wrong. There was going to be a Mass, with all the important people from the government there."

"How do they know he was going to do that?"

"They found plans of the church, lots of technical details."

Having offered this, Sister Damasus leaves as urgently as she came.

IT WOULD BE NO MORE THAN A STORY, a conflation of events — but how we hunger for connections, how we infer them, invent them, assert them. What Damasus brought was a rumour that moved swiftly through the streets, joining — as it approached the convent — a nun's habit with the bomb on the Via Panisperna. In other parts of the city, perhaps, joining the bomb with that man in the alley who was down, being kicked.

She closes her eyes to pray for them all: the man in the alley, the man in the oratory, and now this one, the man with the bomb.

She prays to Christ, who was Himself visited by night. He allowed his feet to be washed by Mary Magdalene, then dried with her long red hair.

In the darkness of her cell, in Great Silence, Sister Tarcisius considers the slither of that copious hair over bare wet feet.

$\mathscr{I}$T $\mathscr{C}$OMES OF $\mathscr{I}$TSELF

When Ellen sees the plume of dust down around Sandy Gully, she'll know the truck is coming from Araluen with the prisoners.

Ellen's in the back garden, working. Doesn't wear gloves, doesn't like them. She pushes at her hair with the back of her hand, then leans over and grubs a spud out. Puts it on an old sugarbag, banging it lightly to shake off the soil.

They were supposed to be here around one. Now it's getting on for five and still no sign of them. Four o'clock by the sun, but they'd brought in daylight saving as part of the war effort. Office clock-watchers down in Sydney thought you'd get more work done that way.

She stops again and looks into the distance. Has to put up a dirty hand to shade her eyes against the light.

How much will these Italians know about working on the land? Duffy told her you couldn't count on them being familiar with anything. "Won't know one end of a sheep from the other," Duffy said. "Good blokes, though. Willing to give it a go."

"They have land in Italy," she'd said hopefully. "Somebody's been doing their farming for thousands of years."

She and Duffy have talked it over. It makes sense that the Italian POWs would welcome a chance to work outdoors, away from barbed wire. They'd been captured early in the war, most of them in Libya, in the desert. They have spent years in POW camps, in Egypt, India, and here in Australia.

Last time she went to Araluen, she'd visited the POW control centre and got a free dictionary of English and Italian. A small, thick book with a grey dust jacket. Still, she will not be able to speak their language, nor they hers.

Duffy told her about a prisoner on one of the other properties. They'd asked him to milk the cow, miming the action. Found him two hours later, staggering about the back paddock, picking up boulders. Duffy had been one of Bill's best mates. They'd been in France together, in the war before this one. The Great War, they used to call it. Now, in the middle of the Second World War, they'd changed its name to the First World War, like they were in some kind of series. Duffy had been best man at the wedding. Pallbearer at the funeral. Bill had asked Duffy himself, when, towards the end, after his major stroke, they'd moved the bed out to the verandah so he could stare at the hills: "Will you do the honours?" Duffy said it went without saying, and Bill said, "Ta very much," and Duffy said, "Don't mention it."

"No sooner blown than blasted," Bill said to Duffy then. His speech was slurred but she and Duffy could understand him. The words were from some poem he'd learned by heart at school. (They knew he was speaking of his marriage.)

"There's your kiddy," Duffy offered, hugely embarrassed. "There's Alice."

Their daughter Alice was eight years old when Bill died, with Ellen not yet thirty.

THE TRUCK DOESN'T ARRIVE until after dark.

Duffy stands on the verandah, his hat in his hands.

"We've got only the one," says Duffy. "As it turns out."

"There's supposed to be two."

"I know. Carstairs wanted one more." Carstairs are the local landed gentry. "Six months ago they were saying they wouldn't touch the Eyeties with a bargepole. Now they're screaming for extras. Can't get enough of them. You know how it is, with that lot, up at Merino Mansions."

She thinks of how it would have been if her husband Bill had been alive. When Duffy said, "Now they're screaming for extras," Bill would have grunted in deep agreement: further proof of the fickleness of people, their narrow-minded contrariness.

"Will I go and get the bloke in?" Duffy asks.

IN THE MORNING, she sees the prisoner before he sees her. He is washing his face under the tap at the tank-stand by the shearers' quarters. Wearing his prisoner's uniform. It is an Australian army uniform dyed maroon. Shirt, trousers, socks — all a deep burgundy. What ugly genius came up with that? Ellen wonders. Dressing defeated soldiers in the colour of dried blood.

She'd been expecting two small, dark young men. This one is tall and pale, with thick brown hair. He sluices the water around, then shakes his head like a healthy dog. He'll need some work clothes, she decides. Some singlets and pants. They only had to wear that uniform, Duffy said, when they were off the property.

They were all enlisted men, Duffy told her. Officer types had to stay behind in camp. Might get dirt under their fingernails, and we couldn't have that, could we?

After she goes down to meet him, she'll look through Bill's things in the big wardrobe.

Duffy, who does most of the work around the place, is getting old Pompey saddled up. A calm, reliable horse, Pompey knows how to work and daydream at the same time.

The Italian walks across the yard with quick, precise steps. Nobody in the bush walks like that.

She reaches out and shakes his hand.

Duffy and the dogs stand there.

Pompey, feeling relaxed, turns to get the measure of him. The Italian takes a step backwards.

He isn't used to horses, Ellen thinks. Their frank, intimate eyes.

His hand is much softer than hers. A desk job, she decides. He's never worked on the land, not with hands like that.

The prisoner nods and says something in Italian, something obviously courteous. He holds himself carefully. Keeps his arms tucked neatly into his ribs, declaring his limits. From the way he stands you can feel his confidence, a genuine, bored confidence that isn't bravado. He is much older than she had imagined at first. Must be in his mid-thirties, she thinks. His age makes her anxious, she doesn't know why.

Duffy is pointing things out to him in that slow, easy way he has. (They are alike, Duffy and Pompey.)

"Why don't you bring him up to the house this afternoon." She isn't stuck up; it is important the prisoner know this. "Come and have afternoon tea when you're done. I'll see if some of Bill's old things might fit him."

"Righteo," agrees Duffy.

"Put your foot in this stirrup first," says Duffy to the prisoner, "then get your other leg over." Duffy winks. "Nothing to it." The prisoner nods but doesn't look enthusiastic.

"Look, I'll show yer," Duffy offers.

"He doesn't ride, then," says Ellen, looking up at Duffy astride Pompey. It is a bit rude, talking to Duffy as if the prisoner weren't there.

"No, he doesn't. But give him half a day on Pompey and he'll be right as rain, I reckon."

"What did he do? What did he do for a living?" Ellen asks Duffy, with the prisoner standing beside her.

Duffy brings his hands up and plays them in the air.

"A piano player?" Ellen asks, incredulous. It would be too good to be true.

"No, typing."

"He was a typist?"

"I reckon so. A clerk or something. Counter-jumper, poor bastard."

She turns to the prisoner, who, like Duffy, wriggles his fingers in the air and smiles graciously. An assured smile. A city slicker smile. Olivetti's pitched up on Ardara, she thinks. Just wait till I tell Ronnie.

He has a pronounced pink mouth with a small vee on his top lip like a child's drawing of a bird in the sky. Poor bloke, having lips like that. In the army.

"Pietro," says Duffy. "From Rome."

"Two kids," Duffy adds. "Boys."

She looks at Pietro, who this time gives a small neck bow. "Roma," he says.

Dear Ronnie, she writes that evening. The Italian arrived yesterday. We got only the one because Carstairs pinched the other. His name is Pietro, from Roma.

Peter from Rome. That would make Ronnie laugh. *Pietro* from *Roma* has pitched up on Ardara.

IMPOSSIBLE, ELLEN EXPLAINED to her daughter Alice, when she was old enough for family stories, impossible to grasp in any plausible way the distance between the convent and ordinary life, even though that life was going on, yards away, immediately outside the high brick walls. "Imagine," said Ellen, "what it meant for Ronnie to go to Rome in the 1930s. To have been to Rome."

On the piano at Ardara there was a picture of the pair of them, Ellen and Ronnie, the twins. Ellen and Ronnie are standing together in long skirts, holding tennis racquets and laughing. It was taken when they were in their fourth year of high school, at Star of the Sea, in Sydney.

When the time came for Alice to go away to school, Ellen insisted on Star of the Sea for her, too, even though they couldn't afford it.

At Star of the Sea, part of every girl's education was the story of Sister Tarcisius's trip to Rome. It had been years ago, but you'd think she'd just stepped off the boat.

On Friday afternoon, Sister Tarcisius held a class called Art and Music Appreciation. When she wasn't teaching, Ronnie — Sister Tarcisius — was in charge of the lay sisters, and she supervised the purchases for the convent.

"They have squandered Ronnie's talent," Ellen said. "Treating her like some glorified quartermaster."

At Art and Music Appreciation, Ronnie dictated from a book about the artists of the Italian Renaissance. She read the book out loud and the class copied down the sentences. *Giotto's cloak was always spattered with paint,* Alice wrote at the beginning of the year.

As the term lengthened, Ronnie loosened up. She started in on The Trip. She'd entered St. Peter's, she told them, and had immediately fallen to her knees. In St. Peter's, you could go to confession in all of the world's known languages. (Should the need arise, thought Alice.) Throughout her time in Rome, Ronnie claimed, she had breathed the air the martyrs breathed. (Must be pretty stale by now.)

They moved on. While in Rome, Sister Tarcisius visited the Cerasi chapel. And there she saw the Caravaggios. Because of the way Sister Tarcisius spoke of Caravaggio, Alice for many years believed him to be a saint.

The climactic lesson came when Sister Tarcisius showed the class a book of Caravaggio's work. Two by two, the girls were allowed to file up and look at the page that Sister Tarcisius was holding open on the desk. In this way Ronnie showed Alice the Conversion of St. Paul, the Cerasi version, in Santa Maria del Popolo.

St. Paul has been stunned by immeasurable, surprising light. It has knocked him right off his horse. He's lying on the ground on his back. Young, helpless, completely vulnerable. But bathing in ecstasy: arms up, legs open wide, head thrown back, eyes shut.

"St. Paul himself explains that his eyes were open but he couldn't see," Ronnie said.

"In that case," asked Alice, "why did Caravaggio paint his eyes shut?"

"So that we would understand," Ronnie replied.

The piebald horse is stepping carefully over St. Paul's body. You can see the veins in the horse's muscular legs. There's an old man in the background, getting ready to lead the horse away. For a feed and maybe a rub-down.

Alice pointed to him. "What's his name?"

"He's just the servant. He doesn't have a name."

Alice could hear her father balking at that. Every man was as good as the next. That old man had a name. Why shouldn't we know it?

Legs are everywhere: St. Paul's, the horse's, the old man's.

The light shines on the old man and on the horse as well as on St. Paul, but St. Paul's the only one getting excited about it.

"YOUR FATHER RETURNED from the Great War.

"That single sentence," Ellen told Alice, "provides your father's entire narrative. Your father was not unusual," Ellen added, in an effort to defend. "Not at all."

Alice already realized that. She could remember sitting at the tea table, listening to the way her parents spoke.

"I suppose you know," her father said (he habitually prefaced news with this cagey phrase), "I suppose you know Duffy's going to take us on."

"Duffy? Take us on?"

Alice knew Duffy was a soldier like her father, a digger from the war. He'd been given a soldier-settler block with no topsoil, a useless pile of wind and stones. Whatever they had done to another digger, they had done to her father, as well.

"He'll be a boon about the place," her father said, in his best-behaved, soothing voice. "You know. Help out."

"How on earth do you suppose we can afford to do a thing like that?" Her mother, in futile dissent.

"He's going to knock up a cottage behind the orchard."

"But, Bill," said her mother.

Before, Bill had worked with Paddy, but Paddy had gone walkabout. (Paddy worked for flour, sugar, salt, and tobacco. No money.) Paddy lived down by the river with his family. In the winter he walked to the coast — they all did, all the blackfellas. Came back in the spring with shells in their pockets to prove it. This year Paddy hadn't shown up.

"Looks like Paddy's gone bush," her father said. Her mother pulled a face and said she thought this already *was* bush.

"They gave those soldier-settlers blocks of land to break their hearts on," her father went on, with a familiar, abiding contempt.

They were the government officials with desk jobs. *They* were the ones who sent men off to hell while they sat at home with their feet up in warm dry socks. *They* were the bankers and politicians and squattocracy — all in cahoots. *They* were the same in Sydney, in London, in Berlin, in Paris, in Rome: dishonest, selfish, sycophantic, stupid, and daily more numerous.

Her mother was right. Her father had not been unusual. Throughout the district there were men just like him, like his mate Duffy. Men who shared wounds too deep and private for anyone except each other. Under their beds they kept books and magazines — *All Quiet on the Western Front*, copies of *Smith's Weekly*, well thumbed — the words that fixed them in their own minds as diggers: doomed, stoic battlers. When they were young, they had gone away to war with bright shining eyes. They had thought someone would be grateful.

They sat on the verandah or in the front room and drank and recited. "Mulga Bill's Bicycle" was her father's star turn. In the first verse his voice would be cheerful and swift, keen to reach the pleasures ahead.

Twas Mulga Bill, from Eaglehawk, that caught the cycling craze;
He turned away the good old horse that served him many days;
He dressed himself in cycling clothes, resplendent to be seen;
He hurried off to town and bought a shining new machine;
And as he wheeled it through door, with air of lordly pride,
The grinning shop assistant said, "Excuse me, can you ride?"

The man who recited always stood. Not in front of his chair, it was too serious for that. He stood on the top step of the verandah, facing his audience. If they were indoors, he stretched one arm along the mantelpiece.

The other men listened, hungry for the familiar lines, their faces soft and attentive.

They always saved the best for last — the sad poems:

"He ought to be home," said the old man, "without
*   there's something amiss*
"He only went to the Two Mile — he ought to be back by this."

Too many of these men, her mother said, had properties that were going to rack and ruin. (It was the first time Alice had encountered this phrase, which she heard as Rackenruin, a mysterious and terrible place up the road from the nearest town, Araluen.)

These returned men were no longer capable of the farmer's casual cruelty. They found the cries of animals unbearable. Some went into their sheds and swallowed poison. It was not considered surprising that they needed even more space, more silence, than the bush could provide.

On the verandah, when they spoke with one another of how things had turned out, their words were subdued. But the sound of their talk, the tone and tenor, was like spitting.

ALICE WAS A BOARDER at Star of the Sea when the Second World War broke out. Alice's best friend, Steph, had a brother who lost a leg at

Tobruk, in the desert. On visiting Sundays he sat in the front garden, wearing his uniform with the red hospital tie. Telling jokes, winning hearts. Alice sat next to him because she was Steph's best friend. Assuming that Alice would surely flutter over Steph's brother, the other girls looked on with envy. But Alice wasn't interested in Steph's brother. She already knew about men who came home with war wounds.

What Alice wanted from Steph was what she saw in the faces of the photograph on the piano at Ardara. She wanted what her mother and Ronnie had. (Though maybe you could have that only if you were twins.)

As soon as third term was over, Steph was going to join the WAAFs, who had the best uniforms. Alice wanted to join the WAAFs too, but her mother was adamant. They exchanged quarrelsome letters.

Your father, Ellen wrote, wouldn't have wanted you to get mixed up in any of it.

Besides, Ellen insisted, we're primary producers. We're exempt.

I won't have you throwing away your education simply because there's a war on, Ellen's next letter claimed. As you well know, the school fees have taken the last of your father's savings. (Everyone in the city assumed that if you came down from the bush you had pots of cash and acres chockablock with stud rams.)

Alice was in her fourth year at Star of the Sea when the drought finally broke in 1942. Thank God for the steady, soaking rain, Ellen wrote. The tanks and dams are all full. Now we can start worrying about flooding on the flats.

The week Alice received this letter, there were, in the middle of the night, depth charges and big guns firing in the harbour. The dormitory windows rattled and broke.

Standing at one of the windows, Alice looked down at pieces of broken glass lying on the polished floor and felt a surge of wounded, stimulating power. *Let them come, let them come and do their worst.*

Alice did not understand, at that time, how much she had absorbed from her father.

DUFFY, PIETRO, ELLEN, AND THE DOGS are mustering sheep. "Let the dogs show you," Duffy advises Pietro. "The dogs know how to get things going. They're the experts round here, mate."

Pietro sees Duffy pointing at the dogs. He looks at them and nods agreement. He turns, catches Ellen's eye, and shrugs. I don't understand, the shrug says. She smiles and shrugs back, gestures with her hand: Doesn't matter, follow me. Amazing, how much they are able to say, she and Pietro, without uttering a single word.

She takes him with her around the edges of the paddock, moving slowly through the dense bush, where stragglers can get mislaid. The paddock isn't an easy one for the dogs. There is no clear, flat ground where the sheep will go, to form eventually into a mob. Duffy and the dogs have to work hard, with barks and answering shouts. At last the dogs get the sheep up to the gate, through it. They get them down across the creek, along the flats, and into the yards.

They pack the sheep into the race. Duffy has the drenching kettle. Ellen grabs a sheep and holds it while Duffy squirts. It's just wide enough in the race for the two of them.

Ellen climbs out. Pietro gets in and has a go. "You'll get the hang of it, mate," says Duffy. "Only a matter of time."

They lie under the trees after lunch. Pietro has had his feet trodden on by several confused sheep, but he laughs and says something in Italian. Ellen can tell it's cheerful swearing. Good, she thinks. He's beginning to relax, to feel at home.

Pietro rolls up his shirt and flexes his arm muscles, pointing to Ellen. You're very strong, he's saying.

Yes, I suppose I am, she nods, embarrassed.

In the afternoon Duffy works in the yards, dagging. He trims around the sheep's arse where the shit has gathered. It's the dirtiest job. Then, fast and expert with his knife, he cuts back hooves that have grown too long.

Ellen works the drenching gun in the race while Pietro grabs and holds. In the powerful smell of sheep, drench, and their own bodies they work through the afternoon. With the jostling of the sheep they are pushed up against each other. The air has become dust. It covers their hair and streaks their faces, useless to stop to wipe it off. They develop a rhythm: grab the sheep's head, force its mouth open — its grassy breath, its anxiety — get the liquid down its throat, push the sheep behind, grab another head.

The kettle drips onto Ellen's hands, staining them brown. *Damn. I won't get that out for days.*

Who was it in the Bible who came in a pillar of dust? Can't remember. She'll have to get a bar of Sunlight, melt it down, stick in some lemon and eau-de-cologne. Where on earth was she going to get the time to do that? Not to mention the eau-de; lemons would have to do. (If she'd been out here with Bill, it wouldn't have mattered a bit, her getting stained hands.) I'll take the pumice to them tonight, she thought. After everyone has been fed.

At the end of all this, they have to take the sheep back to their original paddock. The dogs work on in the dark.

When finally they are riding home, Pietro begins to sing "*La donna é mobile.*" Duffy joins in with his own words:

Ta ra ra boom de aye
Mae West had twins today
Tomorrow she'll give them away
She has them every day

"Duffy," Ellen says. "Duffy, how could you?" Because she has no doubt that in Italian the words are elegant, refined, passionate.

ON SUNDAYS ELLEN DRIVES Pietro into Kelly's Creek to Mass. Duffy doesn't come with them. "You know I gave the game away," Duffy says.

She's wearing white gloves over her tough hands. In the car

Pietro sits beside her, bulky, bathed, and fresh. He doesn't concentrate on the road; he doesn't stare at the trees or listen to the magpies. He looks at her.

There will be talk, no doubt, about her driving Pietro. It would be easier if Duffy had come too. But the major gossip before Mass is that the POWs from Carstairs have rolled up in Carstairs' Dodge, which they've managed to get running on kerosene mixture.

"The old man let them use it," Duffy reports. "They're good workers and they need to get to church."

"He's such a cranky old coot," Ellen marvels. "You'd think he'd be afraid they'd keep right on going."

"And do what? Hit the coast and start swimming?"

Someone claims to have heard Carstairs on the party line announcing it would be a cold day in hell before he'd take up chauffeuring his prisoners to their bloody papist rituals.

In her prayers during Mass she tells Bill that old Carstairs is letting the POWs drive round the main roads in his precious Dodge. Bill gets a laugh out of that.

She sits in her usual place, near the front. There are two rows of maroon uniforms towards the back of the church. *"Dominus vobiscum,"* says the priest. Ellen knows what it means, and Pietro knows, too.

He doesn't believe in priests. She asked him about religion once, and he tapped his head and rolled his eyes, *pazzo*. So why does he come to church?

She is aware of him behind her: sitting, kneeling, standing. She can feel him watching her.

She's never felt watched before.

WHEN RONNIE ENTERED THE CONVENT, Ellen was the one left at home while their mother got on with good works.

Bill came to Sydney occasionally for treatment of a sliver of shrapnel that still wandered in his chest. Sitting on the hospital verandah as an invalid, he was a recipient of her mother's strenuous charity. That's how Ellen met him: her mother had invited Bill home for Sunday afternoon tea.

Ellen, looking back, cannot in any way recognize the young woman who poured tea, who made conversation, who played the piano, the young woman who indicated with every gesture that she was driven not only by the stimulation of a male presence but also by the desire to outwit her mother and *serve her sister right*. Her sister had joined the convent because she was too good for the things of this world, including her own twin.

If her mother assumed everyone would wait upon her good works, if she invited the wrecks home for afternoon tea, if her sister insisted on having herself locked away behind a convent wall for the term of her natural life, she, Ellen, could go one better. She could have one of Mother's wrecks. Have him and hold him. (And who would have the upper hand then? Eh?) The more her mother refused to believe that this folly was indeed taking place, the more intent Ellen became.

After the pleasure of distressing her family, after the enjoyable fuss of courtship, after the wedding, Ellen went with Bill to his property, Ardara, on the slopes of the northern tablelands.

Before that, they spent a week in the Blue Mountains, as newly-weds. They took bush walks in their stiff new clothes. In a Katoomba studio, they had their picture taken.

The evenings lay ahead.

On their fourth day in the mountains, a man came to stay in the guesthouse, another digger.

"It was good to have someone to talk to," Bill said, to Ellen.

ARDARA HAD BELONGED to Bill's father, who'd been wiped out by the Spanish flu. (His mother had died in childbirth when Bill was five.) "You couldn't say we're much of a family," he warned her.

Ellen inspected the homestead. Bare wooden floors. She could see through the cracks to the dirt below. The back rooms didn't have proper ceilings, just a bit of sagging hessian tacked across wooden beams. For cupboards, the bachelors had used butter boxes nailed together. Outside, joined to the home by a small verandah, was the washhouse. It had a tin bathtub. You heated the water for it on the kitchen stove.

It was not that Bill was totally on his uppers. It was just that he didn't care how he lived.

"I suppose it's a man house," said Bill. "When you get right down to it." And stood, hesitant, waiting for her to speak.

"We'll have to see what we can do about that," she replied, making her voice light.

She was going to be brave, and it was just the beginning.

Dear Ronnie, she wrote. It's five miles in the sulky to the nearest railway siding, Kelly's Creek. One has to be careful not to blink. Another twelve to the town of Araluen. As for the homestead, I'm going to be up to my neck in elbow grease. To think! At home we always had Bridie. I could do with an offsider like Bridie out here. You wouldn't believe the disarray.

Disarray. Yes, that was the right word, for the letter to Ronnie.

Ellen thought of her wedding presents: the walnut buffet with lead-light doors; the lamp with the fluted pink glass shade; the wardrobe with double doors and mirror inset; the crossover lace curtains for the bedroom. They were being sent up on the train. They would all be stranded here with her.

Even before the furniture arrived, she was pregnant with Alice.

At Star of the Sea she had read and learned piano music. There had even been talk of her going to the Conservatorium of Music. Now she had married a man who didn't care how he lived.

But they tried. They both tried. She got a Coolgardie safe, to cool her jellies and junkets on the verandah. Bill ran some pipes in from the tank. Eventually there was a sink in the kitchen and an enamel bathtub in the washhouse, complete with taps and a chip bath heater. Trouble was, there was no water left in the tank; there was a drought on. Bill knocked on the tank to see how far down the hollow sound went. Knock, knock, nobody home.

She went with Bill up into the paddocks, learned how to make a sling for stock down in the heat. Together they tried to get to the starving creatures before the crows or maggies did.

One day she saw a crow taking an eye. Ripping it out and flying off with the glistening thing in its beak, pursued by envious others.

It was the way things went.

She thought of the saint who'd had both eyes plucked out by a magpie, who bore them up to heaven. Greedy guts of a bird, how did it manage to fit two eyes into its beak? Through prayer he had his sight restored, this medieval man, despite the fact that he remained eyeless. He had some headaches at first, but enjoyed perfect vision. He later became an acrobat.

She'd told Bill all this while they were boiling the billy. "An eyeless acrobat. Must have been quite the attraction."

"Magpies are different over there," Bill said. "They have amazing great long tails."

There were stories right here, too, on this land where Bill had been born. She asked about them.

"Trouble is," Bill said, "I can't get Paddy or any of his mob to tell me anything. All they'll say is 'Don't go there, mate, you mustn't go there.' I ask if it's blackfella magic, and they just laugh, scared."

Bill's father had been the first white settler. He'd named the place Ardara, after his own father's village, back in Donegal. Beside the creek, he'd built a bark hut. Bill could remember the Aboriginals coming back in the spring, dancing all night until sun-up. He'd gone down to the dancing ring next day, poked about. (They'd let a little kid do that.) Under his bare feet he'd felt the dance still going on. A shuddering, buried deep in the ground.

"You can't force secrets out of anyone, I reckon," Bill said. "Wouldn't be fair." With that, he lay down on the earth, his head against a tree, his hat over his face.

AFTER THE DROUGHT BROKE, Ellen ordered a carpet for the front room. Bought some material and ran up kitchen curtains on the Singer.

She'd had no idea, none, of the work that had gone into the home on Ocean Street: drawers that glided smoothly in and out, bags of lavender and clove apples in the linen press, polished dressing tables, starched doilies that featured embroidered women in full skirts, holding baskets of flowers. Nobody had thought to tell her, nobody had bothered even to mention, what it takes to establish that, to maintain it, to keep it all in clean, well-oiled motion.

This wasn't Ocean Street; it was the bush.

First things first. She conquered the stove, and in time her scones rose high and light, as good as anyone's in the district. She learned to stick a leg of mutton in a barrel of brine and cover it with a plate with a rock on top to keep it from floating.

Carstairs invited them over a few times for cards. Carstairs had a wind-up phonograph and pictures on the wall of nymphs admiring themselves in pools.

It seemed to Ellen that hospitality should be returned.

"We can't afford to entertain," Bill insisted, relieved to have come up with an excuse.

Ellen discovered that the Sydney municipal library would send books out to the bush, on the train. She stood on the siding at Kelly's Creek, surrounded by high, dry grass, and waited for the train to slow. She watched the mailbag drop. The library delivered extraordinary offerings: *Leaves of Grass*; poetry by that German, Rilke, who had an odd middle name, Maria. Ellen pictured Walt Whitman getting off at the Kelly's Creek siding and looking up at the wide open sky — puzzled at first, but pretty soon wildly enthusiastic. (Rilke demanded to be put right back on the train.)

Bill listened to the poetry that Ellen read to him from her precious library books. "Crossing Brooklyn Ferry" was his favourite.

"We're such a long way from Manhattan," she said. "'Manhattan' — can you imagine a more distant word?"

"I reckon it's not all that distant," Bill said. "What that Whitman cove was interested in was the summer and the water. 'Just as you feel when you look on the river and sky, so I felt.'"

He'd ask her to reread that passage; he liked it. "It makes you think," he said, "about the blackfellas. Bet they swam in the swimming hole down at Sandy Gully long before our lot showed up."

So Ellen had her books; she had young Alice, running wild in bare feet. And she could not believe that this was her life, that this was what had happened to her.

What Bill needed was all around him: sky and rocks and grass. The sharp, clear silence. He could relax out there, let what he carried with him from the war drift and dissipate, like gas.

In time, Ellen was able to pick roses from her front garden and arrange them in the cut-glass vase that had been her most important wedding present. Nuns didn't give wedding presents, but somehow Ronnie had managed it, even though she'd been a lowly postulant at the time. (God, what she would have done to have had Ronnie at her wedding.)

Ellen pretended she was in the city. She was walking down thick-carpeted stairs into a dark room where tables were covered with heavy white linen tablecloths. The light from the table lamps was rose-coloured, soft as silk. Ronnie wasn't a nun any more. Ronnie was wearing a smart little blue hat, and waiting for her.

ONE YEAR WHEN THE WOOL CHEQUE was better, Ellen went to town and bought a piano.

"All right now, old thing?" Bill inquired. He stood in front of her and waited.

His wife's desires were like something from the moon. He had nothing against them.

ON THE SECOND SUNDAY OF ADVENT, at the time for messages between the Gospel and the sermon, the priest announces he has good news. Father Ciro will soon visit the parish. Father Ciro, who speaks Italian. Father Ciro will be holding a special Mass for the POWs, everyone welcome.

During the sermon Ellen begins to make plans for Father Ciro. The funny thing is, it was only yesterday that the three of them — she and Pietro and Duffy — were wondering about maybe having some sort of do, asking the others. On Sunday afternoons the POWs are allowed to visit, as long as they keep off the main roads.

She'll make a big meal and invite the priest and the lot of them. Wine, they'll need wine, Italians prefer it. She'll ask Duffy what he can get his hands on. She'll make a trifle. Lashings of cream, no worries. Sugar is a problem though; they're short on sugar, the rations don't go nearly far enough. And there won't be enough canned fruit to go round, she'll have to make do with fresh. Rabbit, she'll serve them all rabbit.

Pietro loves rabbit and he plays the cello. She discovered those two things about him yesterday. It had been an easy day all round. In the afternoon, Duffy and Pietro had gone out with .22s.

"Bloody awful shot," said Duffy later. "No wonder that mob had to throw in the towel."

Duffy showed Pietro how to skin a rabbit, how to pin the skin on a bow made of fencing wire. Duffy promised that, when he took the skins into the hide-and-skin man in town, he'd make sure Pietro got his fair share.

Ellen loves to slip her hand inside those dry skins, feel the fur, sniff the gamy smell. She doesn't particularly like eating rabbit. Mostly she feeds it to the dogs. Yesterday, though, she'd made a rabbit stew and felt apologetic about serving it. Pietro sat up and ate it all, kissing his fingers to say how tasty it was.

"*Perfeto*," he breathed. "*Perfeto.*"

You'd think it would be *perfecto*. But no, that is some sort of cigar. After dinner they'd both looked it up in the dictionary.

"*Perfeto*," she said, looking at the word and attempting to pronounce it.

"*Perfeto*," he corrected, his eyes reaching in.

It is so much, so much more than she expected.

Pietro took the dictionary out of her hands and found the words he needed: *cuocere al forno*, to roast meat; *spicchio d'aglio*, clove of garlic; *rosmarino*.

Roast is easy. Rosemary? That is for remembrance, as everyone knows. They have a bush in the park in town. The school kids raid it for little sprigs on Anzac Day. She can take a basket and gather some.

Garlic. *Aglio*. Duffy rolled his eyes and shook his head. "None of that round here, mate," he assured Pietro.

After dinner they sat by the radio. Pietro couldn't understand much but wanted to listen. Duffy tried to explain bits here and there. They all listened in particular for the news from Italy.

When Father Ciro comes, she'll be able to have a conversation, with Father Ciro as interpreter. That way, she'll find out about Pietro's family, where he grew up, how many sisters and brothers he had, what he typed — all about him.

She'll serve roast rabbit with rosemary and garlic.

Last night, after they'd had the rabbit stew and looked in the dictionary and then listened to the news, a cello piece had come on the radio. Pietro had beamed, opened his thighs wide. As the music played, so did Pietro.

"Can you do that, mate?" Duffy had asked, gesturing. "Can you do that?"

Carefully, Pietro had wielded an imaginary bow. At the end, he had sighed, and she and Duffy had clapped.

Duffy kept the radio on, to listen to the river heights.

Pietro sat there, his shoulders moving slightly. She knew he was playing the cello piece again, in his head this time.

At Star of the Sea they have cellos. They sit in the music room gathering dust. On St. Patrick's Day somebody always gets out the harp ("the harp that once through Tara's halls the soul of music shed"). But when have they last played the cellos? Not at any of the year-end concerts she's been to. Some bright young thing — her younger self, exactly — assaults Chopin's third etude.

She already knows that "cello" is exactly the same word in English as in Italian. Almost. *Violoncello.*

SHE'S IN THE CHEMIST'S. The chemist's is dark, with its wooden counter and, behind, rows and rows of wooden shelves, drawers below. Bottles of red and blue coloured water pretending to be something else.

She has to tell the chemist what she's come in for.

There are two other women in the chemist's. All ears.

Cyril, that's the chemist's name. Cyril lost a son in the desert, fighting against the Italians. He doesn't see why the POWs are being let out to work on the farms. The authorities have gone soft in the head, according to Cyril.

"Do unto others as you have been done unto. That's Cyril's golden rule," Duffy said.

Cyril will know why she wants it, he'll guess right away. By tea time everyone will have heard.

She lifts her flushed face, not to Cyril but to the thin blue bottle on the top shelf. "Some olive oil, please."

It's sold for earache. The only use it has, in this town.

PIETRO FALLS OFF POMPEY. He and Duffy are coming back from sinking some fence posts. They are at the last gate.

Pietro, riding behind Duffy, does what he's seen Duffy do so many times. He bends down, still on Pompey, to shut the gate without dismounting. Loses his balance. Falls heavily, gouges his head.

Duffy gets him back up on Pompey and leads him swiftly home. In the horse paddock, Duffy gives Ellen a *co-ee* to let her know something's up. Ellen, seeing Pietro slumped like that, comes running.

"What's wrong?" she calls to Duffy. Pompey never took fright, never lost his footing in a rabbit hole; Pompey had pigeon feet and no nerves at all.

"Bit of a fall," Duffy calls back.

Pietro, in pain, is breathing heavily. His face has gone pale and he's bleeding. Dried blood in his hair. Fresh bright blood dribbling down his neck and onto his singlet.

In the gums above them, a mob of currawongs are gobble-gobbling. That's how we must sound to him, Ellen thinks, shouting away in English.

Ellen wraps Pietro's head tightly in a tea towel. They drive him in to the doctor right away. The doctor is the chemist's brother.

"How on earth did the silly bugger do that?" the doctor asks, ready to jeer.

"He was on Lightning," Ellen says immediately, to get in ahead of Duffy. "She's so wild, nobody can hold her." Of course, the doctor doesn't know the names of her horses, it's just to put him off the scent.

"You know he shouldn't be out of uniform," the doctor goes on. "I will be obliged to lodge a complaint with the authorities."

"Fair go, mate," protests Duffy.

Who did he think he was, anyway? Doctor High-and-Mighty. It's a relief to get Pietro out of there.

"He can lodge his complaint all right," says Duffy, when they're safely back in the car. "You know where."

"Dear Sir," says Ellen. "Received your complaint and immediately filed it in the garbage bin."

"Where you may rest assured it will get the attention it deserves."

They both feel talkative, a bit giddy; it's invigorating, sharing an emergency. Pietro, in the back seat, sighs and closes his eyes. Detaching himself.

She's being stupid, joking about with Duffy. That's what Pietro thinks, she tells herself. To him we're stupid, just country bumpkins. But she's doing it for him. It's all for him, everything she does is for him. Surely he must know that by now. "Bring him up to the house," she says, when they get Pietro home.

Duffy gives her a noncommittal look.

"He can have the spare room. I'll make up the bed."

SHE SITS BESIDE PIETRO, and they talk with their eyes and hands. He likes being in the house, close to her. It's good to get away from Duffy for a while.

You, he indicates, pointing with his right hand. Me, he adds, pointing to himself with his left. Then he puts his right hand into the left, places his joined hands over his heart and bows his head.

TRAVEL IS RESTRICTED, but Ellen tells the authorities she has to see a man about selling some wethers. She takes the train down to Sydney to stay with her mother, Rose, on Ocean Street.

Alice has just finished school and will be coming home to live on Ardara. (What's she going to think about having Pietro in the house?)

First, a cello.

Ronnie knows about the cellos in the music room at the convent. When Ellen goes to visit, Ronnie lugs one into the convent parlour. "How hard was it to get?" Ellen asks Ronnie. "Did you have to pull strings?"

"Strings for the cello are impossible to replace," Ronnie says. "They have quite simply disappeared."

"Commandos are using them," Ellen says, "for strangling the Axis powers." As soon as the words are out of her mouth, she remembers. Pietro is part of the Axis.

"What an odd word it is," says Ronnie. "'Axis.'"

Ellen drags the cello down the hallway of the Ocean Street home. "For the party," she says, breathless from the careful manoeuvring the cello requires.

"I'd say he's a lucky man," her mother, Rose, says. "This Father Ciro."

Ellen's face fills with guilty alarm. "Cello strings are scarce as mustard. Ronnie says they can't be had for love or money, not even on the black market."

"Since when," demands Rose, "since when does Ronnie know what can or cannot be had on the black?" These days Rose prides herself on her connections in the dingy side streets of Darlinghurst.

Rose is out all next day. Comes home in a good mood with extra tea and sugar, but no cello strings. "That priest of yours had better know what he's doing, that's all," she says.

Ellen opens her mouth to say something, then shuts it again.

When Ellen takes the train home, Alice comes, too. Weighed down with Ellen's purchases. Spaghetti, enough for a battalion. Stinking sausage. Dusty garlic bulbs strung together, tracked down somewhere in the Haymarket. Dominating the entire compartment, the cello. Proof of Ronnie's ability to wheedle and deliver.

"I knew she wouldn't let me down," says Ellen of Ronnie.

From their dog-box compartment on the train, Alice and Ellen look out the window as they pull into a siding to let a troop train go by. To confuse invaders, the station signs have all been painted over. Enemy soldiers would be expected to hop on a train, look out, and not know where they were going. Ha ha, fooled yer.

Alice doesn't want to be going home. Once she's on Ardara, who knows when she'll get away? To pass the time, she begins to argue with her mother.

But Ellen says that if Alice really wants to join up, well then, that's what she should do. She should go right ahead.

Alice, finding the gate suddenly unguarded, draws back. "I thought you said . . ." she protests. "I thought you said we were primary producers and exempt."

"Oh, don't be silly," says Ellen. "That's just men."

ELLEN HOLDS THE BIG DO in the orchard, beneath the apricot trees.

Duffy killed a sheep the day before and left the skinned and gutted carcass hanging overnight, to set. He's up at dawn, putting clean bags in the wheelbarrow, to bring in the carcass before the flies get at it.

They all come, all the POWs. First to the special Mass, then out to Ardara, by horse and bicycle and car. The four from Carstairs roll up in the Dodge with an accordion, and grappa in a milk urn. O'Brien's pair bring a mob of O'Brien kids, two of whom ride around on the Italians' shoulders. Those kids are having a duel, flailing at one another with little arms. The crowd of men laugh and egg the boys on. O'Brien's POWs are both fathers back home. They help Mrs. O'Brien with the kiddies. They're even willing to change nappies. Can you beat that?

"What would Steph's brother say?" Alice demands of Ellen. They are carrying the first course out to the tables.

"Steph's brother?" What was Alice talking about? It would be dreadful to drop something at this stage.

"Why bother fighting and getting wounded and losing a leg when people back home sit round playing silly buggers with the enemy? I mean, there's no point, is there?"

"I won't have you using language like that," says Ellen, without conviction.

"Throwing parties in the orchard," says Alice, with scorn.

"Get those extra glasses, will you? There's a pet. They're on the sideboard."

While Ellen worries, there are preliminary toasts, there is singing. Will they really like the food, or will they have to be polite? Will there be enough to go round?

Father Ciro says grace. Pietro doesn't cross himself and pray. Instead he looks at her and winks. She's too nervous about the food to respond.

Spaghetti, made by Pietro with tomato and onions and garlic, is applauded and gobbled up. Roast lamb and rabbit with rosemary and garlic, heaps of spuds, and pumpkin.

They like it! They really do. She can tell.

Now she can talk to Pietro without being distracted. Father Ciro sits in the middle and acts as translator. The names of Pietro's boys are Francesco and Vincenzo. Ellen already knows that. By now they'd be seven and nine. Good boys, very good boys, healthy and strong.

Ellen is afraid he'll start to talk about his wife, having Father Ciro there. She doesn't want to hear about his wife. Not today. (Not any day.)

At the beginning of 1941, he was held prisoner at Bardia, in Libya. He was kept at camps in Egypt and India. In India, he was in the camp orchestra. He is not a typist but a linotype operator and compositor. No, he didn't work for a newspaper. (So what exactly did he work for? But the conversation has moved on.) He comes from a small town just north of Rome. Yes, he'd been living in Rome. That's why he says he comes from Rome. Really he comes from Orte, the small town where the boys are now. (At this point the priest tosses in a *Deo gratias*; Pietro shrugs.) It's better, much better in Orte, close to the country, more to eat. Yes, his father's mother is alive. She's eighty-five. Yes, yes, it is wonderful. A great age.

Alice, who's been gathering plates with a martyred petulance, has come to listen. "Ask him," she challenges Father Ciro, "ask him who here today supported Mussolini? Ask him to tell us." It's clear that this is a speech she's rehearsed. "Ask him, what exactly do they think they're celebrating?"

Ellen's face grows tight. "Alice," she says. It emerges as a squeaky plea, not the reproof it should be. For such rudeness.

"Come off it," says Duffy firmly. "For these blokes, their war's as good as over."

"Well, ours isn't," says Alice. "I'll have you know ours isn't." With that, she marches across the orchard, managing an exit. It's difficult with the dirty plates, and the way her high heels sink into the ground.

Father Ciro says something in Italian to Pietro, who looks across at Ellen with a gesture of reassurance, parent to parent. "Tell Miss Alice," he says through Father Ciro. "Tell Miss Alice that Bighead is finished."

"He means Mussolini," supplies Father Ciro.

"That's the point I've been trying to make," Duffy says patiently. "Musso's lot have kicked the bucket. That's all over and done with."

Duffy begins to offer Father Ciro his views on the Italian army. "They didn't really want to fight," he explains. "They'd much rather enjoy a good singsong."

Ellen sees columns of Italian soldiers putting down their guns and breaking into song. Out in the middle of the desert. "Desert song," she says.

Duffy gives her a warning look. What's the problem? She's just had the one little glass. Two at the most. Three?

"It was the guards that were tough as guts," Duffy goes on. "Pietro here," he tells Father Ciro, "he was in the camp in Egypt, and you know what this guard did to Pietro's mate? Chopped his fingers off. With a bayonet."

Duffy pauses to let that take effect. "The guard wanted the bloke's wedding ring."

She's gone to all this trouble, and here's Duffy bashing the priest's ear with some yarn he's picked up at the POW control centre in town. Anyway, surely it was just the one finger. That the guard chopped off. For the wedding ring.

Such a shame to be stuck here in this crowd, with the priest parked smack in the middle, when all she wants is to pull Pietro onto the ground beneath the apricot trees and swallow him whole.

SHE GOES TO MASS, hides her head in her white-gloved hands and argues. Weren't you the one who said, "I was hungry and you gave me to eat, I was thirsty and you gave me to drink?" Well, then.

It is what she has to give.

He didn't go in for that sort of thing Himself. Except with Mary Magdalene, the fallen woman. Matey with her, He was.

She knows that as soon as she goes outside and sees Pietro talking to the other POWs, sees his shoulders and the back of his head, the way he holds himself, she'll forget all about God ruling the roost from His little tabernacle. Forget completely. Forget everything except that she's going to drive home with Pietro, alone.

They'll stop by Sandy Gully and make a place by the river, under the willows and casuarinas. The man who planted the willows had been one of Napoleon's guards on St. Helena. He'd probably been proud of his willows, supposing they were making the place more beautiful. Had he been homesick for St. Helena or for England, or both?

She's already told Pietro about the guard and the willows, using the mixture of mime and touch that is now their own private language. Pietro laughed, striding along the sandy riverbed, tucking his arm up his shirt and playing the little general.

Later he murmured, with delicious tongue, "Santa Elena, here, *here* is Santa Elena."

DOING THE MILKING, leaning on the cow's belly, Ellen imagines she's touching him, like this, like this, with persuasive fingers. She's really so skilled, that's the amazing thing.

She's finished the milking, and now she's pouring the milk into the separator. She's watching the cream, thick and rich, coming up the separator's high spout. She's back with Pietro under the willows by the creek.

Pouring yesterday's cream into the butter churn, she's moving with him. She tries to keep every detail distinct, so she can play it over as she turns the handle, again and again, play it with magnified clarity. Washing and salting the butter, she knows she is having it all at once: from initial reassurances all the way through to the final desperate tenderness. Washing the butter three times. Others may have the luxury of one thing after another, but she is having it all at once.

Nothing surprises her now. Music that goes straight to her feet. Frogs coming down with the rain, stars springing across the sky. Yellow butter in a blue bowl. A prisoner who came to her from the war on the other side of the world.

With Bill, she had understood nothing, given nothing. For his gifts, obliquely offered, she had given nothing in return. But it is going to be quite different with Pietro. There is so much to show Pietro, so much.

The beehives beneath the yellow box gums. At night, with the moon full, she leads him across the paddock and shows him how to listen to a hive, how to hear the murmur within. Rashly, he puts his arms around the hive, looking up at her, delighted. (Bill would have liked that gesture; he would have closed his eyes so that he could smile, privately, to himself.)

There are so many things here she wants to share with Pietro.

She wonders if Pietro already understands the cry of crows, mournful and dry. (They know how all things end; they know that the old names go on.) Does he hear the verdict of these birds, feel how it rises from the back of their ancient throats? Gradually — nothing that is subtle can happen quickly — he'll learn to join the crows' voice to the dust, to the bees, to the dry grass and folding hills around them.

In the first years after Bill brought her here, she longed for tight city time, the time of trains and buses and mechanical noise. But nothing on Ardara steps up to say, Get a move on, hurry up please, it's time.

Here, time goes to sleep in the grass.

The trouble is, she doesn't have Bill's granite face, his slow hands. (Those had been her first clues.) So how is she going to share with Pietro the particulars of this place? Of Ardara, which has become her home.

And can be Pietro's as well. Will be his. His, for good.

ELLEN TAKES PIETRO, without the dogs, up to the lambing paddock. Every morning during lambing, she goes up to check the paddock first thing, to see what lambs were born in the night, if a ewe is perhaps in trouble.

On the horses the two of them move as silently as possible at the edge of the paddock. Lambing ewes are easily spooked.

One of the lambs mistakes Pompey for its mother and begins to follow Pietro.

"Stand very still," Ellen whispers. "You have to wait for the ewe to come and find it."

They sit and are silent.

Let him listen to the wind, she thinks. Let him hear it begin at the other end of the valley and slouch its way down the gullies towards them.

He's lived in Rome. ("Ochre stone walls, churches all over," Ronnie said.) He's been a prisoner in Egypt (she imagines desert) and in India (jungle, but she isn't sure). Now here he is with her, out the back of beyond.

It must puzzle him, she thinks. Perhaps, having seen so much, he doesn't see this place at all.

His eyes are on the ewe. She is searching, trotting here, trotting there, bewildered. On and on she goes, from group to group. The other ewes raise their heads and glare at her. She draws back, rejected, confused. She turns away, tries again, getting more and more anxious. Bleating rattles in her throat.

Pietro spreads his arms in distress. Do something. We've got to help her.

Near panic, the ewe makes her way to the fence and comes towards him.

"Don't make a move," Ellen warns.

At last, the ewe smells her lamb and, with exhausted trembling, gathers it in. The lamb begins to feed, butting into its mother, its tail flying wildly.

Pompey, who has been standing like a stone column, turns his head and looks at them in turn. Pietro first, then Ellen. On gentle feet, taking great care, Pompey begins to make his way out of the lambing paddock.

ALICE COMES HOME TO ARDARA on leave from the Women's Land Army. Evenings at Ardara, she finds, have assumed a different, distinctive pattern.

Ellen has taken to blowing out the lamp and lighting the candles on the piano. Ellen's fingers move on the piano, having a go at some Chopin. Then it's Pietro's turn on the cello.

Pietro begins by playing a piece that is wildly popular at the time, which Alice knows as the song that begins, "This is the story of a starry night." Then he plays a bit of Bach. Duffy does his best to look serious.

Ellen's eyes are constantly on Pietro, watching how his legs cradle the cello, how he runs his hands over the cello's neck, its belly, its hips.

Alice looks away, unable to bear it.

It's Duffy who saves the evening from total loony mooning. After a little grappa, they move on to singing. Duffy is teaching Pietro the words; Ellen plays. "The girl I love is up in the lavatory," sings Pietro, in a solemn, unintelligible baritone.

The week's newspapers, with their headlines, lie in the shadow of the lounge chair. Anzio Advance: Allied Air Strikes Accelerate.

DAY AFTER DAY, the allied air strikes continued. The two boys, Francesco and Vincenzo, had gone down to the new part of town near the railway station. They were taking some soup to Pietro's grandmother; the soup was made of nettles. Their mother hadn't gone with them. Every day now she went out into the country in search of food. From a terrace on a neighbouring hill, she saw the silver high-flying planes coming over in their orderly rows.

The bombs seemed to fall in a leisurely way, taking their time in the soft, spring sky. The railway line was a target because it went directly to Rome.

THE CANTEEN COMES TO ARDARA once a fortnight. That's what they call the truck that drives around to the farms that have POWs. The canteen brings supplies for the prisoners: cigarettes, soap, razor blades. The most important thing the canteen can bring is a letter.

Pietro is at Ardara for two years, from near the end of 1943 to the late southern spring of 1945. In that time he receives two letters. The first letter arrives in July 1944, one month after the Allies have taken Rome. It was written in January of that year.

Pietro takes it to the spare room and closes the door.

Ellen stands in the hallway, waiting.

He does not emerge in the afternoon to put the cows up, collect the eggs, and feed the chooks, tasks he has long since taken on as his own. He doesn't come out until ten o'clock at night.

Working with the dictionary, he translates for Ellen: In the small town north of Rome, the weather in October had been clear and still, with no wind. The orange groves had ripe oranges. In November it had begun to rain. Mud everywhere. At Christmas the good weather had returned, cold, calm, and brilliant. Someone — a name Pietro doesn't recognize; he frowns — killed a goat.

Ellen listens to this. Later, she repeats it all to Duffy, who has a genuine, rural respect for weather.

What else did his wife say? Because there must be more than that. Things Pietro won't translate.

The second letter arrives at the end of August 1945. The war has ended: victory in Europe, victory in the Pacific; ruin everywhere. This letter is postmarked five months earlier. Pietro goes to the spare room and sticks the lowboy in front of the door.

He comes out only at night, to eat the food Ellen has left for him in the silent kitchen. On the fourth day, he gets up early and stands before her. With broken gestures, he tells her how his sons, Francesco and Vincenzo, have been killed.

Good boys they'd been, very good boys, so healthy and strong. The soup, the soup had been made of nettles. He tells her how he hopes for a ship as soon as possible. It is this waiting that is intolerable.

Now that everything is settled, over, finished.

IN THE HUNTER VALLEY, where Alice is still a member of the Women's Land Army, a young man called Dick Behan reaches for Alice's hand and produces some sentences about tying the knot.

Dick has come home from the Islands minus a leg, lost to tropical ulcers in the retreat from Rabaul. His words, their cadence and rhythm, are stolen from the pictures last week.

Holy mackerel, Alice thinks, don't tell me I'm going to end up as a *Mrs. Behan*. Dick, the real Mrs. Behan's first of many, has a baffled sincerity and pink, shining ears. There he stands, generously offering Alice his all.

Alice, terrible Alice, has to keep from laughing out loud.

In a letter from Ronnie she gets the news of Ellen's condition. In a postscript, Ronnie announces that Pietro has gone, on the boat home.

RONNIE TAKES CHARGE. She manages to arrange a cottage north of Manly. A refuge, a hideout on the wind-worn coastal heath. Alice, following Ronnie's instructions, moves into the cottage like a good daughter.

It is a night of high, wild winds. There are complications. As Ellen heaves, the wind blows. The bloody-minded heath shudders but will not yield. The wind draws another huge breath, tries again. The whole Pacific Ocean seems hell-bent on giving birth to this child.

There is Ellen's age to be taken into account, the doctor says.

Ronnie, in furious vigil in the convent chapel, bangs on the doors of heaven. I'll do anything, she promises. Take me instead, she challenges. *Go on, go ahead and take me.*

WHEN ELLEN IS WELL ENOUGH, she and Alice catch the bus to Manly and go shopping. They take turns pushing the pram along the street. They buy their weekly groceries; they stick the chops down the side of the pram.

In Manly, where nobody knows them, it is assumed that Alice is the young mother and that Ellen is the grandmother, lending a helping hand. Ronnie hears this and knows her prayers are answered.

Once God and Ronnie have made up their minds, who can hope to escape?

Certainly not baby Bernadette Veronica, whose tiny, demanding spirit cries out for nothing less than post-war plenty: a young mother, a father, a sibling, the lot.

Not Ellen, who opens her mouth and staggers like a drunk.

Not Alice, who swings the baby in the air, high against the vaulting sky, and feels herself to be both powerful and doomed.

Not kind-hearted Dick Behan, who is in every way the least of it. Besides, for him there is the matter of the Ardara acres.

THIS IS SOMETHING ALICE REMEMBERS from her final leave:

She's come home for a few days after working in Victoria. She is about to set off for the Hunter Valley, for the figs, and — although she doesn't know it yet — Dick Behan.

It's a Sunday afternoon. Her mother is sitting on the back verandah, writing to Ronnie. Pietro, in the orchard, is gathering a big basket of greengage plums. Pompey is wild about them.

Now Pietro comes into the yard, making his way across it to the horse paddock. He's wearing the navy cable-knit sweater Ellen made for him, and he's looking, as Ellen would say, rather dishy.

Ellen calls out from the back verandah: "You already fed him some of those today. You're turning him into a total greedy-guts."

Pietro, walking in that rapid way he has, hears the tone of reproof, of caution. He turns and gives Ellen his assured smile. He lifts his free hand to say, Oh, let him have them, he enjoys them so.

There is no doubt in anyone's mind about how this exchange will end.

At the gate, Pompey waits, confidently.

SNUGGED UP INSIDE ELLEN, Bernadette waits with equal self-assurance. She has no premonition of the turmoil to come, has not yet forgotten the single theory of everything.

Her mother tells her what to expect: hills and sun and grass. Flash-harry birds in a wide open sky. Ocean Street, Woollahra. The entire Pacific and beyond.

Pacifica, her mother says. That will be my secret name for you. It means peaceful, pet, full of peace.

Bernadette wriggles her toes; kicks, considers. Good grief. Pacifica. Okay, fine, so when do we get going?

Breathing is easy, her mother says (although later she will be panting and gasping and making heavy weather of it). And love. Love, Pacifica. Love.

Is like breathing.

When the time is right, you will find it comes of itself.

5

I Thought My Heart Would Break

Alice meets Enid Carlson when she opens the compartment door on the train to Renmark. The corridor light is behind her.

"All right if I come in?" asks Enid.

They are in the Women's Land Army, "land girls" from New South Wales, being lent to South Australia for the grape harvest. It is the southern autumn of 1944.

The train has three carriages of land girls, singing songs and playing pontoon. Someone — Monica, probably — has organized a boisterous game of hide-and-seek.

Enid is tall, with pale fair hair in curls that turn inward onto her shoulders. Bet she puts that up in rags, Alice thinks. Alice's own hair is naturally thick and wavy. It was fair when she was little, but now it's turned brownish. Mouse, that's what they call Alice's shade.

"I need some peace and quiet," says Enid, indicating with her thumb the activity of Monny's rowdies.

"Hide-and-screech," Alice says. Enid smiles. "They're thrilled to the back teeth we got corridors instead of dog boxes."

In this compartment, Alice is reading, Betty is knitting, and Syb's doing a crossword.

Betty says something about Monny, how at the last place they'd been, Monny got a football match going. Monny's team played against the men — a motley bunch of young and old who hadn't gone to war. The men decided it was only fair to play in pairs with their legs tied together. Before the game was called off, two of the men had broken ankles and another had dislocated his collarbone. "Monny was in her glory," says Betty. "The injury list grows with each retelling."

"A spectator's leg was broken from merely looking on," puts in Alice.

"You didn't play, though," says Enid. Blue eyes set wide below a broad forehead.

"Heavens, no," says Betty. Then, more confidingly, "Monny reckons we're not joiners."

"You're supposed to be a joiner," adds Alice. "Mateyness is mandatory."

"Don't I know it," says Enid.

They talk about their training in Griffith. Enid went through after Alice and Syb and Betty. Then she was sent to Batlow, to work on the apples.

"You can put your feet up here," offers Alice.

Enid sits down, puts her feet up as invited, and opens her book. She bends her head and reads in such self-contained silence that Alice wants to keep her talking, to get her attention again.

"What's that you're reading?"

"Would you like me to read to you?"

Alice looks over at Syb and Betty. They wouldn't mind. "Only if it's no bother. I wouldn't want to put you to any bother."

"It's no bother. I'll go back to the beginning."

In a rich, smoky voice (like Bacall's, Alice realizes immediately) Enid reads the first sentence: 'I saw the spring come once and I won't forget it."

ENID JOINED THE LAND GIRLS only because she's hard of hearing. She tried for the regular army but they turned her down.

"With me, it's eyesight," says Alice. "The WAAFs wouldn't have me, so I tried the regular army. They gave me the bum's rush, too."

"This country's rejects," says Enid cheerfully. "The deaf shall hear and the blind shall see, in the Australian Women's Land Army."

You can tell right away she's going to be good value.

They bunk down for the night: Betty up on the luggage rack, Alice and Enid on one seat, Syb on the seat opposite. (Syb is pleasantly plump.)

"You don't mind, do you?" asks Enid.

Enid is thin and tall, Alice is small, and under the blanket they fit together. The train says it over and over: She doesn't mind, she doesn't mind, she doesn't mind. They turn the lamps low, and she's lying alongside Enid, beneath the pictures of the Grafton jacarandas and the beach at Ulladulla. Above them, the water bottle sloshes, and its nickel chain bangs against the already clattering windows.

The train is taking them to the border.

SOMETIME AFTER MIDNIGHT they have to change trains. The four of them stake out a compartment and try to recreate what they had on the New South Wales train. They pull down all the blinds. Very late, before dawn, when the train has stopped somewhere in the middle of the South Australian bush, a man shoves a foot-warmer into the carriage.

Enid and Alice work together on the grapes. Enid takes a picture of Alice spreading the grapes on racks, to dry into sultanas. Alice is wearing shorts and looking delighted. On the back of the photo, in Enid's writing: *Something to smile about?* Followed by a row of Xs and a row of noughts.

Alice, examining this photo years later, searches her mind for images. The horses were muzzled, so they wouldn't eat the grapes. They gathered the grapes in wire baskets and dipped them in some kind of solution before spreading them out to dry.

There was some typical Land Army snafu, and they were left down in South Australia for a long time.

What Alice remembers best is Enid's smile. How, with a wary happiness, she had begun to watch for that smile, to follow it around.

AFTER THE GRAPES, they are on loan again, this time to the state of Victoria. Another train journey, a second border to cross. They are going to work on the flax.

Mrs. Beatrice Bennett is there to welcome them. Betty and Syb get the boys' rooms, one each. (The elder Bennett boy is a prisoner in Germany; the other is in New Guinea.)

"Now this is more like it," says Syb. "I'm sick to death of sleeping on a lumpy straw palliasse."

"We'll be in seventh heaven," declares Betty. "A room each."

Enid and Alice volunteer to take the back bedroom, which had once belonged to Mrs. Bea's in-laws.

"Good of you two girls to be willing to share," says Mrs. Bea.

Alice looks at the expanse of the pink satin eiderdown on the double bed.

"We're happy to do our bit, Mrs. Bea," says Enid.

IN LONG PADDOCKS BEHIND THE HOUSE, the flax stretches to the sky. It has already been cut and needs to be turned, to "ret."

"To ret, to rot," says Enid.

"No, well, yes," says Mrs. Bea. "You turn the bundles so they get evenly exposed to moisture. That way the bacteria separates the fibres from the woody tissue."

"You tell us, Mrs. Bea," says Enid. They are having tea. It is a cold evening, and Mrs. Bea has a generous fire burning in the grate.

"Flax is finicky," explains Mrs. Bea. "You should see it when it's young. First it's all soft blue flower, then it turns to a sea of silver silk." She's taken one or two photos of it; she'll have to show them some time.

The flax will need to be turned for six weeks. Then they'll gather it into stooks. The flax is destined for Melbourne, where it will be made into haversacks, webbing, and army stretchers.

"Your work," says Mrs. Bea, "will be of direct benefit to our men in New Guinea and the Islands." Mrs. Bea makes clear, unequivocal connections.

A wounded soldier is being carried over the Owen Stanley range in New Guinea on a stretcher made out of Mrs. Bea's flax. The soldier lies with one arm across his face. Another soldier, walking alongside, puts a lighted cigarette in between his lips. Then he touches the wounded man's shoulder, brother to brother. If you look closely, you will see that the man lying on the stretcher is Mrs. Bea's younger son.

They turn the flax with a special wooden stick. It's endless work, hard on the back. When they come in at dusk, Mrs. Bea makes a point of having a good spread laid out for them. After tea, she encourages them to sit with her in their dressing gowns, in front of the fire. Syb does her crosswords, Betty knits, Alice and Enid read. At nine o'clock, they go to their bedrooms with hot water bottles.

Enid and Alice shut the door. By candlelight, they get ready for bed. Twice a week, Enid puts her hair up in rags, just as Alice suspected.

Out in the paddocks, at smoko, they can count on being together, by themselves. Enid relaxes under the trees, idly drawing in the dirt with a stick. It looks like a random bunch of numbers, but it's really the date of Alice's birthday.

Sometimes Enid will be in a sombre mood. "We aren't just mucking about," she'll say. "You do know that, don't you?"

Having said this, Enid will look at Alice with such serious need that Alice has to lift up her head and shout in triumph; she has to. Shout something, anything, the sillier the better. The words mean nothing at all.

"Monday's wash day! Boots and all!" Alice yells. Feeling quite wild, wild and bubbling.

Syb and Betty stop working, startled. "Alice's gone barmy," they agree, and go back to what they were doing.

You can get away with things like that out in the empty paddocks, nobody around.

Alice and Enid tell each other all about their families, their parents, themselves. Enid's grandfather was a Swedish sailor from Stockholm who jumped ship in Sydney and became a sailmaker in Sussex Street. Alice's mother has a twin who's a nun. Alice's nun-aunt teaches at Star of the Sea, where Alice went to boarding school. Early in the war there was talk of evacuating the school from Sydney to the Blue Mountains. The notion was too far-fetched. In the convent, with its splendid insurance of prayer, who could have any belief at all in the need for such upheaval? Instead, the nuns placed kiddy-sized beach buckets of sand beneath the windows. If they were bombed, they would douse the fire with these small, handy buckets.

They tell each other their dreams. Last night Alice was running with Enid along the sandy shore of a tropical lagoon while bombs dropped all around them; they were carrying out some vital rescue. Then she was resting on the shore, all at peace, only it wasn't sand, it was a huge canvas sheet out on the ocean, which wasn't water but blue roses, tightly packed . . .

The telling, which goes on for hours, reminds Alice of opening parcels, interesting parcels that arrive in the mail, wrapped with brown paper and string.

Alice and Enid will be walking together down the narrow rows of flax, well behind Syb and Betty. There is, in their walking together, a feeling of rightness, of being exactly where you want to be. Then Enid will say, out of the corner of her mouth, "Sugar and spice, mate."

Alice hopes they'll stay here, turning the flax, forever.

ON WEDNESDAY AFTERNOONS, while they are away in the paddocks, Ned-the-Banker comes to see Mrs. Bea, to help with the books.

On Wednesday night, there is the extravagance of leftover seed cake and sometimes the remains of a bottle of claret. "He likes a bit of claret with his cake," says Mrs. Bea. When she speaks of the banker, the blood creeps up into Mrs. Bea's cheeks.

"Seed cake, claret," says Enid to Alice, when they are safely away in their own room. "Quite the Edwardian gentleman."

"I wonder what Mrs. Ned-the-Banker thinks."

"She thinks country women can't do their own sums."

The night before the banker comes, Mrs. Bea isn't herself. Like a schoolgirl, she has laughing fits at absolutely nothing. Despite the shortages, she rolls and lights one cigarette after another. She paces. Stands briefly by the mantelpiece, humming scrappy bits of tunes.

At other times Mrs. Bea hunches her shoulders and says, "Oh, I don't know. I just don't."

Out in the paddocks on Wednesdays, eating their jam sandwiches for lunch, they speculate about what Mrs. Bea will be like when they get back. Will she be curled up by the fire, wriggling her toes in her stocking feet and listening to opera?

When she's really pleased with herself, Mrs. Bea puts Dame Nellie on the phonograph. "*Ah, fose' è lui*" by Giuseppe Verdi. "Immaculate intonation," enthuses Mrs. Bea. "Liquid legato; effortless ascension. Listen to how she holds and floats the highest of notes, like velvet cream." Saying this, Mrs. Bea moves over to the tall sideboard and admires her own reflection in the glass doors.

If the day hasn't gone well, she'll be getting burned food out of the oven, banging it down on their plates. Then going off early to bed, holding her water bottle out in front of her like a log.

Whatever happens, they are not to pass remarks. That is understood.

They never meet the banker. The traces of cigar smoke hanging in the room, the cake, and the claret. Those are the evidence.

Once, in the evening, when they're coming back from the paddocks, they spot an amazingly large black cat. Sitting in the clearing, eyeing the homestead. It senses their presence and moves back into the bush. Leisurely, not in the least fearful. But swift, powerful.

"What was that?" Enid asks, her voice wary.

Alice isn't afraid of animals in the bush. Spiders, snakes, perhaps. Not animals. "Just a feral cat," she says. "They're huge because they have to be."

ALICE IS WAITING FOR ENID in the loft.

Land girls aren't supposed to do extra jobs around the house, but Mrs. Bea is such a good sort that Enid wants to.

The loft is above the shed where they keep the tractors, although the horses think it's for them. The big chestnut likes to get in there out of the sun. He's down there now, eating chaff.

Enid's mowing the lawn in front of the house.

The shed is open to the air, more of a shelter than a shed, with the loft tacked on above, like an attic. The loft has walls of rough timber and a roof of corrugated iron. Through the floorboards Alice can see the big chestnut snuffling in his feed. She can hear the steady crunch of his eating. He brings his head out of his feed, shakes it, and sighs.

Alice can hear the push-me-pull-you lawn mower. Surprising that Mrs. Bea has a front lawn at all, has made the effort; not many do, out here.

Mrs. Bea is in the dunny waiting upon her bowels (Mrs. Bea's phrase).

Mrs. Bea is the best person they've worked for. She insists they have sherry before tea on Saturday nights. When they come in from the paddocks, she's already got the hot water on the stove for their wash. Sometimes she even brings them breakfast in bed.

The loft is full of grey-blue pumpkins, arranged in rows, each pumpkin separated from the other. If one is stored touching another, both will rot.

It's a Sunday afternoon. Alice is waiting for Enid. Blue eyes, blue sky.

She's thinking about Lauren Bacall. In Alice's all-time favourite film, Bacall wears a houndstooth suit with a jacket that comes in at her wondrously tiny waist. To indicate those things that cannot be put into words, there is frequent lighting of cigarettes. Bogey and Bacall are being questioned by a villain whose head is hidden in shadows. After the villain lets them go, Bacall says to Bogey, "I need a drink."

Alice will always be glad to belong to a generation that can say such things, and with a straight face.

THE OTHER TWO LAND GIRLS, Syb and Betty, have gone off on the bikes. They're going to catch crays in the dam. Actually, the dam has no crayfish, and Betty's meeting her young man. He works on the neighbouring property. (He's married.) Alice isn't sure what Syb does while Betty meets her young married man. Sits by the dam and tackles a long, hard crossword probably. Syb's terrifically good at crosswords. Alice can't see the point of them herself. Neither can Enid.

Enid, Alice says to herself. *Enid, Enid.* She pretends she can see the name written in the sky. Written neatly, not breaking up, the lines of the "E" keeping their shape until the "d" has been completed. Skywriting. Would that be possible here, now? Perhaps by one of those planes that went around country towns before the war, taking people up for joy rides. Newsreels showed those white vapour trails above Britain, curling in thin but surprisingly abundant loops.

Soon she'll see Enid, when she comes to join her. About to step into the loft, Enid will stand at the top of the ladder, outlined against the sky.

Alice hears Enid stop mowing the lawn, notes the scraping of the tin shed door as Enid puts the mower away. She hears Enid coming up the ladder with her own blanket and book.

That is what they do up here on Sunday afternoons: they read. Like Betty and Syb, getting crayfish in the dam. In fact, sometimes they do read to one another. Enid likes to do most of the reading; she believes she has the better voice for it. In this story, which is the one Enid first read to Alice on the train, a woman is recovering from a lengthy illness. She lives alone. In the building opposite, lives another woman, alone also. That woman has put a row of persimmons on her windowsill, to ripen in the sun. "Shaped like a young woman's breast, their deep, rich, golden-orange colour," reads Enid.

Sunday afternoon in the loft is the one time they have completely, reliably, to themselves. There is no chance of Mrs. Bea putting her head around the door to ask if they want cocoa. No chance of Syb or Betty dropping in.

Enid is wearing her work overalls because she's been mowing the grass. Enid isn't golden-orange. More pink, really.

Alice hears the car come into the yard. Hears the dogs barking. The car door bangs.

She knows where Mrs. Bea is. Alice does not understand why anyone would choose to linger in an outhouse, even one with a long drop kept sweet with ashes. Mrs. Bea, who — confided in whispers — is having a bit of trouble with her back passage, does just that. Mrs. Bea can put in an hour or two, with the door propped open. In front of her, on the hills, her fields of flax.

Alice, deep in Enid's arms, is vaguely aware of footsteps approaching. Someone must be poking about in the shed below. As if from a great distance, she hears the big chestnut snort softly in greeting. Part of her notices all these things, but she pays them no attention whatsoever. So when she hears the creak of the ladder, she is lying at ease, unconcerned, content, oblivious.

For these Sunday afternoons are times of discoveries that are enormous, far beyond known words, beyond anything that has ever been imagined. And there is a pretence, between Alice and Enid, that all of this is Enid's idea, and that Alice is the one being led. Alice lies sprawled, sated for the moment but soon willing again — more than willing — to be coaxed one more time.

Enid, flushed, damp, and triumphant, props herself on one arm and, to tease Alice, says in a stage copper's voice, "Well, well, what's this, then? What 'ave we 'ere?"

Enid's mouth is closing on those words when Alice — who is lying looking up — sees the silhouette in the loft opening. Sees him fill the sky, substantial, undeniable. Sees his face, sees him disappear.

They look down.

Alice hears herself whispering to Enid, hanging on to her and whispering: "He heard me, he heard me"; feels Enid taking her arms, pressing her, cramped, awful, against the rough wall of the loft and saying: "No, no, no, you must never, ever, *ever.*"

They are getting their clothes on and going down the ladder, and Mrs. Bea, from the outhouse, is running across the yard. Hands over her mouth.

Alice knows immediately what has happened. He thought it was Mrs. Bea in the loft, crying out. An injury. A twisted ankle, perhaps. He was coming to the rescue.

Mrs. Bea crouches, whimpers, whispers.

Ned-the-Banker. He's never shown up on a Sunday before.

Alice stays with Mrs. Bea while Enid drives the truck to town to fetch the police. Mrs. Bea certainly had not been expecting the banker. (Has his wife found out?)

Alice is aware of the return of Betty and Syb on the boys' bikes. How Betty's face goes scared and white, and how Betty and Syb draw together somehow.

The policeman inspects the site. Licks his thumb, opens his notebook. Stands with his legs apart, to steady himself for writing. Pokes at the machinery with his foot. "What do you call this?"

Alice looks at the banker. They all look. Flies are beginning to gather. The banker is wearing a suit of brown serge. Alice has pictured Ned-the-Banker in cream flannel trousers, navy blazer with red-and-blue piping. Walking along in white leather shoes. Lifting his Panama to the ladies. To Mrs. Bea. It makes no sense; she sees that now. She's dressed the banker up as an exotic, a dandy.

"It's a binder," says Mrs. Bea. "A reaper-binder."

"Is it a reaper or a binder?" the policeman asks, swaying on his feet to show how patient he is being.

"Both," says Mrs. Bea. "It's for the flax."

The reaper-binder has serious revolving blades, rows and rows of them. *As ye reap, so also shall ye bind*, thinks Alice. She feels like saying it out loud, for Enid. (But of course it wouldn't do.)

The policeman isn't finished with them yet.

Syb is allowed to fetch a tablecloth and cover the banker. His black shoes stick out. Boring, conventional black shoes, tightly laced.

The policeman sits, grim, in the front room, and asks more and more questions.

What had they been doing in the loft, Enid and Alice?

Reading a book.

What had Mrs. Bennett been doing?

In the outhouse.

He looks embarrassed, but gamely writes it down.

Where were the other two?

Gone to the dam.

Two red patches bloom high on Betty's cheeks. (What if they find out about her married man?)

They were at the dam on their own. The dam at the back of the property. On bikes that belonged to Mrs. Bea's two boys. Nothing wrong in that.

What was the banker doing up the ladder?

That is the one question nobody has an answer for.

He slipped, he fell.

But why? Whom had he come to see?

Mrs. Bea, of course.

The policeman doesn't like it. You can tell by the way his grammar is becoming more careful. He refuses a second cup of tea.

There will be an inquest, he expects.

ON MONDAY THEY ARE BACK on the flax, gathering in the stooks. The flax has gone grey, the retting is complete. It really is an ugly mess, the flax; difficult to understand why Mrs. Bea is bats about it.

Enid stands on the wagon, building the stack. She is catching the sheaves from the stooks as the other three throw them up. Strong and quick, Enid has worked out how to turn the long-pronged fork at precisely the right moment. Alice looks up at Enid, who moves with an assured rhythm, easily keeping up with them, three to one. From a distance she'd look exactly like a recruiting poster. Normally Alice would have said so, made a joke about it.

They go to the funeral in their uniforms. She and Enid stand on each side of Mrs. Bea. They are led to a pew at the back of the church. An Anglican church. Alice isn't supposed to attend; it's a sin to attend the services of other denominations. But what would be the point of standing outside now, after what she's done?

Mrs. Bea, whose cries at night are piteous, is silent in the church. An object not of sympathy but of suspicion. Certainly not one who has any right to mourn.

Enid puts an arm around Mrs. Bea, and Alice puts an arm around Mrs. Bea, and holding Mrs. Bea like that, Alice can trace the chevrons on Enid's jacket and feel her body beneath. And touching Enid (it is the first time, since) Alice is filled with a high, warm feeling of excitement, of moving up into the air. It is such lovely agitation, soaring and swooping like a bird. Like when she looks out the opening of the loft on Sunday afternoon, and all she can see is the deep, ascending blue. A few small clouds wandering about like sheep. Very soon, Enid will be coming up the ladder.

They have to stand for the final hymn. "Abide with Me." Their arms release Mrs. Bea. Alice looks over at Enid. Enid is lifting up her head, and her voice is going up with it. Enid, Enid full of song. Right through the hymn, right through the solemn, silent recessional, with the coffin being carried out — the shuffling of the pallbearers, the wife's weeping — Alice is weak, shameful, and wet, swamped with a most inappropriate desire.

SHE'D BEEN READING IN THE LOFT, Alice says at the inquest. He has pale skin, this man who is asking her questions. Grey, hooded eyes, very careful. He stares right at Alice and asks her exactly what she'd been reading. Impossible to lie.

"A story called 'The Persimmon Tree.'"

The woman in the flat opposite puts persimmons on her window-sill, to ripen in the sun. It is spring, so the persimmons must have come from California, wrapped in sawdust. Persimmons are an autumn fruit. Imagine, Enid says, receiving a parcel, a wooden box. Persimmons, all the way from San Francisco. Imagine opening the box and having some of the sawdust spill out. Put your hand in and feel, hidden beneath the sawdust, the shape of the fruit.

He's already talked to Enid. They are questioning each of the box separately. It is something to do with legal rules. They are witnesses.

"What was happening in this story you allege you were reading, what was happening when you heard him fall?" He asks this casually, as if it were no more than an aside. By now he must suspect that they are all lying: Mrs. Bea, about the banker. Betty and Syb, about the dam and the married man. Enid and her.

"I think we'd got to the end."

He is the kind of man who would be capable of nosing about, going to the trouble of visiting a bookstore, of finding the story himself and reading it to see how it ends.

The woman in the flat opposite lets her gown fall. Her face is in shadow; her body, naked.

My blood ticked like a clock.

The man has gone silent: a ploy. Waiting for more. He hasn't caught the scent, not exactly, not yet. But he knows there's some-thing. He will keep on. He will dig into her story, into Betty's, into Mrs. Bea's. He will find out. He will track them down, her and Enid.

He isn't in any hurry; he will persevere. Remain on the alert.

It's her fault for having shouted in pleasure. For crying out loud, it's all her fault.

"You'd got to the end," he repeats, again as if this were of no particular significance.

LADY FLOREAT IS IN CHARGE of the Land Army for the whole state of Victoria. The big cheese. And she's coming to the property, to see them.

They watch Lady Floreat get out of the car while Mrs. Bea goes to greet her.

"Bet the only work she's ever done on the land," says Enid, "is attend polo matches. I can just see her getting the chicken sandwiches and champagne out of the boot. Such exhausting labour."

She's trying to keep their spirits up.

Lady Floreat declares that the four of them are a bad influence on each other. They are to be broken up, separated. At first she'd had a good mind to dismiss them all from the Army. As it is, they are being returned to New South Wales.

Syb to the peas near Gosford. Betty to the southern highlands and sheep. Alice to the Hunter Valley and figs. Enid to the south coast, to Eden, for the asparagus. Surely she can't mean it. She can't just swan in here, do this to them, and swan out.

Eden is at the very end of the state, on the coast. (It will take days; it will be impossible.)

For the first time, Betty speaks the married man's name. "I won't be able to see John. It really isn't fair," she sobs.

Mrs. Bea gets Betty to lie on the sofa, tells her to curl into a ball, she'll feel better like that. They gather round, to comfort.

"I'll see if there's any sherry left," Mrs. Bea offers.

Betty pushes them away, puts her hands over her head as if expecting blows. "It isn't fair," she cries again and again.

The rest of them finish off the sherry, then all the port.

"I say, let's drown our sorrows, pets," Mrs. Bea urges. "Might as well."

Enid and Alice go to their bedroom, close the door, put a chair against it. They lie down together on top of the pink satin eiderdown.

It isn't fair.

They are stealthy as spiders.

ALICE IS SAYING GOODBYE to Enid at the railway station. Syb and Betty have already gone.

They stay in the waiting room while Mrs. Bea goes to buy two platform tickets. There's a fire in the grate and they stand in front of that, smoking cigarettes. Enid leans one hand on the mantelpiece above the fire. This is something out of a film; it isn't happening to them. (If Enid is Bacall, who the hell is she?)

Outside, the train is arriving, with a huge hissing of steam and banging of doors. Inside, in the waiting room, the fire in the grate burns domestic, cheerful, ludicrous.

Enid has a plan. The one thing, she says, that will save them. In exactly twelve months' time they will rendezvous in Sydney, at Central. At the back of the station, near the Ladies', beneath the mirrors that advertise Pears soap.

"Promise me you'll be there," demands Enid, grasping Alice's hand. "Promise me you'll be there, come hell or high water."

Then Enid says to her, fierce, "You will want me forever."

In the manner of a dream, the floorboards stretch out and the walls fall away, so that there is only Alice and Enid and the fire between them in the cold night.

But here comes Mrs. Bea, holding the platform tickets. Mrs. Bea thinks they are mourning for Ned-the-Banker, and for her. "Oh my pets," says Mrs. Bea. "You mustn't cry for us."

Enid, above Alice, is reaching down from the train. "Promise," she repeats.

"You mustn't weep any more," Mrs. Bea pleads, taking their hands in turn. "You mustn't," she repeats.

You will want me forever.

IN THE HUNTER VALLEY, to help the figs swell, the trees stand in half a foot of water. The farmer's nephew, home from the Islands with a metal leg, drives the wagon through the mud. Alice's job is to stand on top of the wagon, picking the figs. The farmer's nephew, Dick, looks at her as if she were an apparition, a miracle.

"Where in heaven's name did my aunt get a hold of you?" he asks her.

At first, she just laughs.

DICK FINDS HER SHY. One morning, when Dick has to go back to the shed, the horse grows tired of standing around in the water beneath the figs and insists on moving, taking the wagon with him. Leaving Alice clinging to one of the branches, kicking her legs. Then falling into the muck.

Dick comes hurrying stiffly, his face gripped with concern. He helps her up, tender and solicitous, offers a chest to lean into. He doesn't hold back because she's covered in mud, not a bit of it.

After that, the flies and mozzies aren't quite as grim as they'd been at first. And her fingers grow accustomed to the white stinging liquid that oozes from the stems of the figs.

She writes to Enid every second day. The figs are almost done. Did I tell you the farmer's nephew left a leg behind in the Islands? He's got a fake one, but it bothers him so.

After the figs, she moves on to a nearby apple orchard for the grading and packing. She works on the grader. The apples roll along and fall into their little compartments: small, medium, large. The grader clanks, and the apples find their ordained slots, and down they drop, through a little leather trapdoor.

The local women are much quicker than I am at the grading, she tells Enid. Last Saturday night there was a do at the packing shed. Soon, the pruning will begin.

At the dance, Alice is the one chosen by Dick Behan, who is being gallant on difficult legs.

The local women stand along the wall, lamenting the man shortage. After supper they break down and begin to dance with each other.

The thing about Dick is that he thinks she is normal. Out behind the tank-stand after the dance, he tries to touch her. She lets out a giggle. He seems quite convinced by this.

(The coroner who had asked her questions is watching her, though. He knows she is putting it on. He is on to her, he has not been fooled.)

Dick is smitten; soon everyone knows. And it's perfectly all right. People like to gossip and watch and collude. Dick's aunt, on the back verandah sorting clothes, wants confidences.

"Men," exclaims Dick's aunt, holding up a torn shirt. "They're the dizzy limit, aren't they?"

At the pictures, Dick's arm comes creeping across her shoulder, then a paw reaches down. To touch. She brushes it away.

Which seems to be what Dick expects. He waits, then tries again. This is the way it goes, with a man.

Everyone approves.

IT TURNS OUT TO BE SO EASY it's practically a joke. All you have to do is let him, then pick yourself up and shake yourself off. Like a horse getting up in a paddock. None of this implicates her in the undermining way she'd feared it would.

Another thing about Dick: he can't tell what she is thinking, he doesn't have a clue. He doesn't even wonder. Dick has one question only: What is she going to do about his hands, their busy exploring, about his mouth, his enthusiastic mouth?

He doesn't know, you see, he really can't tell.

Alice, pressed beneath Dick, wonders what he did in the Islands. Did he do something which, back here in the predictable light of home, seemed to have happened to someone else entirely? Had he, perhaps, been directly responsible for the death of another? (Although in war that's the whole point, surely?) Even if he had — which is difficult to credit — he still wouldn't have a clue about her. She's a girl at home on the farm, a land girl. What on earth could a land girl get up to?

Alice, letting Dick, discovers a treacherous, isolated freedom. Into that place where Dick can never come because he doesn't even know it exists, there is Enid: Enid, pinning her against the wall of the loft, "you must never, ever, *ever*"; Enid, standing in the waiting room in front of the fireplace, the floorboards stretching out and the walls falling away. In that place inside her, Alice finds she can see the opening of the loft, the sky of Sunday afternoon blue. And Enid, filling all the high airy space.

Dick never suspects even the least little bit of it.

He isn't a bad man, Dick, not at all. Quite the contrary. He's kind, big on respect and marvel. You respect women, you marvel at them, that's what you do.

Respect doesn't fit, does it? Not with what she is capable of.

It wouldn't be fair to tell Enid, though. About her and Dick. Even if it were, as it would be, solely to reassure.

"YOU'RE A VERY LUCKY GIRL, you know," Dick's aunt tells her. They are making jam, stirring it with a wooden spoon. Dick's aunt shows her how to stir until it thickens. Alice already knows how to make jam, but doesn't let on. She is a lucky girl because Dick had been in a mortar section at Rabaul, and when the Japanese invaded he'd escaped through the jungle, over mountain ranges six thousand feet high. For part of the way, Dick's aunt tells her, Dick had carried his mate over his shoulder in a fireman's grip. It was because he was carrying his mate that he fell; the wound turned ulcerous; he lost his leg. Tropical ulcers. Not your normal kind.

So that was what he'd been doing, up there in the Islands.

It's true, Dick's aunt says, every word of it and more.

Dick blushes and looks away, overcome with shyness. Then continues to stare at Alice as if she's just stepped off the train from heaven.

Dick is one of seven children, from out Narrabri way. He'd joined the 2/22nd in Victoria; he'd been down in Victoria working as a rouseabout in the Western District. (When he says "down in Victoria," the blood rushes up the back of Alice's neck into her brain.) What he hadn't realized when he'd joined up, he confides, was that there'd be hardly any other blokes in the battalion from

New South Wales. He'd been dropped right in it with a mob of cabbage-patchers.

He wanted nothing more than to be a farmer. Although with his gammy leg. And no patch of dirt to call his own.

A courageous man, a gentle man. A man who'd been willing to carry his Victorian mate through the appalling jungle.

Alice begins to talk to Dick about her family, about Ardara, the property she'd grown up on, how she's the only child.

Dick takes her arm when they walk down the street in town. "I'm one of nature's optimists, I reckon," Dick says.

(The coroner from the inquest is standing in the shadows of the courthouse verandah. Tonight he will have nothing to go on. Not now.)

She's engaged. Isn't she? Well, almost. She will take him home. Take Dick to Ardara. "Is this your home?" he will ask, unable to keep the delight from his voice. "Ours," she'll say firmly, and take his hand and press it. (And nothing will be able to hurt her after that, nothing.) Surely it's the least she can do; it will be a solid, substantial, honourable thing.

She imagines Dick walking towards the verandah steps at Ardara, pulling his leg along. Mum, noticing, will look sharply at her. She'll look right back at her mother, stare her down.

As for the rest, she is competent. She is tough. She will manage.

ALTHOUGH THE WAR IS ALMOST OVER in Europe, it might go on for years in the Pacific. It's getting more and more difficult to picture Enid, cutting asparagus in Eden on the far south coast. Rising before dawn to get to the asparagus before the sun does. You use a tool like a chisel, Enid writes. Stick it into the little hill of dirt and quick, clip the stalks. Say goodbye to your fingernails.

Eden so far away.

Alice walks down to the mailbox: an old oil drum on a stump at the gate. Mail comes once a week, on Thursdays. Enid's letters are always there, plump and real and demanding.

Alice puts the letter in her pocket and walks back down the track to the farm. With every step, grasshoppers spring up out of the grass. All they want to do is lie there hidden, but she has to go and disturb them.

Enid's letter will be about their appointment at Central beneath the advertisements for Pears soap, how daily the date grows closer. How Enid thinks constantly of working beside her in the fields of flax, and of Mrs. Bea's pink eiderdown, its satiny expanse. Thinks, too, of the candle on the bedside table which they took turns to blow out. How on Sunday afternoons the loft in the blue sky had joined them with the round ocean and the living air. (Enid's letters often run to a spot of poetry.)

Central Station will smell of soot and meat pies and beer and that strong cleaning liquid they use in the Ladies'. And of people coming and going, full of the peculiar elevated tension of having something joyful, something sorrowful, actually happening to them for once and not to others.

We're connected, you and me, Enid writes. You go on turning the pages of your life, and you run into someone and you ask yourself, is this the one? Then you realize you're mistaken and you tell yourself, don't be a dope, who do you think you are? After a while you can't resist trying again. You get your hopes up. Maybe this is the one? On you go, feeling tense at your core, although on top you're pretending you're perfectly fine. All the while you're searching.

That's how it was until I met you. It isn't like that with me any more. You're the one. We're connected, Alice. We are.

At Central they will hug carefully, like sisters. Their eyes, their faces, will do the rest. She'll tell Enid that she was right. About what she said in her letters, and in the waiting room down in Victoria. Anyone passing by won't have a clue what they're on about; might just as well be speaking about a parcel or a port.

When they leave Central, exactly where are they going to go? They'll have to keep their guard up. Until their door, somewhere, is shut. And then she'll say to Enid, joking but not, "I need a drink."

Two single ladies require a room in a boarding house. It is possible. Two single ladies is quite possible. (The other, unimaginable.) But there will be no end to it, the dissembling, being careful. Love's old sweet gone wrong. Not even Enid can change that. Still, they'll do it. One way or another, so help me God. Better keep God out of this.

Alice doesn't care; it's what she wants. And there is something unfair about leading Dick on. She really has been leading him on, hasn't she? She's even thought about taking him home to Ardara. He's a good bloke; he deserves better than this. There are heaps of women around who'd give their eyeteeth to have him.

As for her, she has an appointment at Central beneath the ads for Pears. And come hell or high water, she is going to keep it. All the king's horses and all the king's men won't keep her away. She'll tell Enid. Strong and victorious.

Dead scared, that'll be more like it.

Happy and glorious. That's what she'll say, for Enid. She'll insist.

Alice lies on her bed and reads again the story they shared on the train, in the loft, beneath the pink satin eiderdown, reads it right through to the end.

In the flat opposite, the woman's face was in shadow, her body naked.

I turned away.

I thought my heart would break.

6

That Polio Kid's Come Back

What happens to Bernadette is this: one day in the spring the angel seeks her out. He's bigger than a battleship, this angel, an airborne battleship. He comes into the valley where the property is and hovers over it. His wings cast a giant shadow on the house, on the orchard with its five pet lambs, on the chook run, on the sheds, on her horse, Blazer. The shadow extends from the creek on one side, with its row of quinces, to the cow bales on the other, beneath the stringybarks.

Out of all the properties in the district, he selects Ardara. And within her house, he picks her. His choice makes Bernadette one of those who might rate a mention in the Bible. She's crossed the line and joined the leper, the beggar at the gate.

BERNADETTE'S NOT AS BAD OFF as Terry, who's been in an iron lung. And she's not as bad off as Lynette. (She's heard the doctors say of Lynette's legs, "Quite useless.")

They keep the polio kids at each end of the glassed-in verandah: Bernadette and Lynette at one end, Terry at the other. The middle of the verandah is open to the garden. On hot days they are carried to the open part. Bernadette and Lynette and Terry sit together, looking out at the garden, and beyond, to the gasworks. The garden is a row of leggy geraniums.

"I reckon somebody forgot to water them geraniums," her father drawls, in a jokey, put-on voice.

"*Those* geraniums," Bernadette corrects.

Terry has been down in Sydney at Camperdown Hospital, where they have iron lungs. But Terry doesn't need an iron lung any more. He has a rocking bed, which is like a rocking chair only bigger. When it's switched on, it rocks back and forth, and that helps push the air in and out of Terry's lungs. The rocking bed has wheels; it can be rolled along the verandah. It was donated by the Lions and has a small silver plaque at the bottom: Gift of the Lions Club to Araluen Hospital, April 19, 1954.

One day, when there was no one around, Terry let his sister Jennifer have a turn on the bed. The Giz caught them at it. Nurse Gisborne. The Giz is the day nurse.

Bernadette tells Terry and Lynette her stories, the most important ones. Last year she and Blazer won first prize at the Araluen Show for all-round riding proficiency. Blazer is black with white points.

She explains about the angel, how he came for her. The angel picked her because of her father. Her father came back from the Islands with a metal leg that was covered with fleshy-looking stuff like they use for dolls. The angel saw her father walking stiffly in the paddock and knew immediately that he'd got the right property. Some homesteads have their names painted on the roof, but Ardara doesn't.

She's already told Nana about the angel. "Every angel is terrible," Nana said. And held her tight.

BERNADETTE TELLS MAC about the angel. Nurse MacIlwaine lets them call her Mac. "It's Mac to my mates," she says, in the voice you keep for sharing secrets. "Not when Sister's around, mind."

Mac's the night nurse. When she tells Mac about the angel, Mac doesn't say, Oh, yeah, or, Pull the other one.

"It's called sixth sense. Also second sight," Mac says. "Not everybody who's Celtic has it, but you and I do."

Bernadette tells Mac that there's some English blood on her mother's side. Her great-grandfather was English.

"That doesn't seem to have got in the way, though, does it?" says Mac.

Bernadette is more than eight and a half, Terry is only eight, and Lynette has just turned nine. Terry and Lynette show Bernadette what's expected of kids in hospital. They show her "pretend you're okay," because things are simpler that way. They show her "pretend you're asleep," because sometimes you get to hear things.

Lynette and Terry are both townies. Neither knows how to ride. Lynette even claims to be afraid of horses. "Horses are too big," she says.

Terry agrees. "They don't like me," he explains. "They show the whites of their eyes."

Terry must have done something really stupid.

When Bernadette explains that Blazer has a good hard mouth, they don't even know what she's talking about. What can you say to kids like that?

IN HER FIRST WEEK, Bernadette calls Nurse Gisborne "Nurse Gibbon." She lunges at Bernie and slaps her face with a steady, grim precision.

"Any more of your cheek, and I'll give you what for," Nurse Gisborne says; she has gone bright red, like the geraniums. Then she rushes out of the room and down the hallway.

"Old Gibbon Guts is like that," Lynette says. "Wait till this arvo."

That afternoon the Giz brings them chocolate ice cream for

afternoon tea. Comes in with the tray, thumps it down, not looking at them.

"Oh *thank you,* Nurse *Gis*borne," says Lynette. Rubbing it in.

MAC KNOWS THAT SOON there's going to be a cure for polio. She's seen the words floating in front of her. Mac has a lie-down on Sunday afternoons, before she comes on shift. When she's waking up, she sees the words. The words explain what the cure is. The words are floating, Mac says, "floating in the gloaming."

There is something about that phrase, "floating in the gloaming," that makes Bernadette uneasy. Wasn't it only the Scots who roamed about in the gloaming? (You weren't supposed to say Scotch for people, only for shortbread.) What exactly was gloaming, anyway? Some kind of swamp? Did the Irish have gloaming too, or had it been stolen from them?

One day Mac tells her she's seen the words more clearly. They were in a newspaper. Mac couldn't make the words out, but she knew for certain that they were in a newspaper. She could see that there were other stories as well. All the different stories were going down the page, side by side. Mac has tried and tried to read the type, but it drifts away.

When Mac describes these things, her voice is hoarse. It puts Mac off her tea. She sits by Bernadette's bed, pale and exalted. "The gift takes it out of me," Mac says.

THE FAMILIES COME ON SUNDAY afternoons, Terry's and Bernadette's.

Lynette acts superior because she hasn't got any family. No one who comes to visit, anyway. "I'm actually an orphan," Lynette boasts. An old woman looks after her; Lynette calls her Auntie, although she isn't a real aunt. She doesn't come to the hospital on Sundays because she's some weirdo religion.

Bernadette's family drives into Araluen to ten o'clock Mass: Mum and Dad and Nana, and her brother, Bob, who's not yet seven. After Mass, Mum says, they are forced to twiddle their thumbs until

1:30 p.m. — visiting hours. They have a picnic lunch in the park. Dad reads the Sunday papers, while Mum and Nana get on with the darning.

When it's finally time to visit, the Behans sit beside Bernie's bed, which has been wheeled out to the open part of the verandah.

"We had to hang around the park like a bottle of stale piss," Bob says (when Mum and Dad are off speaking with Sister). Nana laughs and tells him to watch it.

Nana insists on holding Bernadette's hand, stroking her hair. She and Nana have the same rather long face and fine dark hair (or at least Nana's hair used to be black, but now it's half-and-half and wiry). Mac's remarked on it. "You look like your grandmother," Mac said, "the family resemblance is really quite striking." That made Bernadette squirmy. Who in their right mind wants to look like their *grandmother?*

"What have they done to you, my precious little Pacifica?" Nana whispers. Pacifica is Nana's secret name for Bernadette. When you have a secret name, it can be spoken only in whispers. (Mac agrees.)

Mum comes back from meeting with Sister and has her polite-mother face on.

Sometimes Bernadette's best friend, Deirdre, comes to the hospital too. Deirdre sits down and immediately begins to say things she's carefully thought up. Things about other kids, the nuns, even what they're learning in school. Bernadette doesn't want to think about the classroom — she can see Deirdre fiddling with her pencil box, the seat beside her empty. Actually it's probably not empty, they'll have some other kid in it by now. They're opening their readers, they're staring out at the pepper tree, they're thinking about lunch. It's exactly like that poem Mum recites:

The sun was shining on the sea,
Shining with all his might:
He did his very best to make
The billows smooth and bright —

135

And this was odd, because it was
The middle of the night.

Dad's been mustering in the Three Mile paddock, tailing the lambs. Crows are getting at Mum's bantam chooks. Bob took the dray out to get some wood, forgot to put the bellyband on Sailor and had to come back. Then the axe leapt back at him from the tough yellow box, slicing into his wrist.

Bob shows Bernadette the cut. He offers to show it to Terry.

Bernadette can hear the lambs and ewes, bleating. She sees the crows with their clever dark eyes, seizing their chances. They are all far away and very small.

Her mother says, of something, "I was at my wits' end."

Bob, who's forever drawing pictures, has brought her a sketch of Blazer. Blazer, stepping high on slim legs. He's her glamour boy. But she can tell from the alert, interested look Bob has captured that Blazer's taking Bob seriously these days. Blazer's watching with big eyes, trying to figure out what Bob's doing with his pencil and his sketchbook.

"Does Blazer miss me?" she asks.

BERNADETTE'S PARENTS KNOW Terry's parents: the mothers play tennis together every Thursday afternoon. On Thursday nights, Nana gets the tea.

Mum's big on tennis. Comes in late for tea, pink in the face. Walks around the house with her tennis racquet over her shoulder like a rifle, looking pleased with herself. Stands in front of the bedroom mirror still in her whites, practising her serve. Terry's mother's a terrifically good sport, Mum says.

Last year Terry's mother had several shandies too many at the Christmas get-together. Terry's father jumped in the ute and drove off without her. So Mum had to take Terry's mother home. Didn't come back until sun-up. Took that long to get her sobered up, Mum said.

To the hospital, Terry's mother wears a spring-green gabardine suit with a spray of violets on the lapel. She hastens over to Bernadette's mother. They kiss and carry on.

"Alice," cries Terry's mother, "how *are* you?"

"Bearing up, Hazel," replies Mum, putting on her rapid, gushy voice. "Bearing up. But how are *you?*" Mum touches the shoulder of Terry's mother, and Terry's mother lets out a squeak.

They're just the mothers; they're not the ones who have it.

Terry's father is wearing a brown suit and a hat to hide under. He sits by Terry's bed with his shoulders up around his ears. It's the fathers who hate being here the most.

Terry's sister, Jennifer, comes, too, and eats all the biscuits.

Terry's father's a grease monkey. Bernadette saw him when her own father took the Dodge in for a tune-up. Terry's father was out in front of the petrol station, wearing dark blue overalls. Wiping his fingers on his trousers, then putting his hands on his hips. The wind was going after his hair.

Families are a terrible embarrassment. Everyone will feel so much better when they've all gone home.

"I need the newspapers," Bernie tells her father.

He dips his head and looks sideways at her. "What newspapers?"

"All of them," Bernadette commands grandly. Being the way she is, she can say things like that.

The next weekend her father brings the local newspaper. The local will have to do. In a rare show of intelligence, her brother comes with pictures: colour advertisements for drenches, complete with sheep's intestines infested with flukes and worms.

Bernadette plans to show Terry and Lynette as soon as she can.

IT'S EARLY EVENING, and they're going to be allowed to sleep out on the open part of the verandah because it's so hot. This was the Giz's idea. (With the Giz, you never know.)

The air is full of the gum-smell of bushfires. Behind the gasworks, a smoky yellow moon is climbing up.

Bernadette reads aloud to Lynette and Terry. All three of them are on the lookout for the cure. The cure Mac saw in the newspaper.

"Boy Trod on Rake," Bernadette reads. That's the headline.

"Edward Kelly (12) of 82 Beardy Street sustained a puncture wound to his right foot when he trod on a garden rake at his home on Saturday morning."

"Nah," says Terry.

"Baby Drowns in Bucket of Milk," Bernadette offers.

"How could you drown in a bucket?" Lynette asks.

"It'd have to be a pretty big bucket," Terry says.

"Well it *could* be a big bucket," Bernadette points out. "The kind of bucket you keep to feed the pigs."

Bernadette (who is relieved that neither Lynette nor Terry wants to have a go) reads some more: "It's a trend. A suit smartly tailored from Treebark. You'll be intrigued by Treebark. Woven into its weave is the look of the bark of a tree. You'll be fascinated, too, by the new shades, in green, brown, and fawn."

Terry says, "Bark might be a good bet. I'll get Jennifer onto it."

Terry's sister, Jennifer, is already working on a cure. She claims the clue lies in the ruby on the head of a Black Prince locust.

"Their proper name is cicadas," says Mac. Mac's real name is Dora, which is ghastly. Mac made her promise not to tell, cross your heart and hope to die. "Why everyone around here calls them locusts, I don't know."

Bernadette doesn't like the way Mac says "everyone around here."

Mac comes from Sydney. "The big smoke," the Giz says.

Terry's sister is collecting Black Princes. She's waiting until she has a hundred, then she's going to send them down to Sydney. "There's oil in that ruby patch on the locust's head," Terry explains to Mac.

Terry's got a scar over his windpipe. That's where he used to have a tube hanging out.

"You might have to distill it," Terry labours on.

"Well you never know, do you?" says Mac.

138

Mac stands at the edge of the verandah and looks out to the gasworks, dreaming.

Lynette and Bernadette don't have any faith in Terry's sister and her grand ambitions. Terry's sister believes you get polio by chewing on the quills of magpie feathers. Doesn't she realize it's the virus? (It's the angel. Nana knows. Mac knows.)

MAC SITS IN A CHAIR and reads the paper until they are all asleep.

Bernadette wakes up and there is Mac, asleep herself. The newspaper lies open in her lap. Mac had been reading "Royal Romance Rumour." Bernadette can't see what it says because it's upside down. In the margins, Mac has been doodling. Bernadette twists her head around to try to make it out.

Stu, Mac has written.

Stu.

Stu.

Stu.

BERNADETTE ISN'T SURPRISED that Lynette's father survived as a prisoner of the Japanese, only to be run over by a train. Lynette's mother was killed, too, when their car stalled on a level crossing. They'd gone out to get Lynette a bicycle for her birthday, and the new bike was in the car with them. A Malvern Star. Ruined.

Bernadette isn't surprised, because this is exactly how her mother talks. You know that man who was hit in the temple by a golf ball? His brain burst on his honeymoon? Well, his widow was opening a can of tomatoes and they blew up in her face, blinding her. Then, two years later, her new husband was carrying a long irrigation pipe and it touched a live wire.

Her mother, talking on the party line, would tell these stories as if they proved something she needed to be true.

Bernadette wonders what Mum says now.

MAC HAS FOUND OUT what their favourite things are (lime cordial and Nestle's milk chocolate are Bernadette's), and she goes and buys them. She keeps them in the fridge in the nurses' kitchen. If they can't sleep, she'll bring something out to them.

The night light shines down the verandah — heaps of moths are throwing themselves at it. Mac comes into the room and sits by Bernadette's bed. She takes out the chocolate bar, tears off the red covering. Carefully, she peels away the thin gold paper. "I used to go nuts for these when I was a kid," Mac says.

Mac grew up in Watson's Bay, on Sydney harbour. ("Pretty tony," Mum says. "Wonder what's she doing up here in the bush?")

Bernadette's been saving up a story for Mac. She found it in the newspaper: "A woman said yesterday that a tornado blew her daughter and her daughter's pony half a mile through the air. The woman said her daughter suffered some bruising, but her pony, which she was riding, was not hurt. 'The pony just flew,' she said."

THE BIG HOSPITAL NEWS is that the men from the government are coming up from Sydney. Even before "Hospital Half Hour" is finished on the radio, the three of them are moved along the verandah, to wait. The Giz warns them that when the men from the government are here they are to speak only if spoken to.

As soon as the Giz has gone off, Bernadette pulls out the newspaper and begins to read:

There has been more sensational evidence in the trial of Stuart Mitchell Hindmarsh, 33, grazier, of Chandos Station. Hindmarsh, whose wife died suddenly on New Year's Day, is alleged to have poisoned his wife by putting cyanide in some Minties. The dead woman's brother told the court that when a bag of Minties accidentally spilled on the floor of the kitchen at Chandos Station last October, the accused shouted, "No one is to eat any!"

The accused, who has denied all charges, alleges that his wife took her own life.

Cyanide is in Cynogas, which Dad uses for spraying in the orchard. Bernadette's mother says, "If I ever catch you or Bob mucking about with the Cynogas, I'll nail you to the wall for a picture, and I mean it."

The court was told that the accused had formed an attachment with another woman. The accused said that he first realized his chances of getting a divorce were hopeless towards the end of November or early December.

He said: "I thought of leaving the property, putting a manager on the place, and going to Sydney to get a job. I had in mind that my wife might then get a divorce on the grounds of desertion. But I did not take that step."

Reading this, Bernadette looks up and sees the men from the government walking out onto the verandah. Sister is there, and even Matron. The Giz.

The Giz is going to eat her alive.

She turns the page and, without any clear thought of what she's doing, begins to read from "The Week in Wool": "Bradford importers believe that Russia may be stockpiling wool."

The most important man, the one in the middle of the group, advances, beaming. "Current affairs," he says, delighted.

"Those Russkies are at it again," the other man says, quick to catch the tone. He thumps Bernadette on the shoulder.

They have their picture taken. There is Bernadette, holding onto the newspaper. Lynette is sitting on the important man's knee, and Terry is in his Lions Club rocking bed, with the other man smiling down at him. Matron and Sister wear identical, suspicious smiles. The Giz doesn't get in the picture; she has to stand off to one side.

"What about the attachment with another woman?" asks Lynette, as soon as they're out of sight.

Bernadette reads the rest of it:

"You were longing for freedom so you could marry this other woman?"

"Yes, by divorce. I did not anticipate the death of my wife."

MAC SITS BY BERNADETTE'S BED and talks. Mac's in a mood.

Mac's worked with kids in Sydney, kids in an iron lung, like Terry. "An iron lung whirs like a Singer sewing machine," Mac says. "It has rubber-lined portholes. A big rubber collar for the neck. You have to stick your arms through the portholes, quickly, to turn the kid or move a blanket. You have to not let any air escape."

Bernadette doesn't want to hear about the iron lung. Those two words, "iron lung," will pull you right down into the middle of the earth.

"If they're getting better," Mac persists, "you open the iron lung and try to get them to breathe for a few minutes. Frog breathing. You try to get them to do frog breathing." Mac gulps air like a frog.

Bernadette offers Mac some of her chocolate. But tonight Mac wants to be sad. It's as if that's the only honest way to be.

Bernadette imagines Blazer in the shed, his head in his nosebag. By now he doesn't miss her any more. He's got Bob. When he hears Bob's voice, his shoulder muscles ripple.

THEY'RE TO HAVE EXERCISES. A physio has arrived. Giz gets them out on the open verandah to meet her. Above her upper lip, the physio has a line of black hair. The Giz is keen because now she's got the physio to push around as well.

The physio wraps their joints in hot wax.

"We're going to get those muscles moving," declares the Giz.

Arms first. Later it will be legs. The physio sets up a contraption for them, which is like a race they put sheep in for drenching or to force them along to the dip. Monkey bars, the Giz calls them.

Terry doesn't have to do all this. He's still on his bed. It's just Lynette and Bernadette. When Lynette's arms are stronger, she's going to have a wheelchair you drive yourself. (Bernie isn't.) For now, Lynette and Bernadette use hospital chairs, saggy adult ones. They have to be pushed.

"Righto, arms up," the Giz barks. "Reach for the sky. Arms *up*. Open *wide*."

Busy being the big expert, the Giz can't get enough of the physio. Corners her, murmurs in that excited, hushy voice adults get on for gossip they can't wait to repeat although they've promised not to tell a soul.

Bernadette is doing "pretend you're asleep" — which involves some pretty convincing breathing — when she hears the Giz saying to the physio, "That poor man. No wonder he turned to Mac in a big way. His wife'd been running around with the stock and station agent for years."

The physio, who is a quick learner, keeps her mouth shut.

"One day the stock and station agent upped and left for England, without so much as a by-your-leave. The wife couldn't take it, did herself in. Poison's what people use out here in the backblocks. The wife's brother saw his chance and fingered Stuart. The brother couldn't wait to get his hands on the property, you understand, on those big fat stud rams. Stuart isn't one of the local nobs; he came over from New Zealand and did far too well for a Johnny-come-lately. In this part of the world, the landed gentry call the tune, and boy, do they stick together. Everyone knew the charge was a beat-up but nobody stepped forward to say boo. It's the nineteenth century round here, going on eighteenth; you don't know what you're walking into. Mac's in way over her head, I'd say.

"Luckily the judge didn't come down in the last shower, and wasn't a local. He threw the whole thing out, but mud sticks. To be quite frank, Mac doesn't know if Stuart'll ever be the same again. She says it's pitiful. He keeps trying to pull himself together, then he falls back down again."

Bernadette's mouth has gone paper-dry. Her tongue pokes about like it's investigating surfaces for the first time.

LYNETTE AND BERNADETTE ARE PLAYING CARDS. Terry is watching. The physio says it's good for their muscles. They're afraid the Giz will grizzle, but the Giz joins in.

"I'll be Terry," the Giz says. "I'll play for Terry."

How can you be yourself when the Giz's big hand is reaching over the table?

The Giz wins everything. She beats them all the time, even at silly, easy things like Strip Jack Naked. The Giz wants more. "What you kids need to know," she says, "is how to play poker. Poker," she declares momentously, "is the great game of life. Nothing less." She reaches into her pocket and digs out her matches.

"The first thing to learn about poker," she explains, "is when it's best to stick with a pair." The Giz deals the cards, *flick, flick, flick*. "If Sister ever finds out about this," the Giz says, "she'll slaughter me."

MAC'S KNITTING A SWEATER in dark red wool. She has the pattern book open in front of her. All of the sweaters have names: "Simon," "Peter," "Stephen." She's knitting "Simon." It's in moss stitch.

Simon is standing in front of a tree, holding a pipe.

"Is he going to like it?" Bernadette asks.

Mac says, "Oh, I hope so."

Mac sits up on the bed beside Bernadette, and together they look at Simon. Bernadette can see that Mac's there with Simon, beside the tree. He's still holding his pipe, but his other arm is around Mac. You can see only the top half of Simon. So Bernadette dresses Simon in white moleskin trousers and elastic-sided boots (brown, of course, nobody wears black elastic-sided boots). When he goes to town, he puts a tweed jacket over his moss-stitch sweater. The elbows of his jacket are reinforced with suede.

I do have the gift, too, Bernadette tells herself. A little bit of it. That is why she knew to say, "Is he going to like it?" not, "Who is he?" (And certainly not, never in a million years, "Didn't his wife top herself because her boyfriend dumped her?")

THEY'RE IN THE NURSES' KITCHEN, and Mac has given Bernadette a bowl of jelly — port wine flavour (Terry's favourite). Bernie's sitting on Mac's lap, even though she's much too old.

One of the other night nurses is there. It's Nurse Trevor, from what Mac calls "obstets." Earlier this evening, Nurse Trevor reports, there was a baby.

Mac and Nurse Trevor are eating mince on toast. Mac cuts a bit and pops it in Bernadette's mouth. It mixes in pleasantly with the jelly.

To impress Nurse Trevor, Bernadette asks Mac, "Do you think they're getting closer to a cure?"

"Oh, I think they are finding a cure, pet," Mac says. "They're pretty close now."

Mac finishes up her mince, and Nurse Trevor takes her plate. "It will be too late for lots of kids," Mac adds.

Mac starts saying names, in a tender, murmuring way, rocking Bernie as she does so: "Pauline, Nino, Mark, Gosia, John, Veronica, Janet, Beth, Peter."

Bernadette knows right away that these are the names of the really sick kids, those who are having a much rougher spin, those who need to be fiercely brave. (When she heard Mac say the name Veronica, a shudder went through her. It's her own middle name, after Nana's twin, who died not long after Bernadette was born. If only she'd known you, Nana says. If only.) She leans into Mac, burrows into her arms as deep as she can.

Nurse Trevor brings the teapot to the table. "Hear you've got a horse at home," she says crisply, to Bernadette. You can tell Nurse Trevor wants to change the subject.

Nurse Trevor is friendly but cool. (Standing close behind the friendliness, judgement. At all times, one must keep one's head. Let your guard down and you'll cross the line and you won't ever get back.)

Bernadette doesn't think about Blazer as much as she used to. Bob rides him. It's Bob he comes to now, looking for his sugar cubes.

"You know something, Trev?" Mac says. "You know what I think?"

Nurse Trevor stares down at her cup.

"I think I'm living with heroes."

Nurse Trevor looks at Mac as if she's gone too far.

"Living with heroes," Mac insists.

LYNETTE'S CHAIR HAS ARRIVED. It has a posh one-armed drive. Lynette goes about in it like Lady Muck.

"It's a beaut, mate," says Mac. "A real little bobby-dazzler."

Even the Giz acts respectful. Calls it the Rolls.

Bernadette knows how lovely it would be to chuck Lynette out of her new chair, send her sprawling on the floor. Maybe the chair could roll off the verandah and end up in the garden with dirt on it.

Rolls rolls.

Maybe it'd be raining. Lynette's chair wouldn't have dirt on it; it'd have mud. Mac would say to Bernadette, "You'd think she'd take a little more pride."

Terry's got the flu. He lies on his rocking bed and cannot talk. Bernie looks at Terry. Gulping like a frog out of water.

"Mac reckons she's living with heroes," she says to Terry. She watches Terry's face. Sees him soaking up this information like a blotter dealing with ink. Feels the warm lift of power. "Living with heroes," she repeats. Mac gave it to her and now she's giving it to Terry.

TERRY'S FLU TURNS INTO PNEUMONIA and he has to be flown to Camperdown. It's an emergency. Bernadette and Lynette hear the Giz talking to Mac, telling her the news.

"Oh, no," Mac says loudly.

"Take it easy, mate."

Now Mac's really shouting: "Not again. I can't stand this, really I can't." She kicks the wall. It's only a bit of fibro. Her foot goes right through.

"Oh, my God," breathes the Giz.

Mac begins to laugh in a way that says it's funny but isn't. "Looks like I've gone and put my foot in it."

The Giz begins to laugh too. "That's torn it, I'd say."

"Sister's going to throw a tizzy."

They hold on to each other, Mac and the Giz. They giggle so hard their noses run.

MAC TAKES EASTER OFF. On the Tuesday after Easter, she doesn't show up for the night shift as expected. There is a huddle of nurses in the hall.

Sister arrives and there is silence.

Much later a nurse they don't know comes in. They pretend to be asleep and she switches off the light.

What's happened to Mac?

"She was knitting a sweater," Bernadette tells Lynette. "In moss stitch."

"Who for?"

Bernadette won't let on. That might be telling on Mac.

Stu.

Stu.

Stu.

THEY WAIT FOR THE GIZ to come on the next day.

"Ask for a poker game," Lynette urges. "Put her in a good mood."

But the Giz is brimming over with the news; they don't have to do anything to get it out of her. On Thursday, Giz says, Mac left to catch the bus to Armidale in the late afternoon. She'd booked a sleeper through to Sydney on the night mail train. Mac said she'd be back on Tuesday.

"When she left she was perfectly all right. A bit excited, but that's only to be expected." The Giz's voice is okay on top, but underneath, uncertain. "She was going to see her mother and father in Watson's Bay."

The Giz stops talking, and her face flames up. The Giz is fibbing.

"What are you kids looking at?" the Giz demands.

BERNADETTE IS SITTING ON THE VERANDAH with Lynette, reading aloud from the local newspaper. She finds this:

> The coroner's office today confirmed that Stuart Mitchell Hindmarsh, of Chandos Station near Armidale, died on Easter Sunday morning of stomach poisoning. He was discovered by a friend in the early hours of Good Friday morning, and immediately transported to Armidale Hospital, where repeated attempts to revive him proved unsuccessful. Autopsy results revealed that Mr. Hindmarsh had ingested a fatal dose of Bluenic. The substance, a mixture of bluestone and nicotine, is widely used for drenching. Mr. Hindmarsh had been due to leave by train on Thursday night to exhibit his prize merino, Ramses, in the Royal Easter Show.

And here is the Giz, heading across the room.

What happens next is fast at first, then particularly slow. In a single, capable motion, the Giz grabs the paper out of Bernadette's hands and tips her out of the chair, knocking it over as she does so. "You are a stupid, *stupid* girl," the Giz says, and leaves her there on the verandah floor.

Even after the Giz has left, the verandah is full of her anger, huge and focused and strong.

Bernadette lies on the floor, a beggar at the gate.

Lynette in her wheelchair begins to sob.

"Don't, oh, please don't," says Bernadette, for her own sake.

She tries to drag herself to the monkey bars. If she can get there, she'll be able to reach up. (Arms *up*. Open *wide*.)

First, you have to begin.

Next, you have to keep on going. Nothing less.

She's about halfway across the floor, and she believes she's going to make it to the monkey bars. That's when she says, "This should be good for some ice cream, I reckon."

Finally up on the monkey bars, she adds, "Ice cream, bananas, and cream. What do you bet?"

There was lemonade, too.

MAC COMES BACK. Walks out onto the verandah and stands beside them. She doesn't look all that different. Not right away.

"Been playing lots of poker, have you?" Mac asks.

Up close, Bernadette can see Mac's doing "pretend you're okay." Trying to make her face do what she's told it to.

The day after the angel came, Bernadette tried to get her legs to do what she told them to. Her mother was mad at her for not getting up on time to ride her bike to school.

"No," Bernadette says, "we've just been going through the paper."

"Read me something, mate," Mac says, and sits down. Pulls up another chair and puts her feet up. Shuts her eyes, sighs, lets her head fall right back. "Go ahead, do it to me."

Mac is mysterious and brave and exhausted, and Bernadette will love her forever.

Bernadette reads "Cyclist Hits Mailbox." She decides to skip "Triplets All Die." She reads "Rabbit Skins Cheaper."

BERNADETTE'S GOING HOME. Back to school.

"Promise me one thing," says Mac. "Promise me."

Mac pulls Bernadette onto her knee so they're both facing

outwards. They can talk without having to look at each other. More gets said that way.

"What?" asks Bernadette.

"You have to promise me: when you know you've done your best, you'll never toss in your hand."

"Is that like throw in the towel?"

"Yes. Throw up the sponge."

Bernadette smells a possible game.

"I won't drop my bundle."

"No matter what anyone says, you'll stick to your guns."

"Like a barnacle to a rock?"

"Yes."

"Like a bug in a rug?"

"Even better."

Bernadette grows daring.

"Like shit to a blanket?"

"Exactly!"

Mac laughs, then stops abruptly. "Listen, mate, here's the plan. I won't always be there with you, but I know for a fact you're going to out-swim the seas, out-climb the mountaintops. But there's more. Remember what I said about living with heroes?"

"You've been living with heroes."

"Too right I have. And you know what? I want you to be on the lookout for them. You never know where they might be; they show up in the most unlikely places. You won't forget that, will you? To be on the lookout?"

"I won't forget."

She can feel Mac's arms right around her, enfolding her. "Never forget. That's the deal. Cross your heart and hope to die?"

"Hope to die."

BERNADETTE HAS CALIPERS ON HER LEGS. With crutches, she can get about. Within six months to a year, they promise (all going well), she'll be able to throw those crutches away. The doctors say so. Mac says so, too. In Mac's voice there is too much brightness.

Bernadette's mother talks without looking down at the leg braces, the calipers. Instead, she gets a cigarette out of her handbag, lights it, and stares at the smoke she makes.

Bernadette explains that she should stay here with Mac. And with Lynette and — yes — the Giz. She wants Terry back with them, too, in his rocking bed. (The far end of the verandah is dense with silence.)

"Don't be silly," Mum says. "Of course you want to come home."

Her mother produces the David Jones catalogue, pushes it across the table. "Pick out whatever you want, and I'll order it from DJ's."

This is what Bernadette's mother does: she leafs through the DJ's catalogue and picks out dresses. The moment the parcel arrives is best of all. Mum tears at the brown paper, too greedy to think of smoothing and folding and saving. But by the time she's tried the dress on, examined herself in the mirror, she's drooping a bit. It's not quite what she had in mind. It's *very* good quality, Mum insists (she won't hear a word against DJ's, she's terribly loyal). She adds, "It's just not quite how I saw it in the mind's eye."

Then her mother takes off the dress and goes completely still. She's thinking of how she saw it, before, in the mind's eye.

Next week she's leafing through the catalogue, enthusiastic again.

(*Pacifica is walking along a city street. Wearing a navy-and-cream linen suit. What's that smell? Tweed perfume.*)

"I don't want anything from DJ's," Bernadette says. "I think I should stay here. I think I should stay until I don't need crutches anymore."

"Oh, for Pete's sake," snaps Mum. "You may think your family isn't important to you, young lady. You wait. Just wait."

"I don't want to come home," repeats Bernadette, not sacrificing her dignity.

Mum starts in: "Let me tell you something," she says, her voice rising in a dangerous way.

Mum's lips are tight, like they're trying to stop what's about to come out. "When you get home you'll forget all about this, the time you spent here." Mum looks around the room as if condemning it. She's going white around the gills. Jesus. "I know it seems impossible to you at the moment, Bernadette, but you'll look back and it will seem as if none of this ever existed."

Mum pauses, out of breath.

"This Nurse MacIlwaine, this Mac you're so fond of. She's the cat's pyjamas right now, but the months will go by and you'll find you don't think about her any more. You don't believe me, I know, but I'm telling you. You'll find it's your family that counts in the long run. Your family." Mum puts her head down on the table and begins to bawl.

Mum's raving, gone bananas. How on earth could anyone ever forget someone like Mac?

With an unfamiliar feeling of authority, Bernadette reaches over, opens her mother's purse, takes out her mother's hankie. Offers it to her. Watches her push it away, then finally take it.

After Mum calms down, she sits there like a kid in kindergarten who's wet her pants. A scared little kid sitting absolutely still, not daring to look as the puddle spreads.

Bernadette wonders how much Mum knows about the angel. Is Mum aware that the angel is watching her as she drives through a blind intersection and, without looking, pulls out onto the highway?

THERE WAS TALK ABOUT BERNADETTE being put back a class, with a bunch of younger kids. Her mother — her old self again — claims she was forced to have words with the nuns. "I had to put my foot down," Mum says.

Bernadette knows how it's going to be. They'll all look up when she's brought in. She'll have to swing along on her crutches to her desk. (Which is worse: the humiliation, or knowing you've been chosen?) The rubber thump of the crutches, descending together. Then — and this is what they'll all be listening for — the scrape of the calipers as they drag across the wooden floor.

It will be no good telling them: I won first prize at the Araluen Show for all-round riding proficiency. When I galloped Blazer along the back of the lucerne paddock not even Dad could catch us.

None of it exists.

She can hear them already. *That polio kid's come back.*

7

On Another Far Shore

Against the flood noise of the creek, against the croaking of frogs and incessant rain, Dick begins to talk to his wife, Alice, about the war. For the first time in their twelve years of marriage, he speaks of the months early in 1942 when he fled from the advancing Japanese, fled on foot through the jungles of New Britain, up above New Guinea.

In the jungle, Dick tells Alice, things are heaped up. Scrub on scrub, vines on vines, vines on trees, trees on trees: everything dank and clogged and twisted and hidden and layered. And all the same, going on, into the green-dark, forever. You can't get your bearings, can't see the sky, don't know where you are.

Dick found that he could carry a man through the jungle; it was the obvious thing to do. In a fireman's grip, over his shoulder.

As he speaks, Dick gestures occasionally. Sparse, loose-limbed, amiable gestures, designed to deceive. His eyes, deep set, remain watchful. Dick Behan never gives much away, being a man who has learned to carry his burdens quietly. This, especially.

It is strange, Dick's account of being on the walking track, fleeing the invasion of Rabaul. The chronology's pretty much shot.

Trust Dick, Alice thinks, to leave this until they are literally up the creek.

IT WAS TO BE A HOLIDAY at the coast, their first holiday together, ever.

"After all you've been through," said Alice's mother, Ellen.

"All *we've* been through," Alice corrected, to include Ellen.

"Do you and Dick the world of good," urged Ellen. "Now that Bernie's on the mend." Bernie, now age ten, had spent more than a year in hospital with polio.

"Mother's dead set," Alice later reported to Dick. "She wants to take the kids down to Sydney, give us a break by ourselves."

They could afford it. The wool cheque would probably be good again. After the war they'd started getting seven, eight times more for their wool than they'd got before. And Bob, at eight, would be just old enough to enjoy the trip with his grandmother, to take an interest and remember things.

"I'll think about it," said Dick, prevaricating.

Graziers didn't go on holidays: stock could not be left, there were pastures to sew down. You might go to Newcastle for the wool sales, or to Sydney for the Royal Easter Show, but you didn't waste your time fooling around on a hot beach.

At the dinner table next day, Alice's mother took up the case again. In Sydney she and the kids would stay with Nana Rose. "Nana Rose gets about that flat on Ocean Street like a trooper," said Ellen. "She's got the pep of someone half her years."

At what age, Alice wondered briefly, does getting out of bed in the morning constitute a celebrated accomplishment?

Dick considered his mother-in-law and frowned. "There's the stock to see to," he said.

Ellen spotted the beginning of concession. "You could fit it in," she urged. "In the lull between the shearing and the crutching."

Ellen booked a week for them at Port Macquarie in a house

rented out by the Country Women's Association. (Cranky Women's Association, Dick always said.) It was advertised as having wide verandahs with wicker chairs and a fine view of Town Beach.

ALICE AND DICK LEAVE their property and set out along the gravel highway to the coast one mid-January morning in 1956. It is raining.

The boot of their car contains standard gear for any grazier on the move — a rope, an axe, and a small pick that Dick calls his trenching tool. You never know when you might come across a beast caught in the mud or a roo dead on the road. Alice is taking along homemade fruitcake and biscuits in tins, and a pile of their own apricots in a billycan. She puts these in the boot with the other gear. In the back seat she packs the sheets (you have to bring your own linen) and a cardboard box filled with staples: pepper and salt, tea, sugar — it wouldn't make sense to run out and have to buy them when they got there. A can of ham left over from Christmas. In front, beside her handbag, she stacks a pile of books — her mother's, mostly.

Dick drives through the thick rain, looking at the sodden stock, the runoff filling the gullies. "Good job the old Dodge still knows her way round," he says. They have their name down for one of those new Australian cars, the Holdens, but there's a two-year waiting list.

"Port" is what everyone calls Port Macquarie. It will take all day for them to reach Port, going down the Oxley highway. "Named for John Oxley," says Alice, studying the map. "Wasn't he one of those explorers who thought the middle of Australia was an inland sea?"

"The kids would know. Pretty quiet without them, isn't it?"

"Didn't Oxley egg on that other explorer, Sturt? God commanded Sturt to find the inland sea and he went west with a whaling boat."

"You'll have your inland sea right here, if this rain keeps up."

"Mother's the one who should be making this trip, not us."

Alice's mother comes from Sydney, and her idea of heaven is to stay in the surf for hours. Alice, who was born in the bush, is appalled by waves that rear up above her head. Still, they'll go to the beach every day. It's what one does at Port.

Alice supposes they'll go for a swim after breakfast. Back for lunch, then a lie-down in the heat of the day. Green blinds pulled right down to the sill. It should be her period the week they are at Port. Lucky, Dick doesn't mind a bit of blood: "Nothing strange about blood," he says.

Alice has a little black book on the rhythm method. She's heard of some religions where they think you are unclean and you have to stay in a hut for five days, which might not be a bad idea, come to think of it. She happens to be really regular. Not every woman is, although you can't expect the priests to realize that. Who is there to tell them?

Dick does all right with that side of things. He seems happy enough. No, he *is* happy enough. If anyone asked — of course, nobody does — she could hear herself saying, "Fine, thank you. Just fine." At first they'd had a bit of figuring out to do, because Dick lost a leg in the war, up in the jungle. Can't kneel in the way most men do.

Okay, so what will they do after that? Maybe she'll read aloud to him. He doesn't read much himself, but he does like the sound of her voice. In the evenings they'll go out for a walk. Fish and chips. At Port they have ice creams — somebody told her this — decorated with hundreds-and-thousands; you can get all different colours. What colour will she ask for? Green. It will feel very odd, buying ice creams without the kids.

When you add up the swimming and the lying down after lunch and the reading aloud and the walks in the evening and the ice creams, there will still be quite a few hours left.

BY NOON THEY ARE IN FALLS COUNTRY, where the northern table-lands of New South Wales drop away to the coast in steep gorges. Jagged slopes, sharp ridgelines, creeks and gullies. Khaki-and-olive country, open bush where you can see the sky. Rocks, grey gums, rust-brown stringybark. Nobody about, not much stock, just a few cattle, Herefords. Their faces are white, Dick says, because they know what's coming.

They have their thermos and eat their egg sandwiches in the car because of the downpour, and then get going again.

After taking the Dodge through several level crossings already awash with water, Dick comes to a creek too wide and wild to negotiate. The level crossing, if it is still there, has disappeared into swirls of dirty-brown, fast-moving water. Alice and Dick get out of the car and walk down to the spreading water's edge, to inspect. They're listening to the creek's strangely busy roar when the Dodge, behind them, begins to drift. It isn't any fault of Dick's; the brake's on. The road itself, undermined by furious runoff, has begun to break up.

Dick shouts and runs. So does Alice. They scramble up the crumbling bank and gaze, unbelieving, at what's going on in the water. The car is moving sedately along, as if in the hands of a timid, invisible driver. It's stopped only when the debris it's travelling on is caught up in gums a few hundred yards downstream.

Dick and Alice hike and slide along the bank, their eyes on the car. Winded, panting, they stop at a sodden tree trunk. The end of this tree is in the water, and the car has its nose wedged beneath it.

Alice sees that mud has ruined her white sandals and realizes she no longer cares.

They stare.

The car's drowned front end has become stuck beneath a crazy tangle of branches and earth. The engine and the front seat are under water. Alice's books swirl downstream, on their way to the coast. Her handbag, too. (Cigarettes, lipstick, powder, rouge, a bit of money.)

Dick says, "We'd better have a go at getting the stuff out of the car."

He's thinking of the rope, the axe, and the trenching tool.

Thank God the children aren't with them.

Dick inspects the tree and the position of the car, studies the way the current eddies at the bank before rushing away downstream. He inches along the fallen trunk of the tree, pulling himself by his arms so as not to slip.

Alice, behind him, tucks her skirt up into her pants and wades into the eddy.

Dick is astride the slippery branch, taking his time, no hurry. He's creeping up on the car as one would on prey.

With enormous patience, he retrieves his tools, two hessian sugarbags he keeps on the floor of the boot, the tins of cake and biscuits, the apricots from their own orchard. He passes them to Alice, who, knee-deep in water, slowly negotiates her way to the bank and back, item after item, so that their pile of goods grows steadily.

As the cold water goes pushing through her legs, Alice is aware of a sharp, unexpected happiness.

The rain continues. No cars come.

"The level crossing farther back must be washed out by now," Dick says.

"Does that mean we're cut off?" Alice asks. Sometimes she does this with Dick — asks a question to which she already knows the answer. Of course it means they're cut off, a drover's brown dog could have told her that. Washed out in front, washed out behind.

Like any countrywoman, Alice, without so much as being conscious of the fact, has taken note of where the homesteads ran out, where the edge of farms was reached, then passed, as the rocky escarpment took over.

They pile the gear under the thickest tree they can find and Dick begins to push through the bush. Again he's looking, considering. He's after the best place to make a shelter. He selects a shallow basin in a basalt outcrop that has shelves of overhanging rock.

While Alice transfers their cache, Dick sets off, axe in hand, stepping carefully in that stiff way he has. When he finds the right kind of tree, he strips some sheets of bark. He cuts leafy branches from the lower limbs. By evening he's got a fire going and has built a makeshift roof of bark, topped by his slicker. Then he partially dries out some of the cut bark and branches so he can layer bark, then branches, with more bark on the rocky ground.

"Hey, presto," he says, panting. "A floor."

"We should do this every day."

Dick takes one of the hessian sugarbags, slits it down a seam, and sticks it over his head like a cowl. Wearing this, he goes out into the rain again and begins digging a ditch around their camp with his trenching tool.

He's such a *bushie*, thinks Alice. And for once the thought does not disturb her.

"What do you reckon?" she says to Dick. "Do you suppose the secret of happiness is having something sufficiently serious to worry about?"

"I'm going to hunt for firewood," he replies. "You nurse the fire."

Off he goes, looking for bits of dry stuff under rock ledges. He's pleased with himself; she can tell by the way he holds his shoulders.

Alice opens the suitcase, which they've stuck beneath one of the rocky overhangs. Rummages for a pair of Dick's pants and socks and puts them on. Tucks the pants into the socks, slips into her sandshoes. Snakes will be active in the wet, best to watch your step.

Feeling much more comfortable, she walks to the edge of the creek and tosses in the ruined sandals.

Back at the camp (she already thinks of it as "the camp") she empties out the apricots, parks the billycan out in the rain until enough water has gathered to make tea. She sits on a log and makes a roll-your-own from Dick's supply of Log Cabin. Cavewoman waiting for caveman, she says to herself.

A fire, a cigarette, and hot sweet tea. What more does anyone need?

After Dick returns, and they've eaten some ham, biscuits, and fruitcake, they huddle in front of the fire beneath the car blanket (it smells a bit of petrol).

That's when Dick begins to talk.

IN RABAUL, NEW BRITAIN, in January 1942, a garrison of one thousand, four hundred Australian soldiers, outnumbered twenty to one, was abandoned. It was every man for himself. In small groups, they fled the superior invading Japanese force. They moved slowly westward, making for home.

In thick monsoonal rain, Dick and his mates forced the truck along the track as far as it would go.

"Was the rain heavier than this?" asks Alice. (As if she didn't know.)

"The monsoon was a wall of water crashing down on your head."

Dick and his mate Curly abandoned the truck in a hill of mud, but not before they'd put it out of commission. Other vehicles, similarly wrecked, had been driven into the trees.

Dick and Curly were with a few others from the guns. Captain Buggs, the Rabbit, had gone on with some of the officers. The Rabbit was the man Dick would later carry over his shoulder in a fireman's grip. He wasn't with them at first. The foot track went up, over the mountains, two thousand, five, six thousand feet.

On the track, Dick and the other soldiers walked in a shadow world. At the lower levels they pushed through choking bamboo and bush palm; at the higher levels they foundered in treacherous, spongy layers of moss. The constant high-pitched buzz of insects and the fluttering of wings were punctuated by the cries of birds and animals crashing about in the undergrowth. (And always they listened for the enemy.)

The track took them up through twilight that lasted all day, thick and close and fetid. Then rapidly down, into swift rocky rivers and mud. Always the mud. And always the biting insects, bush mockers, little bastards.

Leeches hung like bunches of grapes.

"The worst time," Dick says, "was when it was dusk." It had been half-light all day because the trees blotted out the light. At the quick dusk, even that drained away. "That was when you felt the jungle in your throat."

Dick and the others walked. Walked in the brilliant green of the valley, in the orange-red scars of recent landslides. The haze from the cooking fires in the native gardens didn't plume upward but squatted, solid, in the brassy heat. At the top of the mountains the mist moved like smoke rings. Here and there along the track, copra sheds, or a Chinese store. They came to a store that had already been cleaned out by the enemy; that made them jumpy.

Dick's mate Curly lost the sole of his left boot and kept trying to tie on bark as a replacement.

At one village, the *luluai*, in his official red-banded cap, stood in front of a circle of grass huts, a mob beside him carrying long-handled axes. The *luluai* didn't speak, he simply pointed up the track.

Climbing upward into nothing, they had no sense of where the track was leading. They were walking out into the thin damp air.

Dick and the others from the guns had been on the jungle track eight days when they were surprised by a group of locals coming towards them, talking and laughing, with feathers in their hair. The group seemed delighted to meet them. Their leader was a man called Glorious. A huge man. Everyone called them boys but they were men, extremely fit. Glorious had been at the Seventh Day Adventist Mission. Born on the Sabbath.

Glorious took them to a mission, where a big, pink-faced German priest fed them peculiar steaks. "Maybe it was a zebu," Dick says. The priest claimed it was *bulmacow*, beef.

At first they were cocky, with their tins of meat, condensed milk, packets of biscuits. They had it all doped out. That was in the beginning. Later, after the supplies ran out, the locals fed them.

"Taro, mostly. Pawpaws, pineapple, green bananas. Sometimes a whole village would be deserted. Smart to get out then. Keep going."

At the mission, Dick got busy with a bit of leather from a belt he found at the sawmill and fixed Curly's boot. On the verandah, where they watched the mist come down, there was subdued talk about someone who'd "walked out." A soldier with a broken leg had thrown himself over a cliff in order not to become a burden, slow the others down.

The track followed the spurs of the ridges. The walkers left notes on trees. A note would be found and another left for those who might come behind.

On one tree, a brief account of what had happened at the Tol plantation.

IN THEIR CAMP BY THE FLOODED CREEK, Alice and Dick have let the fire burn out. Alice takes one of the sheets she'd packed for the holiday house. Spreads it over the bark they're about to lie on. Its whiteness flutters in the gloom.

She's too excited to sleep. Dick's cracked open. For the first time in twelve years, the details are pouring out. They swirl in her mind, mixing in with the image of their car making its way downstream, as if out for a Sunday afternoon drive.

I enjoy a bit of danger, she thinks. I bet this country's full of women who'd jump at any chance of disruption. You weren't supposed to ever admit it. Course not. Kiddies, cooking, cleaning, going to town, taking care of your husband when he needed it. All that kept you busy; it was meant to. But was it enough?

They wake to the whooshing of water in the dark. Dick crawls out, digs another trench, adjusts the slicker on the roof, hurries back in. He moves over towards Alice. They're both wide awake now, in the hours before dawn.

This time Dick speaks as a boy, thin as a whippet. This is long before he goes into the jungle, on the walking track.

He's back on the Hay Plain, that immense flat country of south-western New South Wales.

He's building the stack of bags beside the silos at the Henty railway siding, one-hundred-and-eighty-pound packs. He's taking the bags from the trucks, lumping them on his back, flipping them down onto the lift that carries them to the top of the stack, where another man waits to receive them.

There he is, at the top of the Henty bagstack. The biggest in the district. The picture of Dick on top of the bagstack was in the Dalgety's stock and station office in the town of Henty for years. Behind the desk it was, for flies to wipe themselves on.

Alice imagines the young Dick pictured from a distance: lanky, underfed, skin tight on his frame. She sees his long legs, clouds heaped huge between them. The things he remembers about the walkout from Rabaul have stayed with him because he was the boy who lumped the wheat, who built the stack beside the silo at Henty, the largest stack in the district.

Kunai grass, for one, growing straight up out of the stony soil of the walking track. How the sun beat down, got trapped in the stones, then jumped back at you from the flat grass. The stubby banana plants, and the place where the coconuts stopped growing.

Alice understands that a boy from the bush would take note of such things.

IN THE MORNING, THE RAIN CONTINUES. Dick's already been out and up the hill. This time he's brought back denser, slow-burning bark, stripped from some of the smoother gums.

Good lord, thinks Alice, next he'll be finding goannas to bonk over the head and toss on the coals.

"The birds are quiet," she says. "The rain's made them miserable. They're lying low."

"That's what we're all doing, I reckon. Lying low." Dick sits on his haunches and patiently feeds bits of bark into the fire. Alice cuts pieces of fruitcake for breakfast.

The creek will run high like this for only a few days at most. When the waters have subsided, she'll put on a frock and her high heels — the only shoes she'll have left — and step out along the road. It'll be a small story around the falls district, how, after days in the bush, there she was in her frock and high heels. I'll be sure to wear my gloves, too, she decides. Make the most of it.

Mid-morning, Dick announces that he's going to walk back along the road. She watches him disappear, sugarbag cowl over his head.

He isn't just off for a stroll. More of a reconnoitre of the area, looking for abandoned huts, bridle paths, ridgeline trails. Maybe he'll run into some old codger who pans for gold. There'll be Aboriginals, too, bound to be. Moving on their ancient tracks to the coast — although maybe that's seasonal. Down in the autumn, up in the spring. She isn't sure.

She pokes at the fire, eats an apricot, sucks its pit. Being stuck in the bush during a flood has brought Dick's memories back.

"*Flooding* back," she says aloud, to amuse herself.

"WHEN THE ARMY TELLS YOU it's every man for himself," Dick tells Alice, "you can count on its being a prize snafu."

After they'd been released to make their own way, Dick says, some went down through the mangrove swamps. Dick was with a group that reckoned they'd do better going over the mountains. On that route there were more missions, more plantations. The walking track climbed steadily through the slopes of kunai, then gave way to the trees, then the rivers. When they had to make their way across, they sank to their waists in the soft ooze. Higher up, where the riverbed was more solid, fine gravel worked its way into boots.

"Your feet went soggy on you and would not unwrinkle. Hard to get a fire going. When you did, an enemy scout plane came over. Had to kick the fire out in the hurry."

One morning, Dick had looked up, and there was the Rabbit stumbling towards them, winded and bawling at the same time. Dick's first thought was to wonder what trouble the silly bugger had gone and got himself into.

"What happened to the Rabbit?" Alice prompts. It's the Rabbit he wants to talk about.

"He'd been left for dead. When the Rabbit came to, he was in a pile of bodies, all stacked up. His group had agreed beforehand: if one of them were captured they'd all give themselves up. Stick together.

"At the Tol plantation the Rabbit had been bayoneted six times. Using a bayonet saved on ammo, you understand. Finish off with a bonfire. The Rabbit was in pretty bad shape. He'd wandered for three or four days, couldn't say how many. He'd been going round and round in circles. Early in the morning, he'd smelled the smoke. He walked towards our smoke."

DICK HAD ALWAYS FELT A BIT SORRY for the Rabbit. With his tight, pale face and concave chest, the Rabbit hadn't been much of an officer. Hadn't quite known how to handle himself. Had to huff his way up the steep track to the artillery on the point. When he finally got there he'd lean over, winded.

The Rabbit liked to sit on a rock at the point and look out over the bay. "New Ireland to the east," he'd say. "To the south, gentle-men, the Duke of York Islands." The Rabbit would announce the names as if he were putting edges around them. Something a man like the Rabbit did to protect himself.

That was earlier, in the empty blue time. They'd pissed away the day cleaning the guns and staring through the Rabbit's personal telescope at the civilian shipping and local canoes. Right on the rocky point, where they'd placed the guns, the sea light had a fierce brightness — it was almost a relief to step back into the thick green air of the jungle that stood like a solid wall close behind.

Below the guns, in a gully that caught the sea breeze when there was one, they'd rigged up a platform on stilts, roofed it with coconut-palm thatch and canvas to withstand the brief, intense rain that arrived promptly each afternoon at four o'clock. Perched with the rest of them on the makeshift platform, Rabbit would ramble on about stuff he read in those books he carried.

The Rabbit's family was posh; he'd grown up some big house in Toorak, the most la-di-dah suburb in Melbourne; he'd been to the university.

In his kit, the Rabbit carried sweat-stained books with words in them like crochet. Greek words. Dick had imagined someone writing very fast with a small, light nib, writing with the morning light over his shoulder. Exactly like his mother trimming a hankie, her hook in and out, quick quick quick.

The Rabbit tried to read them bits. Sometimes they'd let him, out on the point, staring at the sea.

A woman turned herself into a cow so she could get away from some god who was after her. So the god turned himself into a bull and guess what. Curly said it sounded pretty silly, the things they went to uni for. "It's a *story*," protested the Rabbit, with a small smile of ownership. Dick, who knew a thing or two about bulls, shrugged his shoulders.

On New Year's Day, when the colonel declared there would be no retreat, Dick and Curly went to Mass. (The Rabbit was C of E.)

You could tell by the way the Rabbit gestured that his stories were more important to him than being an officer with the 2/22nd Battalion, Australian Infantry Forces. Which was being hung out to dry.

They were sitting on their hands waiting for the invasion. The enemy's superior force was well on its way. The Yanks were planning to get them out of there within twelve days, the Rabbit announced, distaste in his voice.

"The Rabbit wasn't too keen on the Yanks," Dick explains to Alice. "And of course it was only a rumour. Nobody came to get us out."

"Sounds like the Rabbit would have preferred to have a winged horse come down and scoop him up," Alice says.

Every morning at around five, Dick and his mate Curly would drive the ration truck to HQ and make themselves useful: a tin of meat here, a can of condensed milk there.

Dick added a bolt of cloth to their cache. Native tobacco. Trade goods, he explained to the Rabbit. They all laughed. Where on earth had Dick got a bolt of cloth? Not at HQ, surely?

Dick went on getting stuff together. Within three weeks he'd scrounged quinine, water-purifying tablets, string, matches, coarse salt, a couple of billycans, a pack of cards, folding nail scissors, a pile of newspapers for rolling the native tobacco in, some rope, a can of talcum powder, and a light axe. Oh, and some ulcer tablets — you stick them into a tropical ulcer and bind it with a bit of mozzie netting.

The Rabbit asked Dick about the cards. What was he planning on doing with a pack of cards?

When they'd let the Rabbit get out a book, his nose twitched with pleasure. There was a watchman on the roof, the Rabbit told them. (This would be back in one of the Rabbit's ancient Greek cities.) The watchman was waiting for a signal. At last! Finally! The fleet is coming. The signal, the Rabbit said — leaning forward, letting the book sit open on his lap — the signal is a relay of fire, from peak to peak. Victory, or a warning?

"What was that story really about?" asks Alice.

A woman jilted her husband and ran off with her new lover, a foreigner. The husband's brother decided to go get her back and there was a ten-year war.

They let the Rabbit tell them that story the day the air raids began. They listened to the Rabbit while they watched the Catalina flying boats taking off from Blanche Bay.

Close in, the sea was turquoise. Farther out, it turned a sharp purple-blue. The Cats were in the air, flying with their slow, dependable beat.

Dick liked to hear the big Cats.

DURING THE INVASION ATTACK, Dick worked on the ammunition, pulling out the trays to unclip the shells. The shells were long and grey and had a red band at the base. He had to wrench at the tin that held the shells tight.

Dick swung the shell over to Curly, who rammed it into the breech. Curly's shoulders swayed and his right leg went through a series of tight little steps as the shell went home at the end of the rod. Curly's movements — the shoulders, the feet — reminded Dick of standing along the wall, watching Curly on the dance floor back home, down in Albury.

Curly turned to the next man, who had his hand on the firing level, his face clapped against the rubber eyepiece of his telescope. The telescope stuck out through the gun shield, low down. It worried Dick for some reason, the way it poked out like that. Useless as tits on a bull.

The army thought they'd be going to the desert, with German soldiers coming at them across the sands. (Dick had been looking forward to the trip over, to staring out a porthole and seeing a bit of the world, the way his father had.)

But quickly, don't muck about, get the shell case out, slam the breech, load again.

It was the aerodrome the enemy was bombing; they were going for the Wirraways, the flimsy Australian fighter planes. They were smashing those little Wirras to pieces.

After the order came to demolish the gun, Dick's first thought was that they wouldn't be cleaning the finicky thing any more. But as he watched Curly cheerfully reducing the gun to wreckage, he didn't like it at all; the clanging sounded ugly to him.

They were used to taking the gun apart twice a day, cleaning and oiling it against the soft black pumice dust from the three volcanoes.

The volcanoes, according to the Rabbit, were a mother and her two daughters.

AT FIRST THEY TOOK TURNS carrying the Rabbit on the walking track. Then Dick did it, most of the time.

"Why was that?" asks Alice.

Dick shrugs, looks away, modest. "I suppose I had the knack."

Dick was the one who was able to run through the rivers with the Rabbit over his shoulder, not stopping to get his breath, not once. If you stood still, you'd lose your balance from the stones rolling away beneath.

Funny, with all that heat, the streams were cold. Fast and cold.

Get in and get out, quick. Everything wet. Blankets and kit. Wake up and find yourself lying in water. Not just under a damp blanket, but lying in water.

Boots and groundsheet rotted from being constantly wet.

At last the clouds swept away, and far ahead, between the high, deep tiers of mountains, they saw the open blue cleanliness of the sea. Reminded Dick of the paddocks of the Hay Plain.

"I thought: I could walk across that. If I wasn't so buggered. If only I could get down to the sea I'd take a long soda bath then walk on that wide open plain, carry the bloody Rabbit all the way home."

Walking downhill with the Rabbit was more difficult than climbing upwards. The mud was in Dick's boots, the water was in Dick's boots. As he moved, he saw muddy water spilling out of his boots. What else could be in those boots? The army had done him the favour of telling him about hookworm. Best not to think.

"At least I had boots."

BEFORE THEY WERE SENT UP to Rabaul, Dick had been at Bonegilla down near Albury, on the border of Victoria and New South Wales. Dick and the other recruits had marched all the way from Melbourne to Bonegilla. Marched through the bush in springtime. Lots of silver wattle and little white flowers called traveller's joy.

"City blokes complained it was miles and miles of bugger-all, but it was lovely country; they'd had some rain. It was marvellous, really, with your legs carrying you along. Pretty different from the jungle.

"The best thing about Albury was the dances. And the best thing about the dances was the suppers. The sponges. The cream puffs."

Alice wonders what Dick was like down in Albury. Before the jungle, before he lost his leg. Tough, lithe as a lizard.

"Things made of jelly. Red and green with bits of fruit hanging in them."

"I bet you and your mates were lords of the dance floor."

Alice imagines a younger Dick wading into the pack along the wall, reminding himself not to be put out by the panicky giggles. Selecting one. Leading her to the middle of the floor, where she wriggled like a sheep trying to bolt.

"Nah," says Dick. "I was never much of a dancer. But Curly was pretty good."

What is required of a man at a dance, Alice knows, is the confidence of a crack shearer. Put your hand on the girl's waist, pull her slightly, lead her out. And pretty soon the girl stops protesting, gives herself over. And having done so, is amazed at her own body, her sureness, her success. Begins to laugh in nervous triumph. And that's the moment to move in close, face diving into the sweet flutter of her neck, right leg quickly in out, in out.

No, Alice decides. Dick wouldn't have been like that. He would have taken the girl out onto the floor, treated her kindly — but it wasn't kindness she'd have been after, even though Dick was in uniform and not a local.

Dick: uncertain, standing on the outside of the group.

Like her.

BY THE TIME HIS MATE CURLY FELL, Dick was already carrying the Rabbit.

"*Walk about big fella water?*" Glorious asked. Glorious and his men were taking them over the mountains to the coast. They were stopped by a narrow ravine with a fast-flowing river in its depths. It would be a steep descent all the way down, then a stiff climb back up.

Build a bridge if we can, they agreed. Glorious nodded.

Dick had to hang onto the vines to haul himself over. He had to hang on with both hands, with the Rabbit sort of tucked up between the top of his arm and his face. He expected the Rabbit to cry out, but he didn't at first.

Later, the Rabbit joked that he now knew what it was like to be a violin.

Lawyer vines, they called them. Twisted, lengthy.

Dick had malaria. Well, they all did. Nothing to write home about.

Across the ravine, Glorious strung up a cable made of vines and bits of rope. Dick went first after Glorious, out over the precipice, hanging in the air, clutching the vines, with the Rabbit tucked between his arm and his face.

Curly went next. Probably his boot tripped him, even though he was agile. Like a sail in the wind, he was swept out on top of the water. Curly, who had been carrying their water-purifying tablets, billycans, string, coarse salt, matches, folding nail scissors, newspapers, can of talcum powder, ulcer tablets, and light axe. The pack of cards.

Dick looked down at Curly and their kit, spread upon the turbulent waters.

ALICE, HALF AWAKE, feels Dick's fingers. He's quietly stroking her hair. At least it feels quiet to him. The thin sound so close to her ear irritates her.

She could try to keep sleeping, get back into the dream. But she's close enough to the dream to know it was something anxious; best let it go. She could sit up abruptly, act aloof. He'd draw back then, he never pushed. Or she could turn into his chest, let herself drift in his warmth and disappear.

She turns towards him. Pulls the car blanket over her face.

DICK WAS BACK on the walking track: three days after Curly had fallen. Dick, carrying the Rabbit, slid sixty feet down a cliff face. Conscious, he was able to joke about taking the shortcut. Was able to say, in his limited pidgin, "*Leg belong me e bugarap.*"

The Rabbit had dropped free at the beginning. Slid onto a small ledge and did not tumble the whole way.

That's how they ended up in a hut together, the carrier and the carried. Glorious set Dick's leg with bamboo splints. (Dick passed out, lucky.)

The hut, on small stilts, had no windows, only a little entrance about two feet high that you had to stoop to get in through. There were fleas and more, but it was an almost dry place. Dick and the Rabbit were there together, swimming in and out of fever, for a long time. Glorious's boys cleaned up their messes in buckets they made daily from dead vine leaves. "My stinking green shit is the jungle itself," the Rabbit said, and turned away in disgust.

Glorious brought them each a piece of sugar cane for a toothbrush, and a strip of bamboo, about five feet long, with clean water, stoppered with a banana leaf — Dick admired that, very much. Glorious's boys brought them the milk of green coconuts: fizzy and fresh.

As well as bayonet wounds, the Rabbit had his left shin open with tropical ulcers. "During his fevers," Dick says, "you could actually see the Rabbit's bones shiver."

FOR A LIGHT, one of Glorious's boys set up a strip of cloth in a shallow dish of dripping. Comforting to have that in the night, when the rain was, often as not, preceded by crazy thunder, lightning, and a stupendous crashing of trees.

From what they could hear, they knew there was a cooking fire in front of the hut and a larger fire in an open space, probably in the middle of the village. Dick and the Rabbit listened to the talk-place, the local language. To Dick it sounded energetic, like steam coming out of a kettle left on the stove.

The Rabbit was always trying to say some of the words, repeating them to the boys who came to care for them. The boys giggled and ducked their heads, embarrassed. These were real boys, the youngsters who tended them. They were eleven, twelve years old, at the most.

"Weren't there any women around?" asks Alice. "The only women I've heard about so far have been the volcanoes, the mother and her daughters."

There must have been women out there in the world beyond the hut, carrying things on their backs in string bags, held by a band across their foreheads — sweet potatoes, firewood.

"The women never came into the hut; it was always boys. '*Me fella come up now*,' a boy would say quietly, announcing himself." Once a boy brought a freshly killed and cooked pigeon for them to eat.

"I bet one of the women cooked that," Alice says.

The hut was about a foot, maybe a foot and a half off the ground. The floor itself was made of mud, hard packed. Dick wasn't sure how they'd managed that.

The thing about malaria is everything gets jumbled up. The Rabbit's voice ebbed out of the spinning darkness. What was amazing about the Rabbit was how he could be there in the hut, but somewhere else all the time.

The king, the Rabbit said, got a fleet together to make war against the man who had stolen his brother's wife. But the goddess got pissed off and dashed the fleet against the rocks. She was the goddess of the hearth. As in home and hearth. Before she'd let them sail away to war, they had to realize what killing really meant. The king had to murder his own daughter.

The little Rabbit kept yakking away, nose aquiver. Dick wasn't sure if he should push back a question or two, the way you do in a bar, to keep the storyteller going. Dick never felt completely at ease in a bar; you didn't know when the attention would focus on you, and you'd have a crowd of men suddenly gone quiet, looking at you to say something. They all knew what they were expecting, but did you?

The king's daughter came down the coast, saw the altar ready for sacrifice, and asked, "Why is the altar empty?"

When she learned what was needed, she stepped up to the altar, lifted her hair, bared her young white neck.

DICK AND THE RABBIT HAD ULCERS on their backs and the smell in the hut was much worse; it kept them both awake. They could hear the pigs snoring down below. The Rabbit reckoned they must be the last two left. Surely everyone else from the garrison would be gone by now. One way or another.

Eventually the Rabbit was able to crawl out of the hut during the day, sit in the shade, and talk with some of the men in broken pidgin. He tried out his few words of local talk-place. It seemed as if the Rabbit was getting better. "Soon you'll be the one carrying me," Dick joked.

But one night Dick awoke to find the Rabbit vomiting blood into the vine-leaf bucket. Acting furtive, pretending nothing had happened.

THE WHOLE VILLAGE HAD GONE utterly mute, birds and pigs included. Dick heard rubber-soled boots, then a man's voice shouting threats in pidgin. Another voice — this one immensely nervous — translating into talk-place.

No boys came to them that day.

Neither the Rabbit nor Dick could follow the talk-place that erupted outside the hut at dusk. But they could pick out Glorious's voice. The Rabbit said it was obvious that Glorious was being pushed onto the defensive.

How were the villagers going to get rid of the pair of them?

They left that night, in the rain. Glorious and his men were carrying the Rabbit and Dick on copra bags. Once again into the steaming tangle; they were battling down the track by night, making for the coast.

Something had gone badly wrong with Dick's leg: stinking, putrid, poisoned. The Rabbit could gimp along for a few hours, but Dick was good for nothing after only twenty minutes.

Glorious and his lot were approaching the edge of their territory; they had to find other carriers willing to take them on.

No trade goods left.

One sick white man was a liability. Two, impossible.

After hours of being hauled from rock to rock, from one cliff ledge to another, all in the dark, Dick lay on the leaf mould on the wet ground, waiting for the light. The insects and frogs had packed it in, which meant dawn wasn't far away.

It was the movement that startled him. The Rabbit, stumbling to his feet. Swimming against the strong current of fever.

"Time to walk out," the Rabbit said. It wasn't an order, more like asking permission. "I think you'd better let me walk out now."

OF THE DEFEATED RABAUL GARRISON, Dick says, one thousand, one hundred and thirty-six have no known graves.

"Of course we didn't realize that," Dick says. "Towards the end there, it felt like it was just me and the Rabbit."

Dick claims not to remember the rest of the journey down to the coast, the pearling lugger to one of the small islands, the small boat into Morseby. He does remember the hospital in Cairns, where they finished off what was left of his leg, and his head began to clear.

"It was like the end of the rainy season," he says. "Welcome end of the wet."

"I THINK YOU'D BETTER LET ME WALK OUT NOW."

On the jungle floor, Dick listened.

At last, something: *swee, swee.* A little cry, but persistent. It was a relief when that was drowned out by layers of *grut grut grut* — the bigger birds, getting up.

Just after he'd heard the big birds, he must have fallen asleep, because when he woke, it was full daylight and he was looking at a bunch of palm leaves, immediately above him. Huge butterflies, with emphatically triangular wings, were busy depositing goo on the fronds. (Their shape, extremely sharp. He couldn't remember their colours.) His efforts to move set off a cloud of trembling silk.

THE FLOOD IS OVER. The sky has cleared. In their bark shelter, Alice is listening to the outpouring of song that happens when the rains end and morning light is upon the bush. The dawn is dry enough for magpies. Butcher birds, bellbirds, whipbirds, currawongs, lorikeets. In the distance, lyrebirds (those fabulous, shy, dying poets) are laying on virtuoso impersonations of the lot.

Dick's full of energy today. After their hot tea and a bit of fruitcake, he hunts about and finds a stone to play with, like a cricket ball, trying to spin it in his hands.

"Give the ball plenty of air," he says. He makes a stiff run-up, throws it. Scurries down the hill to bring it back, throws it again.

When he's finally winded, he comes back to the fire. "Used to do that when I was a kid."

He sits on his haunches and speaks, in an easy, happy voice, about his father. Back before the war, a long time ago, Dick and his father would do odd jobs, they'd do anything. One time they were down in Victoria, cutting the gum timber, fine big wollybutts along the ridges. Stayed in a hut behind a pear orchard. A storeroom really, with a floor of cow manure smoothed over and dried to a fine, dark-green, smooth surface. His father laughed when he saw it and said some things never do change.

There were rabbits to eat, and in the creek, small blackfish his father called greasies.

Late summer, early autumn more like — they'd sit on the bench outside the hut and watch the evening come in. Flowers, lots of them: wild violets, billy buttons. Grew near the wash bench; they must have appreciated the extra drink.

Dick walked across to the well and drew up water using a windlass and a bucket. While he was doing this, his father was sitting on the bench throwing a pear into the air.

His father was trying to make the brown pear spin like a cricket ball, although of course it wouldn't. From the shelter of stringybarks, a small roan wallaroo stood up and watched.

Between himself and his father alone, all of those things.

"What was the pear like?" Alice asks.

"Brown. Brown skin, sort of tight looking."

"The taste?"

"Well," says Dick, "crispy, but easy. When you bit into the brown skin you were surprised to find it so white inside."

"And the aroma? The smell?"

"Light. Sweet and light."

"Ah," says Alice, satisfied. "A gift of the gods."

"You're as bad as the Rabbit," Dick says.

DICK IS HERE NOW because the Rabbit had walked out. Perhaps it hadn't been necessary. "Greater love hath no man than this, that a man lay down his life for his friends." Was that a fact, or romantic rubbish? Maybe Dick and the Rabbit could have both got down to the coast. Maybe the Rabbit's sacrifice was worthless.

Dick looks over at Alice, sees her considering him. He glances away, like someone who's caught an unexpected sight of himself in a mirror. "Today's the day, I reckon," he says, gesturing towards the sky.

She's put the billy on, is making tea.

He's shocked that he's told me so much, Alice realizes. The murmuring in the hut, the gestures and words from the war a decade ago. The time he dropped down into the deep.

In the Islands. New *Britain*. Now there's a laugh.

Would something ever happen to her that would make Dick really look and see?

A strong orange flame flares in the fire.

Would she ever have the courage to let him?

"Tea's up," she says.

AS SOON AS THE SECOND WORLD WAR was over, Alice remembers, the mood of the times changed abruptly. Overnight, the resolute partying disappeared. In a desire to signal decisively the transition to peace, there was a lengthy queue for the altar.

She and Dick had joined the lineup. In the midst of the wedding fuss — even though it was hurried — she'd had time to puzzle at the effort people made to claim that all couples were filled with identical enthusiasm. Men were supposed to be thrilled to desert their mates, while women couldn't wait to get at all that housework. Bliss. That was the cant word. Married bliss.

"Marriage is in some ways a simplification of life." Alice had read that in one of those books now on their way to the coast. (Maybe they'd just sunk into the mud.) Was that true for the women of her generation? Married young, many in haste, to men who had good reasons to guard their secrets. What happened in the walkout from Rabaul was a form of madness. To speak of such things is to pass contagion along.

"Between even the closest people infinite distances exist," the poet said. It had been a relief to find someone who'd finally got it right.

DICK DOUSES THE FIRE, packs his tools into the one good sugarbag. Alice tidies the stuff into the port, and they go down to the creek together, to look at the receding waters. Drowned animals (wallabies, a few cattle), stiff with death, are stuck in the mud and beginning to smell.

They walk back up to the camp, aware it's the last time.

"I suppose we'd better push off," Dick says. His voice has gone very quiet.

"Yes," she agrees.

He makes two roll-your-owns, hands her one, lights it for her. "Wasn't so bad, was it? Roughing it for a few days?"

"Not so bad, Dick."

"We made a pretty good go of it, I reckon," he says. He stirs the ashes with his foot.

"I'd say. A pretty good go of it."

They stand close to the remains of the fire, neither wanting this to be over.

ALICE IS THE FIRST TO TURN AWAY. Fishes out a pad and her belt. (Her period's just started.) Changes into a dress and brushes her hair. Lucky, her hairbrush was too big for her handbag and she packed it.

She carries her high heels down to the road.

She's wearing her best dress, the one meant for church on Sunday morning in Port Macquarie. Cream, with marigolds around the yoke, around the short sleeves, and around the hem of the skirt.

Dick slings the sugarbag of tools over one arm and carries the port in the other. Alice slips her right hand through his arm. Together they walk down the road, back the way they came.

The sky shines brilliantly in the puddles. Rainbow lorikeets sweep in and out of trees like mobs of drunks.

Today, the bush has flashes of unexpected green.

BEFORE THE FIRST TRUCK COMES sputtering down the road, Dick tells Alice his final story about the war. (She knows he will not speak of it again.)

The man in the next bed in the Cairns army hospital had also scampered out of Rabaul with another group, taking a different route, moving south from island to island.

In sight of the enemy, they were waiting for a canoe to take them to another island. As they sat on the beach, two fox terriers came along, walked steadily into the water and began to swim across the channel. Where had they come from, and with such assurance? What were they doing there? From time to time, the larger dog would stop paddling, look around, and wait for the little one to catch up. A croc came alongside, inspected, but lost interest.

When he heard that story, Dick says, he knew what he'd do if he ever had a wife, if she ever asked about the walkout from Rabaul. He'd tell her about the two foxies. Tell her about them as if he'd seen them himself.

How they'd both swum safely across and reached another far shore.

8

WATCHING THEM

For the first three or four days that Bernadette is home from boarding school, either Alice or Ellen, catching sight of her, will sing out, "Bernadette's home!" The other woman, hearing that in another part of the house, will take it up. "Bernadette's home, Bernadette's home."

Her mother and grandmother first started this when she came home after thirteen months in hospital with polio. The tune is the same as the one for "Oranges and Lemons," but always upbeat, *con brio*, as her grandmother likes to say.

Everyone should know a few words of Italian, her grandmother claims.

They call it "Song of Bernadette." (What else?)

Bernie's mother, Alice, is singing right now in the car on the way back from Mass in Kelly's Creek. Not "Song of Bernadette," not a hymn from Mass, but a hit from the radio. "Oh, what a beautiful mornin' / Oh, what a beautiful day."

Bernadette joins in, although not invited to do so.

On this Sunday morning in May, there was an early frost, but its dusting has long since disappeared. The air that rushes into their new Holden sedan is crisp. The paddocks stretch out in broad, clear light. This is sheep country. The finest wool, Bernadette's father says, grows snug around the heart.

"Smell that," commands Alice. "So pure, so utterly clean. Autumn on the tablelands." She says this as if she were some kind of returning world traveller, catching the scent of home after many years away. (Bernadette has definite plans to become a world traveller herself.)

THE BEHANS ALWAYS HAVE BACON and liver on Sunday morning when they get home from Mass, hungry after fasting for Communion. After breakfast, Bob and Bernadette read the Sunday comics while Mum puts the joint on. (Dad reads the sports pages, then "Uncle Joe's Horse, Radish.") Nana has a lie-down.

Today Mum lets Bernadette and Bob leave liver on their plates, lets them stand by the warm stove and dip their bread directly into the bacon pan. Joins in herself.

"Delicious," Mum cries. "Isn't this just delicious?"

Yesterday Mum cleaned with the new Hoover, her head tied up in a scarf. The front room smelled of lemon furniture oil. After the cleanup, she cooked a sponge cake. This morning she's going to fill the sponge with cream, laced with fresh passionfruit.

"I want everything to be just so," Mum says, anxiety beginning to creep in.

"What's got into her, having visitors?" Bernadette asks Bob, who's in primary school and still at home. "Usually it's just the Hogans." Mrs. Hogan is a nutter and a Pom, but Mum seems to like her. Deirdre Hogan is Bernadette's best friend in the entire world.

Now that Bernadette's packed away with Deirdre at boarding school, doing homework and getting chilblains, her mother has begun to throw card parties. On Thursdays the Larsens come to Ardara for what Alice calls her euchre night.

Now they're showing up on a Sunday as well.

Bernadette knows the Larsens. She was in hospital with Terry Larsen, before Terry was taken away to Sydney on a plane and never came back. "Why's Mum getting so sociable all of a sudden?"

"Dunno," Bob replies, bored. He has more important things to think about. For his birthday, he got a set of proper paints, the ones that come in tubes like toothpaste. Besides, Dad's promised to teach him how to use the rifle. To shoot rabbits. Bernadette wants to learn, too.

THE LARSENS ARRIVE IN THE FORD. Tom Larsen runs the garage at the top of north hill, on the highway. "Poor old Tom Larsen," says Bernadette's father, "having to get matey with spark plugs." For no machine could ever give you the big-hearted stamina and unnerving prescience of a horse — everyone on Ardara knows that.

Tom Larsen parks the car in the yard outside the gate. There's a fence all around the homestead, to keep stock out of the garden. Bernadette hears the car doors slam three times. Damn. They've brought Jennifer with them. She'll have to stop reading *Reach for the Sky* and join in.

Hazel is wearing her winter overcoat and a hat with a tiny veil, as if she, too, had been to church. But the Larsens don't attend church. They go to the Methos for Christmas and Easter. The rest of the time, Bernadette's mother reports, the Larsens are happy to give the whole thing a wide berth.

Jennifer, at thirteen, is two years older than Bernadette. She goes to the high school in the nearest town, Araluen. The school bus comes out and picks her up from Kelly's Creek. Today she's wearing small heels and lipstick, which Bernadette neither desires for herself nor admires in others. She can see how they are making Jennifer nervous, uncertain.

Tom Larsen has fair red hair cut short at the sides but surging thick on the top of his head, making his narrow face look even longer. His is a face that belongs on top of an old-fashioned cricket blazer, the kind with stripes on it. In an outdated Boy's Own adventure story.

Tom Larsen claims to have had one of life's great adventures himself, right here in Kelly's Creek. For it was at Tom's garage that the cars from the Redex Trial stopped to refuel. They were on a race around Australia: from Sydney up to Townsville, over to Darwin, down the Centre to Adelaide, and around to Sydney again. When Tom recites the itinerary, he repeats "down the Centre to Adelaide" several times.

The night the Redex cars went through, Bernie's father took them into Kelly's Creek to watch. (This was the winter before the polio; Terry was at the garage, standing close to his father.) The sound the Redex cars made as they pulled into the station was deeper and stronger than the noise any ordinary car could hope to come up with. These trial cars, covered with advertisements for motor oil, were equipped with screens to prevent insects from splatting into the engine or onto the windshield. They had bull bars to fend off beasts. Most had a mechanic/navigator and two drivers so that they could drive all through the night. They would push on through swollen rivers, through sandstorms, through plagues of locusts and stony desert heat.

When they hit Kelly's Creek, they were at the end of their first day out. It was all still ahead. The men emerged from their cars, wearing sweaters and leather jackets in the cold wind. They stretched their legs and strode like the champions they were to the men's toilet.

Hazel Larsen supplied the Redex men with tea and biscuits. She'd got a little booth going, decorated with fairy lights, the ones they use on semi-trailers. There were plates with two sorts of biscuits: oatmeal with butter, and macaroons — the ordinary and the exotic. (A jam jar for donations to Legacy, for kids whose fathers died in the war.) Dressed in an old-fashioned double-breasted coat with a blouse done up severely at the neck, Hazel looked at once perky and military.

Tom Larsen worked the petrol bowsers, Terry beside him. The

petrol flooded into the glass tower at the top of the bowser then down into the powerful cars. Tom Larsen talked with the drivers, with the mechanic/navigators. His stocky hair stood up against the chilly westerly. During one of these exchanges, a Redex man put his hand on Terry's shoulder.

From where Bernadette was watching, she could see the talking and the gesture but couldn't hear the words.

It was on this night that Tom spoke with, and actually shook the hand of, none other than Jack "Gelignite" Murray.

At the euchre parties on Ardara, Tom Larsen tells this story, slowly working his way up. "Gelignite went on to win the trial with his Ford V8. He was just an ordinary bloke you know, not up himself at all." With that, Tom sits back and rolls himself a smoke.

Bernadette wonders if perhaps she'd seen Gelignite Jack, too, and not even known it.

TOM LARSEN STANDS AT THE GATE to the homestead, talking to Dick Behan, Bernadette's father. Her father doesn't have much to say to Tom Larsen, a townie who knows nothing about the land. But the Ferguson's on the blink. This is the new tractor, which sits in the shed, an old horse blanket over its engine. On winter mornings it won't start.

Would Tom Larsen like to take a look at it?

Tom Larsen's face opens with pleasure. He would indeed. Off they go, Bernadette's father and Tom Larsen, with Bob tagging along.

Down the path come Hazel and Jennifer, up onto the verandah. Jennifer is holding her silly handbag over her arm, pretending she's at least Princess Alexandra. Hazel says something about the cotoneaster, its bright red berries. Although she must see it every time she visits.

Bernadette's grandmother has emerged from the hallway, and waits beside her mother at the top of the shallow wooden steps to greet the guests.

Bernadette's mother, Alice, is responsible for what happens

next. "You girls can go for a walk," she suggests, waving her arms tentatively.

Bernadette, who has been torn away from her book, decides to take Jennifer, in her Sunday heels, to the culvert.

What you do at the culvert is this: you wait for a car to go over. Doesn't happen very often, but you've got a better chance on Sundays. There's heaps to do while you're waiting. In the culvert on her own, Bernadette conducts Beethoven. Her grandmother recently bought a recording of the Egmont for the gramophone. It's fabulous. Bernadette slashes her arms about, scraps of music roaring through her brain.

In the culvert there is the waiting, followed by the drama of certainty (yes, it is a car; it is), then the steady, approaching noise. And in that instant when the car is going over, when everything is shaking, you shout your head off. The fact that the driver of the car doesn't know you're there makes it so much better.

You can almost stand up in the culvert. It helps if you pretend you're a bent-over prisoner who's never before seen the light, and who is now crying out, demanding freedom.

At the mouth of the culvert, Jennifer hesitates. Clutches at her handbag, tries to hold her coat in.

"Watch your head," Bernadette warns. Bernadette knows that Jennifer is reluctant, repelled by this game, afraid she'll get dirty. If Bernadette were some other girl, Jennifer would stand there, full of confident scorn. But Bernadette was in hospital with Jennifer's little brother, Terry, before he went to Sydney and died.

Bernadette was there with him and Jennifer wasn't. This is why she can demand that Jennifer crouch in the culvert, holding herself away from the dusty sides.

She wants more.

In the culvert, Bernadette keeps a supply of charcoal from a burned-out gum. With it, you write your name backwards on the cement wall.

"Take some charcoal," Bernadette commands. "Do your name.

Here, I'll show you." *Naheb Ettedanreb*, Bernadette writes quickly. An ancient Egyptian name. She can see Jennifer trying to work out what her own name would look like. "Begin with a capital N for Larsen," she instructs. "Then work your way back."

There are other things that Bernie likes to do, but wouldn't share with Jennifer. Special things. Like lying in the river beneath the weeping willows (not here, over on the other side of Ardara). Lying back in the water with her best friend Deirdre and reciting:

Or when the moon was overhead,
Came two young lovers, lately wed:
"I am half sick of shadows," said
The Lady of Shalott.

When Jennifer gets out of the culvert, Bernadette sees her reach into her handbag and take out a small mirror. She stares into it, inspecting her face for damage.

Not a single car had gone over, although they'd waited and waited.

"We'd better be getting back," Bernadette says. "Get a move on. You'll be late for afternoon tea."

THE NEXT TIME BERNIE COMES HOME from the convent in Armidale ("Bernadette's home!"), there are brochures in the kitchen, in the lounge room. For Port Macquarie, South West Rocks, Nambucca Heads.

Years ago, Mum and Dad tried to go down to Port Macquarie, but got caught in a flood and had to camp out beside a creek. The way they talked about it, you'd think it'd been something brilliant, sitting out in the wet.

The brochures offer cottages called Surfside, Emohrou, and Orana.

"What are these in aid of?"

Plans are being made for a fortnight's holiday after Christmas. They're going with the Larsens.

"Who else?" Bernadette says. "Without the Larsens, wherever would we be?"

"No need to be cheeky, young lady," says her mother.

Bernadette is pleased with herself for being ironic and challenging. If you're brave enough, she is discovering, you can make your own claims; you just have to find the precise words. There are times when Bernadette sees herself commanding the Red Sea to part and leading the people through. The sand is white and miraculously dry, with a few fish tails sticking out of the walls of water.

"Your father says the two of us should go," Mum says.

"Why aren't Dad and Bob coming?"

"Your father says he can't leave the stock, not with the drought on and having to put out feed. And Bob's off to the Scout jamboree. It'll be just us and the Larsens."

"Does that mean Jennifer's coming, too?"

Bernadette already knows the answer: Jennifer will be coming, and Jennifer will be a pill. And guess who'll have to share a room with her (maybe even a bed, *très* revolting). "I don't want to go with Jennifer. Who says Deirdre can't come? I want Deirdre to come."

"Hazel's barracking for Southport," says Alice, ignoring her.

"Southport? But that's in Queensland."

Even to her parents, Queensland is an unknown. (Her mother was a land girl during the war. She's been to Victoria and South Australia. But not Queensland.)

Bernadette makes a list of what will be different in Queensland: the railway gauge, the newspapers, the school system (four years of high school, not five), the times of school holidays, state parliament, daylight saving, houses up on stumps.

She shows this list to her mother, who shows it to the Larsens on euchre night.

"Beer," says Tom Larsen. "Forget your Grafton lager; you can drink four-X. Up there, a pony isn't a pony, it's something else."

"That's quite enough beer talk, Tom," says Hazel.

"The Gabba," continues Tom. "The Creek. Roma Street Station."

"Pineapples, bananas," says Alice.

"Mangoes," says Hazel, "fall out of the trees."

ON THE DAY OF THE TRIP, Tom Larsen drives up in his Ford with its recently installed V8 engine. He's rigged up a special grasshopper screen and he's got a water bag hanging off the front bumper in case they are in danger of dying of thirst.

Jennifer's in the back seat, surly.

"Looks like Tom plans to keep right on going," Dad says. "Down the Centre to Adelaide."

"Queensland," Bernadette says to herself, as the car bumps through the gate, over the cattle grid, and out onto the highway, turning not south, for Newcastle and Sydney, but north. As she says the word, "Queensland," she can feel something inside her, opening, expanding.

For weeks, the two mothers and Bernadette's grandmother have been running up holiday clothes on the old Singer sewing machine. Her mother's foot flew, while her grandmother was responsible for the decisive act, taking scissors to cloth. Hazel tried on, and made Mum burst out laughing, although her mouth was full of pins.

Tom Larsen is decked out in one of their lairy new shirts with yellow yachts on it. As soon as they get going, Tom pulls the shirt off, to relax in his singlet. His arm dangles over the car door, and the hot air pours into the back seat, where Jennifer and Bernadette stare out opposite windows.

They stop for lunch at Tenterfield. Devon luncheon meat, fresh bread rolls from the bakery. "We should look at the School of Arts," Bernadette says. "That's where Sir Henry Parkes began his plan for federation. He issued a clarion call."

The School of Arts turns out to be pretty boring: a few pictures of old men in beards, sitting and standing around tables in meeting rooms.

"That was quick," says Tom Larsen, lighting up a cigarette. "So much for the clarion call."

Jennifer uses the toilets in the park. "They *stink*," she reports, fretful and offended.

"Lavatory in Parkes's park not up to scratch," says Tom Larsen.

HAZEL AND ALICE SIT IN THE FRONT with Tom, Hazel in the middle. From the back seat, Bernadette can study their heads. Hazel is even older than her mother and has grey hairs growing at the back of her head. Does she know about them? Can she see them in the mirror? For the holiday, both mothers have had tight new perms. ("For easy care after the surf," Alice said, poking at her perm with a finger. "Anyhow, it will grow out," she added. "Feels like steel wool," Bernadette said, touching it. And suddenly her mother had looked quite helpless.)

In the car, the women tell each other stories. Hazel contributes a long yarn about her family.

Hazel was born after Hazel's father went away to the First World War and got himself killed. As a new widow, Hazel's mother moved up to Murwillumbah, on the far north of New South Wales. She worked in the Imperial Hotel, serving in the dining room. Hazel lived with her mother above the hotel — you wouldn't believe the noise on Saturday nights.

In the Imperial Hotel in Murwillumbah, Hazel's mother invented a completely fictitious past for herself. While Hazel's mother actually came from some dumpy part of Sydney, she always said she was from Brisbane and had grown up in a big house right on the river. She even threw in lengthy descriptions of floods. Claimed that she had, as a child, been swept away by the Brisbane River on her way home from school.

"Imagine having the nerve," concludes Hazel, "to make the whole thing up."

"It would be like starting your life over again," says Alice, her voice timid.

"Why would your mother want to make up a new past for herself?" Bernadette asks Hazel.

"Do you think that would really be possible?" Alice goes on. "To start again? A new life, somewhere different?"

It's no big mystery why someone would want a new life, Bernadette decides. She can imagine moving up to Queensland, getting her own mango crop (mango plantation?). She'd do all the repairs on her own Ferguson tractor, then ride around on it while fruit fell out of the trees.

TOM LARSEN KEEPS HIS EYES on the road and does not take part in the storytelling. When the women sing songs from the musicals, he groans. He joins in, however, when they sing that they were "dancing in the dark, dancing in the dark." And he thumps the dashboard for "Run rabbit — Run rabbit — / Run! Run! Run! / Don't give the farmer his / Fun! Fun! Fun!"

All the adults love these songs. At home on Ardara, these are the songs that bring Bernadette's grandmother from her room. She'll sit at the piano and play for hours. It takes you back, she says. Doesn't it take you back?

Around tea time, they come to the border. There are exciting signs about agricultural products being forbidden, but the other side looks disappointingly like home: paddocks, apple orchards, gum trees, granite boulders. In the homesteads, lights are beginning to come on.

"We'll stop when we're through the Gap," Tom Larsen promises.

They drive on. Hazel falls asleep, her head dropping onto Alice's shoulder. Tom glances over at Alice. Bernadette can see them smiling at each other. It's a glance she's seen exchanged over the sleeping heads of children: comfortable, familiar.

Bernadette watches Tom Larsen lighting a cigarette. You can tell he loves this: the smooth ribbon of highway, himself at the wheel — alone, now that the women are quiet — the darkening country, the green light on the dashboard.

They make camp at the edge of the rain forest, which Bernadette thinks of as scrub. But it's scrub unlike any she's seen. While the others are getting things out of the boot, she takes a closer look.

There is the smell, the completely dominant smell, of dank earth. This scrub is a dense, busy breathing in the night. Coming up from the ground and down from above. It's like a living thing that enters you; you are sucking in its earthy air. The ground feels springy underfoot. Reminds Bernadette of the perms her mother and Hazel have.

"Be on the lookout for leeches," Tom Larsen calls.

"All hands on deck," cries out her mother, summoning her.

Tom Larsen puts down the tarp for a groundsheet. Alice and Hazel get the old army blankets out for what Tom calls the bedrolls. They lie down, discreetly and partially undressed, on and beneath the army blankets. Tom folds the ends of the tarp around them.

"This is the way to go," he says. "The hotel of the stars."

But Jennifer is taking her quota of blankets to make a bed in the back seat of the car.

"Get out here this minute," barks Tom Larsen. "I'm warning you."

Hazel says something to calm and distract him. The stage Jennifer's going through. Then she murmurs with Alice, something about men. The mothers laugh together, privately.

Jennifer gets away with everything. Too hoity-toity to sleep on the ground.

The stars are visible directly above, in the gap the clearing has made. Bernadette is familiar with stars that begin at the horizon, but here they can be seen only through a dark, tumultuous tunnel. That is how she'll describe it to her best friend Deirdre, to whom she is going to write every single day. *Tumultuous.* Very pleasing, all those instances of the letter "u." *Tumultuous,* she says to herself, searching for Orion, the Irishman who owns all the pubs in heaven.

SHE WAKES TO SLABS OF LIGHT and rising heat. The breathing of the night has turned into a wall of cries from particularly forthright birds.

Tom Larsen is getting a fire going with green, spitting twigs.

Bernadette's father would know better than that.

"Black tea," Tom Larsen declares. "The only way to beat the heat."

Studying the map, Tom Larsen leads them off the range, down perilous back roads to Southport. They break out into full sunshine, absurdly green paddocks packed with cows, dams full of water. Dairy country. Not their kind of country; not like Ardara at all.

The coastal morning has a strength that is dizzying. The sand shimmers and begins to bounce. The sea pumps back an immense bright light. Pelicans manoeuvre on prodigious wings. The sky, the sky is blazing like a blue bushfire out of control.

Looking out from the back seat of the Ford, Bernadette knows that already she is sharper, more experienced. This place is like a radio that has been turned up as loud as it can go, and she is in it. This is what it was supposed to be — intense and foreign.

This is Queensland.

THE HOLIDAY FLATS ARE ON THE ESPLANADE, facing the broadwater. In the morning, before breakfast, Bernadette gets up after Tom Larsen (gone fishing), puts on her togs, goes down the steps, and crosses the road to the water, where she swims among the small boats and local squadron of pelicans.

"Probably only bushies swim in there," Mum says. "Dick thinks if it's wet and more than half an inch deep, you jump in and go for a swim," she adds, to Hazel. "A boy from the black soil plains."

Bernadette doesn't like the way her mother gets when she talks to Hazel about Dad. Cagey, a bit nervous. You'd think Dad was on trial and Mum wasn't sure what the verdict would be.

When Bernadette goes out, there's nobody else around. Just a few pensioners, up early for the newspaper. She sniffs the morning smells. When she gets back, the two mothers will be in their housecoats, dawdling over toast, having cups of tea, finishing off the pot. The front and back doors will be propped open for the through breeze, because the day's going to be a scorcher. After breakfast the mothers will put on their swimming costumes for a surf at the main beach.

Alone in the broadwater, Bernadette pulls herself up on the sides of the small boats, to look in. There isn't that much to see — a bucket, a few big brown XXXX beer bottles, someone's sandshoes, a rusting tin can that once held bait. Some of the boats have cabins. These are the best: little houses on the water. She can climb up onto the side of the boat and look in through the salt-stained windows. The most attractive of these boats is called *Skipper*. Its name is on the back, lettered to look like handwriting.

Skipper has been painted a tough, thick white. It has a line of royal blue, just near the top. And beneath, the bit that's in the water, that's royal blue, too. She likes to run her hand over the smooth, fresh paint. These cabin windows are clean, unlike the ones on other boats. Sparkling.

One morning, when Bernadette hauls herself up to take a look into the cabin of *Skipper*, there are two drunks inside. They are lying on a blanket. One is young; he is wearing shorts and sandals. The other is an older man, his hat over his face. (It is still the era of hats for all men.) He's in his singlet and underpants. He has taken his suit off, folded it carefully over the wheel. He's the one who owns *Skipper*, she decides, he's the tidy one.

The men are sleeping wrapped together like cats.

AFTER BREAKFAST, THEY GO DOWN to the beach, Alice and Hazel, Bernadette and Jennifer. One of the mothers carries the beach umbrella while the other brings the thermos and biscuits. Under the umbrella the mothers sit, staring at the waves and endlessly patting suntan lotion onto each other.

Working on her tan, Jennifer lies out in the sun and gets fried.

Bernadette, in the water, studies the other kids. Watches them flatten their arms against their sides, their heads well down, kicking off just before the wave begins to break. She tries it again and again, letting the water boss her around, feeling its toss and push.

Coming back for lunch, Bernadette checks the broadwater to see if *Lurline* or *Sunset Sails* or *Skipper* has gone out. She has become aware that she knows nothing about boats. Right and left are starboard and something, green and red. How can she find out? Is there perhaps a book she could read?

She asks her mother.

Alice laughs. "Why do you have to know all of a sudden?" she asks. "No need to go tying yourself in knots."

"Knots," says Hazel. "That's a good one. Take a bow."

"Don't be stern, take a bow," says Alice.

The mothers giggle. They think they're being incredible geniuses.

The mothers lie in cane chairs on the front verandah, to catch the afternoon breeze from the water. The verandah at this end is shaded with a climbing vine over a trellis, enclosing them in bright green light. There are fat, velvety yellow flowers all over the vine, but neither Alice nor Hazel knows what they're called. You'd think that Hazel, who grew up just over the border, would at least have a clue.

The mothers go back to what they were discussing before Bernadette showed up and started asking about the names of things. On New Year's Eve they are going to a dance at the club.

"Send us reinforcements, we are going to advance," says Bernadette. "They passed this message down the line, the soldiers did. At the Battle of Waterloo. By the time it got to the last person, you know what it said? 'Send us three and fourpence, we are going to a dance.'"

Nobody is paying her any attention whatsoever.

THE MOTHERS, IN A GOOD MOOD, buy cream buns every day for lunch, and fish and chips for tea. Jennifer and Bernadette drink Tristram's soft drinks, which are absolutely terrific. The adults have beer.

"This is the best fish ever," says Bernadette's mother.

"Shark," says Tom Larsen.

Off Tom Larsen goes, to the horses, to the dogs. He likes to have a flutter, that's Tom Larsen's idea of a holiday.

The flat has a large front room with a wooden floor and not much furniture. Ranged around the edges of the room are a divan, a few cane chairs, and a Laminex table with a squat radio. White sand sifts in everywhere — it seems to fall from the air. At the end of the day, either Hazel or Alice takes the broom and sweeps it up. The broom makes a slithery sound on the floor. One of them sweeps, while the other holds the dustpan. Together they take the sand out the back, dump it over the verandah railing. That's all the housework they do.

The humidity is getting to them, they say. Their shoulders slouch, they drift into the bedroom, where they lie down in their underwear.

"You go," they say to Bernadette, who proposes an afternoon trip to the main beach. "You go."

"Why don't you take Jen with you?"

"Mind you stay between the flags, now."

"You'll be all right on your own, darling, won't you?"

Bernadette doesn't even bother to ask Jennifer, who is shampooing her hair yet again. When she's finished that, Jennifer will go round with her head in a turban and her face covered with cold cream. Ridiculous. Then Jennifer will lie on the divan, reading old copies of *Woman's Own* that Hazel found at the op shop. Jennifer laps up soppy stories about young women falling in love with the village locum. Jennifer, take note, didn't even know what a locum was.

While Jennifer's in the shower, Bernadette swipes a couple of copies of *Woman's Own* and leaves for the beach. She plans to read the letters asking for advice. They sometimes make mention of periods. *Woman's Own* has a most peculiar-smelling ink, as strong in its own way as fresh bread. (Bernadette prefers the smell of the *Women's Weekly* herself: more cheerful.)

In the afternoon surf, Bernadette manages to catch a few waves right into the shallows, where toddlers are paddling. Feeling large and powerful, she runs back into the surf, diving under the waves she doesn't want. Once, when she is catching a wave, she brings her head up at precisely the right second and looks down the inside of the tube of green water, spinning and stretching away, secret and strange.

IN THE EVENINGS, after the fish and chips, when Tom Larsen has set off to the club to play the pokies and the mothers have gone for what they call their constitutional along the broadwater, Bernadette is free to investigate on her own. She takes a circular route along the broadwater: down to the main pier to inspect the war memorial, past the bowling club, over to the campground, then home along the broadwater again.

In the campground, a mob of children are playing at a tap, their water wings still on. Behind them, you can hear whistling coming from the men's shower block.

Sitting at a card table outside a caravan, a pregnant woman is peeling potatoes into a basin of dirty water. Seated next to her, a man smoothes his rounded belly, as if he has a baby in there, too.

By the light of a kero lamp, a woman inside a tent is taking off her dress. You can see her shadow, huge in silhouette on the canvas wall. In front of the tent opposite, some men have gathered. They are quiet. Watching.

Smells of chops and baked beans drift in the bushes along the fence. The bushes themselves are full of improbable large flower trumpets that have now shut down for the night.

Coming home along the broadwater, Bernadette spots the mothers. They are sitting on the steps of the jetty, low enough to dangle their feet in the water. Bernadette sees her own mother bring one foot out and study the water spilling off. Slowly, her mother lifts her leg up, wriggles her foot, still staring at it. Hazel, beside her, is talking intently. Bernadette can see the frequent glow of Hazel's cigarette as she inhales, emphatically, rapidly.

Hazel is trying to persuade Alice of something. Anyone could see that. Anyone who looked.

BACK ON THE FRONT VERANDAH of the flat after her tour of the neighbourhood, Bernadette sees Jennifer coming down the street with a boy. Walking along, embarrassed and proud.

Bernie knows who he is; she's seen him before. He's staying in the top of the back flats. Bernadette's mother has spoken to his father, found out he's a schoolie.

This boy has a huge jellyfish in a wide net, the kind of net you hold in your hand and scoop with. As they're walking along, he's thumping this gelatinous thing on the footpath — and it really is big, it's massive, it's about three feet across. Jennifer is pretending that the jellyfish isn't there, which is absurd. People are turning their heads, and they're not looking at Jennifer, who's convinced a boy to walk along beside her, they're all looking at the jelly.

The boy and Jennifer are making for the path into the flats.

It might still be alive, that blubbery jellyfish. The silly cruel boy is in the process of pulping the poor thing to death. It isn't very attractive, but it probably quite enjoys its life, floating along like an umbrella and having a good look at everything going on down below.

Or has the boy killed it already?

Up the path they come. *Thump*, *thump* goes the jellyfish.

Bernadette's at the top of the steps. She opens her mouth, and, to her surprise, she screams: "Put that thing back!" She's yelling, and finding her voice wonderfully ugly. "Put it back right now. Do you hear me?"

A crowd has gathered. For the jelly, for the row. Somebody laughs. Are they making fun of her?

Then a stern voice. A terrible, headmaster-getting-out-the-cane voice. The boy's father, coming around the side of the front flats. "Take that *disgusting* thing away *right this minute.*"

Jennifer crumples into tears. At the top of the steps, Bernadette stands over her, getting ready to block her way. Even as she's doing this, she's wondering how Jennifer pulled it off. Without seeming to make any effort at all — apart from preening and lying about all day — Jennifer has managed to attract a boy's attention.

NEW YEAR'S EVE. Tonight, Tom, Hazel, and Alice are going to a dance.

Alice and Hazel are taking turns to have a shower and get dressed in the bedroom.

Bernadette has been down under the house. She enjoys under-the-house, which has exotic plants — heaps of them, with coloured leaves — and a big cactus that her mother says is forbidden in New South Wales. Even bigger plants called monsteras grow huge on the house stumps.

In the late afternoon, a very old man comes over from the house across the lane and hoses everything down. As soon as he turns on the hose, lime-coloured frogs emerge. They are bright green, exactly like the colour in the Derwent paint box. The old man talks to the frogs in a confiding voice. He reminds Bernadette of her father, his easy gentleness with animals.

The old man has dumb names for his frogs: Joey, Blowie, and Nits.

"Do you think they like it?" asks Bernadette. She wants him to talk to her.

"They've come to count on it," he says. "When you get used to something good you want it to keep on going, I reckon."

This old man has false teeth. Pushes them around in his mouth and clicks them to horrify the little kids from the other flats, who've come running to stand beneath the hose.

Bernadette, having watched the frogs enjoy their shower, goes up the back steps. The door is wide open.

Her mother is sitting on the divan, painting her toenails. She's wearing one of the new sunfrocks. This one has a grey background: a windmill, trees, the Arc de Triomphe, pink roses scattered here and there.

Hazel comes out of the bedroom. (Hazel and Tom's bedroom; Alice bunks down on the divan.) She's got her evening dress on. "*Tarrraaa*," she says, twirling around so that the full skirt swings out. She's all dressed, except for her shoes.

The evening dress is satin. Midnight blue, they call it. Shoulderless. She's got a push-up bra on underneath. (Bernadette's mother has one too. "I feel like a *tank* in this thing," her mother says.)

Bernadette's mother stands up, goes over to Hazel. Hazel takes her arm and they begin to dance. Hazel's feet, in nylons, slide easily on the wooden floor. Her mother, in bare feet, moves more slowly. They do a sort of waltz around the front room.

"Shall we dance?" Hazel sings, and her mother joins in. They're not singing actually, they're whispering the words. But in a loud, spirited whisper. Their feet slide: slow, quick.

"Shall we dance?"

Her mother takes up the *pom pom pom* bit in a lower voice.

Shall we dance? (pom pom pom)
On a bright cloud of music shall we fly? (pom pom pom)

Around the room they go, midnight blue satin and the Parisian street scene. Hazel breathes out the words emphatically.

On the clear understanding that this kind of thing can happen,
Shall we dance?
Shall we dance?
Shall we dance?

They pause, giggling and panting.

"Pom pom pom," whispers Bernadette's mother. And they're off again. It's the kind of song that could go round and round forever.

Her mother looks up, sees Bernadette in the doorway. Stops. "What are you doing hiding there?" she says sharply, with misplaced irritation.

"Nothing," Bernadette says, relieved somehow at having a chance to be offended. "I wasn't hiding. I wasn't doing anything at all."

BY BERNADETTE'S NEXT HOLIDAYS, in May, Tom Larsen has burned his house down and Hazel is living at Ardara.

IN KELLY'S CREEK, Bernadette hears things. (All you have to do to hear things in Kelly's Creek is ride in on your bike, sit in the bakery-café and have a spider: ginger beer or lemonade with ice cream in a tall glass.)

Goes up so easily, weatherboard and fibro.

Burned his bridges as well, I'd say.

Nothing but the clothes she stood up in.

You'd never get over it.

Left standing in the ashes.

No, you wouldn't.

Husband, child, house — gone, all gone.

One Thursday night, when Jennifer was playing softball and Hazel was out at Ardara (euchre night), Tom Larsen took a fifty-gallon drum of petrol from the garage and poured it throughout his house. Leaving the blaze to gather force behind him, he drove to the high school, where he picked up Jennifer. They were last seen driving south.

Going like bats out of hell.

AT ARDARA, HAZEL WEEPS for her child and her husband, gone. She weeps for her home, up in flames. She weeps from the core of her body.

Bernadette's mother cries quietly, constantly, like a dripping tap.

Unbelievably, Bernadette's father weeps, too. Bernadette sees him saddling up his horse, sees him push his face into the horse's neck. The horse nudges him, makes a small wickering noise of sympathy. Hearing that, her father begins to weep openly, with terrible, rasping cries. He runs his hands up and down the horse's neck in an overwhelmed, tormented way. Her father, who never cries.

When they are together the adults move carefully, as if nervous of each other. Wary, like exhausted animals.

Bernadette rides her bike back into Kelly's Creek to inspect the ruins. The fireplaces are all that's left: one facing into the lounge room, the other facing into the kitchen, joined into the large central chimney reaching up to the sky.

She tries to picture Tom Larsen turning the fifty-gallon drum over, hauling it from room to room. Wouldn't he get a jug and use that? A watering can would be good, that way you could sprinkle it everywhere. His biggest mistake, of course, was taking Jennifer with him. She'd be turning the rear-vision mirror to put on her makeup. She'd be complaining about how she needed to shampoo her hair. (Jennifer didn't just wash her hair, oh, no.)

How long before Tom Larsen took a tumble to himself and left the whingeing Jennifer in a ditch beside the road?

Bernadette pokes about in the ruins and uncovers a bit of old mattress. The neighbour, who's been spying on her from over the fence says, "You're the Ardara girl, aren't you?" Gimlet-eyed.

The Ardara girl. Aren't you? Aren't you?

For by now Bernadette has figured it out. For her father to be crying, something terrible must have happened between her mother and Tom Larsen.

Bernadette crosses off the days until she can get back to boarding school, where none of this exists.

WHEN BERNADETTE COMES HOME AGAIN, in September, Hazel has set up camp (Dad's phrase) in the cottage. In the main homestead there is a small sense of reprieve, a tentative lightening of mood.

But Hazel has emerged, and is walking up through the orchard.

Bernadette's father, sitting on the verandah, sees her coming. "Uh-oh," he says. "Here comes trouble."

Bernadette's mother stands beside him. "Once more into the

breach," she mutters. She pats his shoulder. He reaches up, covers her hand with his. She pushes it quickly away.

Dad has begun to refer to the cottage as "the waterworks."

Tea is over, and Mum is putting food on a tray for Hazel. Anchovy eggs with pickled onions, tomatoes from the garden. Fresh bread. Lemon sponge for dessert. Lovely.

Bernadette and her mother carry this down through the orchard. They go into the cottage and place the food on the kitchen table.

"Hazel," cries out Bernadette's mother, "Haze."

Hazel dawdles into the kitchen, housecoat rumpled and smelly. Surveys the food.

"I did the eggs specially," offers Bernadette's mother.

Hazel takes the covers off, sniffs. "You don't expect me to *enjoy* this, do you?" With that, she hurries back into the bedroom, slams the door.

"Hazel," pleads Bernadette's mother. She stands at the bedroom door.

No answer came the stern reply. Dad always says that, it's something he learned at school.

From inside the bedroom, sobs, designed to be heard.

Her mother begging, Hazel denying. It will go on for ages.

"You'd better go on up," says Mum.

Back at the house, Dad is sitting by the fire reading the newspaper *The Land*. Bernadette's grandmother is playing the piano in a cheerful, slouchy way. She sees Bernadette, gestures to her to come and sit beside her on the piano stool. "Blue Moon. You left me standing alone," the two of them sing, with a steady, defiant cheerfulness.

Without a dream in my heart,
Without a love of my own.

THE NEXT HOLIDAYS, the long summer ones, they are repairing the cottage. All of them.

Hazel and Alice are painting. Hazel, her head wrapped in a scarf, is working in old jodhpurs. Alice's. (Nothing but the clothes she stood up in.) Carefully, they pour the paint into the pan. Hazel has a roller. Alice comes after with a brush, doing the tricky bits. "Buttercup yellow for the wall," says Alice. "Mother's going to run up some blue-and-white curtains."

Sure enough, back at the house, Bernadette's grandmother is getting the old Singer set up, threading the cotton through, making the treadle fly.

Bernadette's father is also working on the repairs. When he comes in from the paddocks and on Sundays, he clambers onto the roof, hammers sheets of corrugated iron. Fixes the tank with dabs of creosote.

The three of them go to town — Alice and Dick and Hazel. They bring home a roll of new lino for the cottage hallway. As they manoeuvre it out of the ute and into the cottage, Bernadette can hear the three of them laughing.

Bernadette's mother, uncharacteristically, does not tell her she has to help. But before long, Bernadette, too, is down on her knees in the cottage, scrubbing out mouldy old cupboards.

Bernadette's grandmother comes with afternoon tea. "It hasn't looked this good in years," she says, looking around, delighted.

Hazel and Alice hug each other, as if they've both come top of the class. Then spring apart, alarmed.

BERNADETTE DIDN'T PUT HER FINGER on what was wrong with this story about her mother and the Larsens until she herself had left her first husband.

This was in the early 1970s. She and her husband were teachers in northern New South Wales, on the coast. While others were storming around speaking of revolution and getting excited about the moratorium, Bernadette and her husband lay abed. She read to him from the weekend papers while he admired her breasts.

She taught herself to entertain with proper wines. When she went down to Sydney, she stocked up on what the cookbook called Egyptian beans, pomegranate molasses. To eat all this fine food, Bernadette invited many guests (including her short-lived new lover). They cleaned their plates and asked for more. They lingered in the garden, thanking her. And her husband put his arms around her, approving. Husband and wife, they stood at the gate, waving bye-bye together in the warm night. Then he lay down beside her and listened to the sound of the surf. And he did not know, he did not suspect, any of what she was thinking or feeling.

Until one day she told him.

Her husband walked down the hallway of their house, their small, white wooden house, beating his fists on the walls and looking surprised to find himself doing this. "It was so good," he cried out to the walls, "it was so good." Really, it was, he declared with his fist. It was. Or had he been mad, quite mad?

When her husband had finished smashing his fists into the walls and stumbled off, Bernadette sat in a chair and thought about Alice and Hazel and Tom Larsen.

The perpetrator doesn't burn the house down.

Doesn't need to.

TWENTY YEARS ON. Bernie's just back from overseas. Home again. She feels the cool of the verandah tiles on her bare feet. Looks out to the bony slopes of Ardara.

"Bernadette's home!"

She carries these clear, clean, hungry hills in her molecules. They move in the blood and gather in the heart.

She's walking out on the verandah very early, before dawn. They're in the sleep-out, the three of them: Dick, Alice, Hazel. Three single beds. Sheets, no blankets needed at this time of year. It's a new sleep-out Dick's put on. Floor-length sash windows you keep down all summer long — just wire mesh to stop the blowies. In winter you leave the windows up and it's a sunroom, snug against tableland frosts.

Bernadette is wide awake, in another time zone. This time yesterday it wasn't yesterday and it wasn't this time.

After she and her brother, Bob, left home, to go to university, Hazel moved from the cottage into the homestead, taking one of the back bedrooms.

Here, in the sleep-out, there is Dick in the bed nearest the wall, his leg lying beside him on the floor.

In the middle bed, Alice, curled up.

Closest to the sleep-out windows, Hazel.

When Bernadette first attempted to talk about these three, she found herself unequal to the task. (What will people think? What does *she* think?) Her version of their story was a mixture of her own uncertainties and a narrative that veered off into the reliability of pathos, or, less often, into an embarrassing form of braggadocio focused on sexual novelty.

But now she finds herself less interested in the complexities of the arrangements. What absorbs her is the capacity for accommodation. How they got out the cards, opened the piano, sang a few songs. How they went into town. Fixed the roof. Bought new lino.

As she watches, they turn in their sleep with the habit of years. Dick first, then Alice, then finally Hazel, who throws her arms into the empty air. Reaching out, while her husband, in a pillar of orange dust, drives on.

Birds are stirring. Sparrow fart, Dick would say, if he woke.

Dick, who had one day dried his eyes and resolved not to cry again.

Alice, who had run between cottage and homestead and realized that they were both going to be there with her, hearts cracked open wide.

And Hazel?

Hazel, who'd had nowhere else to go.

Bernadette stands at the edge of the verandah, watching them.

$\mathscr{O}$PEN $\mathscr{W}$IDE

Alice reaches out a hand and makes a gesture for silence, although neither Bernie nor her brother Bob is speaking.

"I should mention right away," announces Alice, "the staff here aren't real. They don't fool me, not for one minute."

Alice is in Canberra's Odin Hospital, which is not what it used to be. Years ago — back in the 1950s, when Bob and Bernadette were young — nurses swept along in ice-bright white, confident little battleships. Now they go slopping about in tracksuits, searching for supplies they cannot find, shoulders hunched with their own considerable grievances.

"Don't worry about the nurses," says Bob, reaching out to stroke his mother's hand, "they're neither here nor there."

"Certainly not here," says Alice.

"Not compared to the real Odin," says Bob. "The real Odin kept a pair of ravens perched on his shoulders."

Bob, who'd seemed destined for a life on the land, has turned himself into an artist instead. His most recent project is a series on ravens, each painting dominated by weighty black birds, with a gloss of purple and dark green. In thick paint that sweeps downwards, Bob's going after the falling final note of the raven's *ah-aah-aahaah*.

"The ravens were thought and memory," Bob continues. "By day they travelled the world. At night they returned to Odin and whispered into his ears all they had seen and heard. And that's why Odin was omniscient, a god."

"We could go for a bit of the real Odin round here," says Bernie.

NEXT MORNING THEY HOLD a conference in the hospital corridor: Jen the busy Canberra bureaucrat, jet-lagged Bernadette, and Bob down from the bush.

"What are we going to do about Hazel?" asks Bernie, leading off.

Hazel, who is Jen's mother, lives with Alice in the Canberra suburb of Chifley. Hazel claims that Alice has ascended into heaven. From Mount Taylor. She's written to the *Canberra Times*, describing Alice's ascent. Witnesses are coming forward to offer eager confirmation. It isn't even the silly season; it's a chilly autumn and taxes are due.

"We have to talk to Hazel," Bernadette goes on. "We've got to get Hazel off this kick about Alice ascending."

When Hazel and Alice went for their walk up Mount Taylor, it would have been one of those coppery, autumn Canberra days. No wonder Hazel heard the thin sound of trumpets in the air.

"I wouldn't give a stuff if it weren't for Mum," says Bob. "She's got more than enough to worry about."

"What do you think I've been doing?" Jennifer replies, looking at Bernadette. Reminding them all who is the negligent party here, the one currently living overseas. Who had to rush home on a plane when she heard the word "metastasized."

"Keep telling Hazel that Alice is in the hospital," urges Bob.

They have arrived at the door to Alice's room.

"I've tried," says Jennifer, becoming pointedly patient. "But she won't take my word for it. She sees what she believes."

"She can't go on like this, with her head stuck in the sand," says Bernadette.

"Stuck up her arse," puts in Bob.

Jen's pager rings, and Jen announces, "I simply must fly."

"I thought she'd have to *buzz*," says Bernadette to Bob, as Jen disappears into the lift.

"Power morning tea," says Bob. "PM's put the kettle on."

"YOU PAIR LOOK LIKE YOU COULD DO with a good story," says Alice, as soon as Bernie and Bob reach her bedside.

"A hospital yarn for you," she goes on. "A woman comes into casualty, bleeding profusely. All over the floor, up the walls, you bet. Fibroids, she tells the nurse. Fibroids, she says again, to the doc this time — weeks have gone by, now at last it's her turn. 'Five boys?' the doc says, scribbling busily. 'Right,' he says, finally looking up. 'And now what seems to be the problem?'"

"Mum, you'll wear yourself out," says Bob.

"I'm already worn out," says Alice. "I believe that's why we're gathered here today."

Bernadette reads the piece in the *Times*.

Martin Moon, level-four economist with DETYA — Department of Education, Training, and Youth Affairs, so help us all — was looking out his window at three-thirty on the Sunday afternoon in question. Although his mind was on his long-service leave in Tuscany, he noticed the two elderly women in matching cherry-red wind-cheaters, stepping along the path behind his home that led to Mount Taylor.

Francis Nguyen, pigeon fancier, employed in a photocopy room at Defence, was out talking to his birds (probably illegal in that backyard). He saw them too, the old ladies. So said his girlfriend Debbie, who works at the Belconnen Country Rest. She'd been bringing in Frankie's wash before the damp got to it.

From these anecdotes, the readers of the *Times* were able to trace Alice's movements: along the paved cement path among the gums, across the road, over the stile, onto the gravel path, slipping finally through the gate and up the mountain. At this point, the path is no wider than a sheep track and is at times a little steep.

The ascent itself was witnessed by a participant in a Butt Out program who'd sneaked off for a few cigs behind the reservoir. Also witnessing liftoff was his dog, Bowler. He saw the two ladies going up the mountain track. Had been impressed by their amount of puff. Just before it happened, Bowler began to growl; his hair stood up in a ridge along his back. Then one of the two senior ladies stepped into the air. Up she went, he claimed, with a calm, relaxed expression on her face, despite the chill wind from the Brindabellas. Maintained her cool (his wording) when one of her sandals dropped off.

Bowler barked.

He kept looking up, he said, as the woman disappeared behind the clouds, then came out again, still going, on into the sky.

Until she was only a wash of blue.

The article includes a photo of Hazel, holding up the dropped shoe in a triumphant gesture of belief. It was a shoe, not a sandal, Hazel explains in the caption. Being winter weather.

"What do you make of this tommy-rot?" asks Bernadatte.

"Tommy-rot is right," says Alice, then adds, "But it's a poor sort of memory that only works backwards."

The morphine drip gives a reassuring little burp.

"Does the morphine round out the edges?" asks Bob.

"Rounds out the edges, my foot," says Alice. "More like being dumped in the bottom of an old bathtub."

"Is there anyone," asks Bernadette, "you want us to talk to about this?"

"Bear with Hazel," Alice says, wearily, "bear with her. That afternoon we walked up Mount Taylor was our last outing together."

A nurse happens to come in. Not for Alice, but to rummage for something in a cupboard by the window. Not finding it, she leaves.

"Is this normal?" asks Bernie, running after the nurse. "Isn't she wearing herself out talking so much?"

"I suppose it's the treatment." The nurse shrugs, and walks away down the corridor.

"I'm lying on the bottom of my bathtub," Alice is telling Bob, "and over me are the Odin Hospital blankets. You can call it sleep if you want. But it's much thicker and murkier than that, believe you me.

"Dick," Alice goes on, referring to her husband, "now he was the lucky one. Dropped dead filling his water bag before he went out to the paddocks. Not much call for water bags anymore, but Dick kept his. Liked the baggy taste, he said. I found him by the tank-stand, the tap still running. At first I thought, what a grim way to go, unattended and unwitnessed. But now I know it's the best, the Indy of exits."

After Dick died, Alice left the property in northern New South Wales and came to Canberra to join Hazel, who had already moved there to be with her daughter, Jennifer.

"Looks like the women in this family go in for the big C," Bernie says to Bob, when they are having lunch — soup and grilled cheesies — in the Odin Plaza. (Alice's mother, Ellen, had died five years before of the same disease.)

IN ODIN HOSPITAL, Alice is reading what she announces will be her final book. Grave as a high priestess, she sits up in her bed and recounts a recent passage.

From a distance, a young girl glimpses a woman being driven down a private lane in an elegant, highly polished touring car. She has red hair, this woman; she is pale, indolent, languid, unapproachable. She belongs to the colonial class, the class that hides itself from the locals and the fierce damp heat in villas set behind fences covered with dense, flowering vines. The officials don't like her, the ambassador's wife. She drinks too much in embassy drawing rooms. In the torpor of this particular afternoon, the woman appears to be dreaming, far away, removed, consumed with an overwhelming ennui, utterly indifferent, utterly passionate. (She isn't English, she couldn't be. French.) She has no friends, it is said, only lovers.

Recently a man killed himself out of love for her.

Another man falls in love with her. (This is in a different city, but the woman is the same; it is always she.) He sees her bicycle beside the tennis court, but she does not come for it. The bicycle stands beside the tennis court, untouched, while he waits. He waits for her so intently that yet another man falls in love with her, compelled by such longing. In the half-light, within the exaggerated, febrile smell of frangipani, she plays the piano. The listeners, those who are desperate with love, must wait for the return of the melody.

And forever she is walking up the wooden staircase of the deserted, darkened ballroom. Wearing an evening gown with pale spaghetti straps that cross in the front and reach around her neck.

Consider the satin, the expanse of bare shoulders.

In the gloom, she goes slinking up those stairs. We can see only indistinctly the burning movement of her hips as she moves into the shadows that close behind her, going right to the end. She's taking the stairs out over the edge of the world.

When she grows up, the young girl writes about this woman she glimpsed, writes about her in novels and plays and film scripts, writes repeatedly, brilliantly, obsessively. She has forgotten the woman's name; she has given her another one.

One day, fifty years on, the writer receives a note from the woman, inviting her to afternoon tea in the old folks' home. This is the real woman, you understand, the one she glimpsed in the touring car, going down a private lane, such a long time ago, in another country.

"So what did the writer do?" Bernadette asks.

"Didn't go, of course. Didn't even reply," says Alice promptly.

"What would you have done," asks Bob, "if you'd received an invitation like that?"

"She couldn't go," says Alice, becoming more thoughtful. "If she'd gone, can you imagine?"

ALL THE TIME ALICE IS TELLING this story, Bob is looking at Bernadette and remembering how, when she was younger, Bernie loved to gaze at others when they didn't know they were being watched. To see who they were when they believed themselves to be alone. Bern also enjoyed examining their things. She had a hunger for how they hung their clothes, how they arranged things on their dressing tables. She would stand at the open doorway to other people's rooms. Becoming bold, she would venture in. Just to touch something. Not personal papers or a diary, although she would probably be capable of that, as well. A towel, a pencil, a dress — a dress was always good, or a shoe, or underwear. Anything close to the body.

She wanted to know how life was for them, how it would be to look out through their eyes.

"I WANDERED AROUND AND FINALLY FOUND . . ." Alice sings.

Bob and Bernie are sitting by the bed, carefully nonchalant. They exchange glances. Alice is bombed on drugs this morning. What's next?

"Turns out the joker is a tiger. 'Open the door and the tiger leaps.' Who said that? Can't remember, not for the life of me."

It's almost noon when the doctor shows up.

"She's more than holding her own," says Dr. Ahearne. "You're more than holding your own, aren't you, Alice."

Alice gets a highly responsible look on her face when Dr. Ahearne is speaking to her. Dr. Ahearne is genial but rushed, hirsute but closely shaven, with small, bright-as-a-berry eyes.

"In his spare time," Alice says a moment later, when the doctor has left, "he's a spelio. That's what he says, anyway."

"He does look rather like a bat," Bernie says. "He'd be a natural for a spelio."

"I bet he goes down into those caves on the Nullabor," says Alice. "Imagine how soothing and cool it must be. There'd be shade down there thousands of years old."

They consider the doctor wading through subterranean waters. Does he perhaps carry an inflatable dinghy?

THE TIGERS COME DOWN THE CORRIDOR and stand at the doors, looking in to check. Precise and careful, but not in the least shy. Naturally, the protocol is to pretend you've not seen them, to look the other way.

One of them has his eye on me. Always the same one. He comes to my door and looks in. I pretend I'm asleep.

I'm his, you see.

He's chosen.

BOB IS DRIVING BERNIE BACK to the motel in the early winter evening. They admire Mount Ainslie turning purple up behind the war memorial. "Thank Christ for the Canberra hills," says Bob.

This is no real rush hour, just privileged commuters drifting easily across the bridge, with time to enjoy the view.

The first day, after they'd been to the hospital, Bernie and Bob went for a walk through the botanical gardens and up Black Mountain. As Bob stopped to stare at the smooth white bark of the brittle gums, the rough brown of the stringybarks, Bernie carried on about the crisp air and said that if anyone ever did make a break for heaven, this quiet city would be the logical launching pad.

"Let's get Chinese takeaway," says Bernie. They're sharing a room at the motel — cheaper that way.

"Why do you think Hazel's wedded to the idea of Alice going up into heaven?" Bernie asks, as they hang about for the takeaway. She's been waiting for the right time to chew this over.

"Hazel's no big mystery," says Bob. "If you can't bear the truth, best rearrange it."

"Do you think we'll go nuts, when we're old and something happens that we can't endure?"

"But what about the others? That's what I'd like to know. The guy from the government? The Butt Out dropout? The pigeon fancier? How come they wanted to get in on the act?"

"I suppose nobody ever went broke overestimating the hunger for belief. The question is not, 'What do you believe?' but, 'Is there anything you *don't* believe?'"

Takeaway in hand, Bernie and Bob drive to the motel, prop themselves up on their beds, and watch TV while they eat. Hyper young things pour blue liquid over sanitary pads, then the evening news. The aftermath of a mass murder in America somewhere. Katharine Hepburn comes on and says that, any day now, she is going to join Spence. "I have waited over thirty years," she says.

Then it's back to the mass murder. "When can the healing begin?" the journalist asks.

"First the tragedy," Bernie says, "then the healing. Just like that. How about a spot of mourning in between?"

OVER AT ODIN HOSPITAL, Alice sleeps.

Oh, how I rode with Father, lifted up and up by Mother, who was saying something about precious cargo. Me wrapped in Father's arms and the warmth of the horse — it was a winter's morning, there was frost — and the smell of the saddle and gums and us racing, and the magpies rinsing their throats and Father roaring with pleasure. It was one, all of it one precious cargo.

It was being alive and moving over the face of this earth.

You can't ask for more than that.

WHEN THEY VISIT THE NEXT DAY, Alice is at the top of the morphine.

"Whenever I think of Mother," Alice says, "I hear Massenet's

Thaïs on the old record player at Ardara. Remember *Thaïs?*"

Bernadette nods. She does remember. The besotted violin floated out over the tough paddocks and evaporated.

"'When you hear something as lovely as that,' Mother used to say, 'you realize you just have to hope for the best.'"

Jennifer arrives, cellphone sticking out of her briefcase.

"Were you able to sleep last night?" Bernie asks Alice.

"I was trying to sleep, but the priest arrived. Decked out in civvies, not so much as a collar in sight. Flyboy began to talk about anger and forgiveness. 'What I'd appreciate from you,' I said, 'is something smart about the last things.' Then a nurse barged in and Flyboy looked up, prayers answered. Slunk out, fast."

"Haze's begun to sort through your clothes," Bob says. "She's taking them to the Vee de Pee." The St. Vincent de Paul.

"Can we intercept her?" Bernadette asks. "Maybe I could talk Hazel into giving me your clothes."

"No point in playing along with the deception," says Alice. "Hazel's going to have to come to terms with facts."

"Fact one," says Bob. "You don't ascend into heaven from Mount Taylor like you're taking a lift."

"It's assumption, not ascension," Alice points out. "Christ ascended; Mary was assumed. *Assumpta est, alleluia.*"

"It's an assumption all right," says Bernie, getting fed up.

"Deep in the heart of denial," says Bob, humming a little tune.

"Denial," says Jennifer, who's just been paged and has to run, "is step one in any trauma syndrome."

"Spare us the syndromes," says Bob, as they listen to Jennifer's shoes *clicky-clacking* away.

"Hazel's going to lead Jen a merry dance," says Alice. "This business about travel to heaven is just the beginning."

Bernie says, "Everything Jennifer reads has tabs and numbered paragraphs. It's the fate of lofty bureaucrats."

"I wouldn't worry about Jennifer. She'll be rolling in the bucks when she retires," says Bob. "Rolling."

"I believe she could run the entire country with one hand tied behind her back," says Bernie.

"Does in fact run the whole country," adds Bob. "And look around."

"You know what Jennifer reminds me of?" asks Alice, looking exceptionally pleased with herself. "That bit in *Alice in Wonderland* where the King says, 'The horror of that moment, I will never, *never* forget.' And the Queen replies, 'You will, though, if you don't make a memorandum of it.' That's Hazel's Jennifer for you."

I WAS IN THE SHEARING SHED at Ardara. Sitting under the classing table, watching. One of the shearers had put a packing case there for me. "Alice's throne," he called it.

Outside, all around, the bush, stiff with heat. From the pens, incessant bleating. Slipping through the sapling rails, leaping along the sheep's backs, were the dogs, drunk on work. And the sheep themselves, so many sheep, their nervous squirming. Swiftly reduced to trembling bare.

Inside the shed, corrugated-iron shimmery. Wool and dust, ammonia, tar, and sweat.

The first run after lunch, usually the fastest shearing of the day. Everything going full bat: the fleeces falling thick on the board, the picker-upper scurrying, and the shorn sheep skittering down the chute to the counting out pen. From there, at a right angle, I could see the shearing board, see Father at his stand. Father had the style and patience that made fast look easy. (He was old mates with the head shearer, he paid proper rates, so they'd let him take a turn at the stand.)

Above me, on the table, the picker-upper, with expert wrist, had just tossed a whole fleece as if it were a dirty cream tablecloth.

Father had the sheep in a sitting position. They were both down on the shearing board, the ewe and Father. Father's arms were around the ewe. The handpiece, caught in the thick neck folds, was biting its way in.

The picker-upper rushed to pull the stand out of gear.

The ewe's neck bled in orderly spurts. Steadily soaking the wool, ruining Father's final tally.

BERNIE AND BOB VISIT HAZEL and Alice's home in the suburb of Chifley. "The bijou bung," Alice calls it.

As he parks the car, Bob signals for Bernie to listen: the deep, brown sound of a thornbill, and above that, wrens, singing in the garden across the street.

Hazel answers the door. Takes their hands, draws them solemnly in. The miraculous event has made Hazel more stately than ever, her still-thick hair even whiter. Like a countrywoman on her day in town, Hazel has dressed. A dove-grey polo neck, a knitted navy-blue jacket, over a long skirt of dark purple. A necklace sits on the polo neck, blue polished river stones.

"Nothing expensive," murmurs Bernie to Bob, "but everything works."

Bernie, thinks Bob, is the kind of woman who loves good clothes on others but can never remember what she herself is wearing.

The room is warm, with wide, sunny windows looking out on first-class sheep country ruined with tacky houses. While Hazel makes tea, gets out a packet of biscuits, Bernie lies back, turns her face to the sun.

"Do the harmful rays come in through the window," she says to Bob, "or does the glass stop them?"

"You should have seen her, my dears," says Hazel, when tea and biscuits have been served and conversation can begin. "So peaceful."

"Hazel," says Bernadette, sitting up. "I know that Alice's sudden illness has been a great shock for you."

"And so light on her feet."

"The news is not all bad," puts in Bob, keeping his voice calm, full of tolerant understanding. "In fact, the news is quite good, really."

"I know, dear," says Hazel. Her hands — soft old parchment —

seize Bob's and will not let them go. "God works in mysterious ways His wonders to perform."

"Hazel, I want you to listen to me now," says Bernadette. "I want you to listen to me for a moment."

"All we need to do is listen. If I listen, I can hear her voice. And she's happy. A little sad perhaps, but happy." With this, tears begin to make their way down Hazel's grooved face, among the small, benign sun cancers.

"Sad, but happy too," Hazel repeats, busy being brave.

"I know this is difficult, but when you see Alice, you'll feel so much better yourself."

"But I do see her. I look up and I see her. I say to myself, how beautiful upon the mountains."

"You know what I think we should do?" says Bernadette, pretending to be on the point of leaving.

Bob stands up.

"Alice would love to see you," Bernadette says. "Now that we're here. Look, we'll all go together. Bob'll drive you. Alice will be thrilled."

"She does see us, dear." Hazel has wiped her eyes. "You mustn't worry about any of that."

Sensing defeat, Bernadette begins to behave badly.

"Once she's settled in heaven, I'll be able to pray to her," Bernadette says, assuming the believer's attitude of trust. "We all will." And for a moment, Hazel's face is startled into openness. (*Gotcha!*)

Hazel draws back, dignified. Sinks into her polo neck.

JENNIFER HAS A PLAN. Alice will phone home on the cellphone, her mobile. Mobile phones are forbidden in the wards, they muck up the kidney machines.

"Takes the piss out of them," says Bob.

"But needs must," says Jen. She dials the number, hands the phone to Alice.

"Hazel," says Alice, taking the phone in a trembling hand, "just what do you think you're playing at?"

"No," says Alice, "I am not, repeat not, calling from the Vale of Bloody Beulah." Hazel's tedious Methodist tendencies are showing up, an unfortunate childhood legacy.

"Haze, this can't go on," Alice insists wearily.

Hazel has hung up.

"She tires me out," Alice complains.

"What's she going to say when you arrive on the front doorstep?" asks Bernadette.

"Behold, the Second Coming," Alice suggests.

THE NEXT DAY, someone who calls herself Merle-Next-Door arrives at the same time as Bob and Bernie.

"Who is this woman?" asks Alice, turning to Bob.

"Mum," he says, "Mum, it's Merle, from next door. In Chifley. Merle-Next-Door."

"Hazel's sticking to her guns," Merle tells Alice.

"Merle," Alice says firmly. "Let me tell you a story."

She'll fix her, Bernadette thinks: adult content; some violence.

Merle-Next-Door looks up, expectant.

"In the 1950s, Hazel lost her son to polio."

Merle puts on a mandatory sad face. But the 1950s were a long time ago, weren't they? There must be more to it than this.

"Her only son," puts in Bernadette.

"Bernie here had it, too," Alice adds. "But she pulled through. They were in the hospital together. It was the longest thirteen months of our lives, I can tell you that. Then, a few years after, Hazel also lost her daughter."

"I had no idea," murmurs Merle-Next-Door in humble, delighted horror. Hazel's daughter, Jennifer, is expected any minute. Alice is perhaps rambling?

"Stories within stories," Alice promises foolishly. But is losing interest. Having come this far, Alice shuts her eyes, exhausted.

Merle leans forward. As if Alice's breathing itself might yield secrets. "No idea at all," supplies Merle-Next-Door, in further encouragement.

IN THE 1950S, Jennifer's father took her away from their home in New South Wales, all the way to Western Australia, took her as far from Hazel as was possible. Depriving Hazel of the crucial years of her daughter's adolescence. Hazel spent much of the 1970s — that bubbling, fractious decade — hunting for Jennifer: beating the bushes, creating a hullabaloo, going on talk shows. Her first taste of the media.

"She appears not to have made a complete recovery," Bob observes.

While bright young men prophesied the death of the family, Hazel would natter on about the permanency of the bond between parent and child. A child separated from a parent lives with an absolute sense of loss, Hazel explained to the cameras.

"And then," Alice says, "O frabjous day! Callooh! Callay! Hazel found her daughter."

HE HAS SUCH FINE PADS. Forget leather; forget velvet. This boy is something else. I haven't touched his pads yet, but you should hear them, coming along the corridor. They're the softest things. Living quietness. *Pad, pad, pad.*

He comes into my room regularly now. Sits under the bed, washing his fur. I wake up and wonder what the noise is. It's him, purring and cleaning himself at the same time. Last night he got up on his hind legs and took a long look at me, inspected the bed. He has yellow eyes, a bit poppy. A thyroid condition, genetic probably.

How do you describe the golden eyes of a big cat? Gold-bright, gleam-garnished, light-filled amber, crushed butterfly wings? The black tunnel at their centre opening and closing, making the finest, most crafty adjustments.

He was quite small at first. Did I tell you that he's getting bigger?

I know he's thinking about me more. Stands up, front paws on the blanket. Looking at me, considering. Sizing me up.

Hides under the bed if nurses come in. They never see him slipping away. For who can disappear as easily as a cat? Who can vanish as convincingly?

He's an all-black marsupial tiger. The special kind.

THE NURSES ARRIVE with their vague good cheer, pushing and probing and chirping.

"And the city of God was pure gold, like unto clear glass," Alice tells them.

"Was it, dear?" they say, ramming in a needle.

"Don't count on it," Alice says.

Dr. Ahearne comes on his rounds. "You're looking well this morning," he says.

"We who are about to die salute you," says Alice.

The doc gives a brief laugh, no extra charge, he won't even note it down on the bill.

Abruptly, Alice closes her eyes, shutting them out.

THEY WERE GATHERED ON THE ROOF last night, the tigers of Odin. (Not my boy, he was beside me all the time. Some of the others.) Jumping up and down, as a matter of fact. Rejoicing, or fighting; I don't know which. I suspect they had a body up there and were quarrelling over it. Bickering: hallmark of the animal kingdom, and that includes us. Limb from torso, like the early Christians in the coliseum. We who are about to die are not particularly enthused about it.

I lay in my bed in pain and terror; he was down below, on the floor alongside. From the way he carried on, you'd think nothing unusual was happening. He simply put his head down on his paws and went off to sleep.

In pain and terror. Lead blankets, heavy and cold. (Hospitalspeak — "resting comfortably": drugged insensate; "experiencing a little discomfort": in pain and terror.) Experiencing a little discomfort, I lay under my blankets, Odin Hospital in red stitching on the side, in case you're planning on swiping them.

BERNIE HAS SMELLED THE TIGER, understands the great game's afoot, wants to get things said while there's still time.

Bob couldn't come today; pity. Jen had a meeting; fine. Merle-Next-Door apparently met with sufficient excitement yesterday.

"How did you *feel?*" Bernie asks. They are talking about some forgotten family story, something that happened years ago. Surely none of it matters now.

"I simply can't remember how I felt," Alice replies, to annoy. Then she relents, because what will it matter? "My life is yours," she says. "Help yourself. I suppose you're having the coffin wired for sound."

Bernie wants to know if Alice has any regrets.

"We're all sisters under the skin," Alice says. "The sisterhood of man."

"And the roads not taken?"

Alice doesn't have the heart to tell her that pouting about roads not taken is a luxury of the middle-aged.

"Father had a gelding called Regret."

Bernie is not to be put off. "Give me the names of all the animals," she commands. "As far back as you can remember."

"Jennifer will have Hazel," Alice tells Bernie. "Something to go on with. It'll be Bob who'll say, 'Last one out turn off the light, so where's the fucking switch?' It'll be you who maunders, who stumbles into doors, who asks, 'Where have you gone?'"

I WONDER WHAT BOB WOULD MAKE of my tiger. As an artist, in a purely professional sense, I am sure my son would admire his strength, his symmetry.

Tigers, like all cats, are carnivores. You can feed a cat all the brown rice you like, but what a cat craves is animal flesh. Warm and fresh is naturally preferred. So there is bound to be a certain amount of tearing and grabbing and rending asunder. Nobody gives up without a fight, we hang on; we hang on for dear life.

My tiger hops into bed with me every night now. Paws-paws a spot, gets into the crook of my arm. We lie curled together like lovers. I am permitted to kiss his face, stroke his head between his ears. He purrs to me; he listens. And he does understand that so very much has fallen away. He realizes how distant they are becoming to me and he knows that that doesn't mean I didn't love them, not for one minute.

My mother. Hazel and Dick. My son Bob. And Bernadette, who will need to remember these things, who will not be able to forget.

None of that feels particularly close now. Not compared with the plaster spotty dog Father brought home from the show in 1929. It was about eight inches high, an impressive size. Spotty Dog wore a red polka-dot collar and looked mournful — as well he might, that year. I had him on the dresser beside my bed.

Yes, yes, the tiger says, I remember Spotty Dog. You were four.

THEY'RE STANDING BY THE BED, Bernie and Bob.

Looking at me like I'm a sheep down in the heat and they're determined to haul me up, make me go on until I grow weak again, thanks for precisely less than nothing.

A CROW CRIES IN THE EMPTY HALL of summer. Cicadas have sung up the heat, which stretches across the boulders, lies deep in the dry grass.

At night we look up and remember that the stars, too, are burning, made of fire.

It was the end of the New Year's Eve party. We had a barbecue after it got dark and the flies died down. The kids had gone. It was just us: Dick, Mother, and Hazel. Mother opened the piano for a few last corny songs. "It had to be you . . . And even be glad, just to be sad, thinking of you."

I learned all the best songs from Mother. Really, I did.

That night Mother put on a Bach cantata: "*Herr, gebe nicht ins Gericht.*" A change of pace. "I'm not quite sure," said Mother. "I think it's, 'Lord, don't judge us.'" It was about two in the morning of a new year. Where we were that night, there is now nothing. There you have it. No need to go on about it.

And here's Bach, blasting away with such elegant, uplifting confidence, and I'm listening to the recitative near the end, listening to the line, "God will open wide the gates of heaven." And I'm looking around the room, thinking that I don't really believe a word of what Bach is saying, not in any literal sense, not in any sense, but what a splendid, ambitious, mysterious idea it is: perfect happiness, perfect love, forever.

I tell the tiger.

Open wide.

$\mathcal{P}$OSTSCRIPT, $\mathcal{A}$RDARA

Bernie's taking early retirement. "Post-polio syndrome, PPS. A post-postscript from the Fifties," she tells people. "Consider my life an epilogue to that maligned decade."

To tell anyone she has PPS is to press a free-advice button. For the fatigue, has she tried evening primrose oil, drum therapy, a bracing enema of cold licorice tea?

"It's just," she says, growing resentful at having to explain yet again, "that my nerves are having a hard time regenerating sprouts."

Keep it simple. Sprouts are something people can get their head around, out here on Canada's west coast.

CREAMY-YELLOW BEDROOM WALLS shift into focus. She's stiff this morning, but not too bad. It must be late because Patrick's already left. Has he gone to work, or is he off on a run? His grey sweatshirt's on the chair, so he's gone to work. Eleven o'clock, or later? Still morning, though, she can tell by the light on the wall. When she retires — soon, soon — this room will be her full-time study as well. For six months of the year. For the other six months, they'll be on Ardara. Northern summer, southern summer. Paradise, here we come.

She's got her desk in the window nook — a laptop, a notice board. She's put her list of names up there: her family on her mother's side. All dead now. The way they lived then, forever gone.

Today she's feeling happy, but why? — *Yes, got it!* Her brother, Bob, is coming in on the plane. She looks at the clock. Christ, he's here now. That's where Patrick's gone. He's out at the airport picking up Bob.

BERNIE AND PATRICK ARE PLANNING a party in their Vancouver home for the friends who, in this same city twenty-five years before, celebrated their non-wedding. Naturally, not all will be able to attend.

Patrick's daughter, Zoë, living in Donegal, has sent regrets.

But Bernie's brother, Bob, will make it. It's been five months since she last saw him. She and Patrick were back in Oz at Christmas, staying with Bob on Ardara. They were there for the centenary of federation celebrations, January 1, 2001. Bob drove them into Kelly's Creek. A small crowd had gathered at the sports ground for the ringing of the bells in the afternoon. People were doing this across the country to mark the exact moment of federation, one hundred years before.

The instructions were quite specific. They were to start ringing at 3:55 p.m., Eastern Daylight Time, and ring for at least five minutes. Right on time, the crowd got stuck into ringing. Cow bells, small silver bells, a few school bells, the local fire truck's bell. About six minutes later, the bells petered out. People stood about in the dry, yellow grass, looked around, and wondered what they were supposed to do next.

Bob said it was reassuring to live in a country that didn't know its arse from its elbow when it came to ritual.

"I HOPE YOU'RE TAKING IT EASY," Bob says to Bernie, as soon as he gets in the front door.

God, can't they ever forget? "I'm doing good," she replies. "The neurons are napping, not dropping."

"Not dead yet, then," he says, giving her a bear hug.

There's something shambolic about Bob in middle age. Pink complexion, wild white hair, and cranky opinions. A face like Van Morrison's. Looking at him reminds Bernie of how neat and tidy and *North American* Patrick has remained. This, despite the fact that he's an ornithologist, keen on creeping around in swamps, hiding in trees.

To be fair, Bob has had to sleep in his clothes, and has been up for approximately two days. But already he's opening his carry-on and scattering things around, messing up the living room.

"I've got the house plans," Bob announces, tapping his suitcase.

"Excellent," says Bernadette. "Let's take a look, as soon as you've recovered."

Bob and Patrick settle into the best chairs with the duty-free bottle of Scotch Bob brought with him.

One of Bob's paintings dominates the wall above them. It's the view from his shed on Ardara, where he paints: granite boulders, parched grass, khaki bush, the dead stumps of gum trees, blue-haze hills behind. His style has matured since he painted that one. Now, behind the stumps, he includes the outlines of what the trees once were. There is a suggestion of trunk, rough, friable, refusing to be forgotten. At their most successful, Bob's shadow trees drift in the air, insubstantial but persistent.

Lately he's started painting these trees — the stumps and their abundant former selves — on some kind of thick tissue paper, which he arranges to have backlit.

Fragility is what he's after, these days.

THE DRINKING DOESN'T AGREE WITH BOB, who took sleeping pills for the long, cheapo charter flight. Rather than go upstairs and take a nap, he follows Patrick into the kitchen.

No mention of the house plans.

Bob paces up and down beside the counter, where Bernie is preparing food for the next day's party. "The ugly surprise of it," Bob says, "waking one day to find the land you belong to is stolen and the thief turns out to be you."

Lord, here we go. The litany of family sins. The land he lives on has something urgent to say to Bob. He isn't much interested in what he calls the invasion cities of the New World.

"Say what you like. *Mea maxima culpa* doesn't cut it — mind you, we could do with a bit of that from the government — but here's the worst thing, what you come to realize is this: you can make nothing right."

"Your problem," says Patrick, "is that you can't do the blood and the love without the rhetoric."

"I hope he doesn't plan to have his knickers in a twist all weekend," Bernie says in an aside to Patrick, when Bob goes to the bathroom. "There's only so much truth and intensity I can take."

Saying this, she feels a familiar wash of guilt. Ardara was her home, too, and will be again. The house plans that Bob has for the moment forgotten are for a yurt she and Patrick plan to build. The yurt — wooden, round, smallish, on low brick piers — will be in the rocky southeastern part of Ardara. That's all that's left of the property. Bob's sold the rest. As he became more engaged in his artwork, Bob's skills as a grazier deteriorated. (Sometimes he claims he lost interest when his wife left him — one of those brief, ill-matched 1970s marriages. At other times he says he could no longer bear to go on ruining the delicate soils.)

Before their family arrived, a little more than one hundred and fifty years ago, the land belonged to people who spoke Aneuwan. They had been there over five thousand years.

A sudden fog of fatigue comes rolling into Bernie's brain, bone, muscle. Fog is just a cloud on the ground, Patrick says. A cloud of unknowing.

She can't lie down yet, there's food to prepare. Patrick's doing most of it, but she's been looking forward to cooking the glamour items.

"*Terra nullius*, my arse," Bob says, coming back into the kitchen. "Nobody owned the great south land; it was an empty place. Now there's a handy legal fiction for you. Don't set sail without it."

Ardara is a name from Ireland.

PATRICK HAS BEEN CHOPPING VEGGIES, heaping them into piles under Bernie's supervision. A managerial job at last, Bernie says.

To deal with the potential challenges presented to their guests by red meat, wheat, dairy, tomato, oil, vinegar, soy, Bernie is organizing inoffensive vegetables stuffed with other vegetables, vast salads. For the reprobate and the truly fortunate, she plans a tremendous Brie soufflé followed by strawberry pavlova.

Tonight she's going to bake the meringue for the pav. She's got the yogurt draining — with yogurt instead of cream, pavlova really isn't all that wicked.

Patrick decides they need some white asparagus.

"Take Bob to the market with you," Bernie says. "It'll give me a chance to get on with the egg whites." She's not as ambitious as she once was in the kitchen. But she's been doing well since Bob's arrival, taking it easy, pacing herself.

They can inspect the house plans later.

BACK FROM THE MARKET, Bob's in a milder mood. Patrick goes upstairs to check his e-mail; Bob sits at the kitchen table.

"Too bad Zoë can't make it," Bob says.

They've been discussing Zoë, Bernie notes. I wonder what Patrick said.

Zoë's the reason that Bernie and Patrick rush back and forth across the Pacific. (Bernie likes to call herself a mid-Pacific woman.) Zoë's mother — who was a bossy little Maoist in her day — is now some kind of junior judge in Washington State. Zoë grew up in both Seattle and Vancouver.

Zoë's adolescent world-view, according to Bernie: You owe me one. Nervy, assertive, ambitious. But in her twenties Zoë's changed, has become smiling and meek and (in Bernie's opinion) way too willing to accommodate her peers.

"She didn't get that from her birth-mother-the-judge," Bernie says to Bob. "I suspect she may have picked it up from me. My fear is she may not realize that it's just surface, a way to navigate."

"When did this start happening?" asks Bob, who can cope with gossip.

"I think it was when she first fell in love, really in love, and discovered that bareness you feel when you'd do *anything*."

"Lie in traffic," supplies Bob. "Sever a few choice body parts."

"It went down in flames."

"Was she the dumper or the dumpee?"

"Dumpee."

"Don't worry too much. She'll get her nerve back. When she hits thirty she'll realize, it gets easier."

"And as for working, she seems happy to just skate along."

"Time enough," Bob says. "Zoë's young. She can afford to fool around."

"That's not what her mother-the-judge thinks. She's dead keen to have Zoë opposing globalization, saving the environment, either or both. She wants her daughter speaking truth to power, or at least knowing the language. But Zoë isn't a scrap interested. So far, she's not thrown so much as a single teddy bear over the barricades."

Zoë's a composer. That is to say, she has the appropriate degree in music. She's staying this northern spring and summer in a Donegal cottage, rented from its German owners at considerable parental expense. God only knows how many freeloaders are there with her.

"She's supposed to be getting on with her requiem, is our Zo," says Bernie.

"*Dies irae, dies illa*," intones Bob.

"I doubt if she knows what the words mean."

"You wouldn't have wanted her to. You were dead set on a secular upbringing."

"Christ, yes."

Bob remembers a joint trip to Europe when the gorgeous Zoë was eleven. Zoë sloped up to a painting of the Last Supper and asked who those guys were.

"Of course it's all so different in the Church now," says Bob, who calls himself a Christian Brothers survivor. "The robust sadism ain't what it used it to be."

"I don't see that it matters," says Patrick, who has come into the kitchen, bearing the bottle of Scotch he's retrieved from the living room. "About the Latin words. She can look them up in a dictionary."

"You don't have to be tolerant," says Bernie. "You're the one paying the rent."

"I promise you, it'll be a requiem to die for," says Patrick.

"Of course it will, my darling," says Bernie, and kisses his bald head.

Bob rinses his drink in the bottom of his glass. Bernie watches him play with the heavy glass base, enjoying its heft in his hand. Their best glasses. She'll have to make sure they get washed again. "I thought you were saving the rest of that bottle for the party," she says to Patrick.

"Sit down and put your feet up," he replies, pulling out a chair.

The meringue shell is in a low oven, won't be ready for hours.

"Give us a story, Bern," says Bob. "Tell us something from your project."

Bernie's working with an old friend, a woman she's known since childhood. Together, Bernie and this friend, Deirdre, are writing Bernie's family history on her mother's side: all the way back. Bernie boasts that this is the ultimate intimacy — being willing to share your imagination with someone. Deirdre, who currently lives in Sydney, has been going to the Mitchell Library and digging about, coming up with dirt.

Bernie talks about what Deirdre has been sending in recent e-mails. "You know how they used to say the Aboriginals were no trouble in our district? No trouble."

Bob nods.

"Well, it turns out this guy, who would be your great-great-great grandfather, came from England to work for the Land Commission. As a junior member of the Land Commission, he lived in Port Macquarie and travelled widely on the mid-north coast. This would be early to mid-nineteenth century. He was a small man, with a hunchback."

"A hunchback," says Patrick. "That's so Saturday afternoon at the movies. I wonder what caused it?"

"Anyway, the Baryulgil had once had a beloved chief who'd been a hunchback too. So they welcomed this guy, made much of him, treated him with honour. He spent a lot of time with them, he learned their language. And he had a child by a woman he called Mary.

"Then he was transferred down to Sydney. A few years later, he showed up on the tablelands. A full commissioner this time, no longer an assistant. He would have been the one who parcelled out the land to our family.

"All the reports he sent back to Sydney said that there were no problems in his district. Nothing ever went wrong, it seemed.

"He wasn't palling about with the local Aboriginal people any more. No mention of that. But — get this — there is a mention of a massacre at which he was present. Not on his turf, mind you. Down near the coast.

"The thing is, he prospered, built himself a big blue-brick house in the posh part of town, married well, had one son, and hanged himself on a tree in the front garden.

"And this is the man who said there were *no* problems."

"Maybe," ventures Patrick, "maybe he became ill in middle age. Depression set in."

Bob stares out the window at English Bay.

IT'S THE AFTERNOON OF THE PARTY, and Patrick is in the hallway, sticking up mementoes that include pictures of the original gathering in the late 1970s.

These photos show a spring evening in May, a month in Vancouver when the light is long and the weather falsely warm. Bernie and Patrick, youthful and hippie-ish, stand in front of hanging golden laburnum and deep purple lilacs. (Patrick is wearing glasses with only one arm; the other has fallen off and it has not occurred to him to replace it.) Behind them, out of focus, the vague splendour of water and mountains.

When they first picked up these prints and Bernie saw their faces set against laburnum and lilac, she thought, Those are not my trees. This knowledge went to her heart as a stab of pleasure, for it was the proof she needed — of the lengths to which she'd go, for Patrick.

She remembered that because later the same day she received a letter from Bob. It was the first letter to describe a mysterious disease that was attacking the trees on the property. The letter spoke of the loss of living trees, and the sickness of the yellow box gums, the dominant large tree on Ardara. It was the start of the tableland dieback.

At first the scientists pointed a hesitant finger: an infestation of the Christmas beetle. Later the theory became infinitely more complicated: one fungus, brought in on the tires of vehicles, had activated another already there, which by itself would have remained entirely harmless.

Bob's letters focused on the history of cutting, poisoning, ring-barking. Our family walked onto that land with their terrible innocence, he wrote, and the first thing we did was chop-and-destroy. We ruined the fragile soils; they drifted away on the wind. The trees, living on longtime, were slower to react, but now they, too, have given up, and are dying back.

At home, Bob became known in the district as a bit of a ratbag. When the cause of the dieback was finally established, he stopped chuffing round the paddocks on his motorbike, to the disgust of his top sheepdog, Nellie. She'd taken profound professional pleasure in riding pillion.

Bob, who had always drawn and painted, began to paint the dying trees, and in a few years his troubled paintings were making their way into galleries. A grazier-artist, the journalists wrote, in their swift, fifteen-minute commentaries, unsure whether sneering was in order, but hoping it might be.

"WHO'S COMING TO THIS SHINDIG?" asks Bob. He's been vacuuming with the laborious care of one unused to such tasks. Bet the old house doesn't see much housework these days, Bernie thinks.

As she begins to arrange the nibblies, she tells Bob they have two sets of friends: the biologists on Patrick's side, and the exhausted feminists on hers.

"Or maybe it's just me that's exhausted."

God, it will be good to move into a place that doesn't have stairs. Many miles to go today. Take it easy.

"Just before the guests begin to arrive," she says, "I always doubt that anyone will actually show up."

But friends do arrive, drinks are passed, the talk builds and establishes itself. (Zoë, waking in Donegal, resolves to phone her father, then forgets.)

It's the same kind of May night they had for the original party; laburnum and lilac bloom once more in Vancouver backyards. With a jacket, sitting out will be quite possible, although Bernie feels the cold.

In cheery party mode, the guests mill about. The volume rises; the nibblies rapidly disappear. Bernie is carried along, buoyant, excited, bubbling with easy talk. The party has been launched; the mood is happy, the food is good, the night will be a success. A ring at the door: more guests, with a pair of sociable black Labs, leaping delight. Patrick gets down on the floor to play with them, while others make space, spill their drinks, laugh.

The dogs subside, go off to work the deck.

Abruptly, without any warning, Bernie's energy evaporates. She's just walked out of a bead of light. In a matter of seconds, this party has become distant, remote, irrelevant, strange. Her life's taking place completely off stage. And the trouble is, *she doesn't care.* Hoping no one will notice, she sits by herself and closes her eyes. If she's quiet, maybe this will pass.

Patrick brings her a blanket. "It's the blasted-heath number, isn't it?" he murmurs, tucking the blanket around her. She nods.

"In your mid-fifties," someone is saying, "you wake up one morning and find your libido's turned into a lazy pussycat."

"Not men," another voice puts in. "More or less the same horny fuckers they've always been. Look at Michael Douglas."

"Let's keep this classy. Look at Picasso."

Bernie tries to concentrate, but the words are floating, refusing to attach themselves. I should go upstairs and rest, she tells herself. When I feel better, I'll come back down, be able to join in.

"So what's the right word? 'Companionship' is too wishy-washy. Like you're sitting next to somebody on a bus."

"How about 'toughing it out together'?"

"Grim, gratuitously grim."

"You need a word that captures the shared years."

"Okay. An expression that gets at 'joined memory,' with the physical stuff thrown in."

"That term does not exist."

"Didn't the Greeks have all those different words for love? 'Philadelphia,' and so on."

"That was brotherly love, wasn't it? What about sisterly love?"

"Philafilia? To coin a word."

"Doesn't *filia* mean daughter, not sister?"

"Same thing," Bernie finds herself saying.

"The physical being the sex *and* accepting the notion that your body's on a one-way trip."

"The paths of glory lead but to the grave."

"Please."

Bernie pulls the blanket up to her neck. Christ, listen to us, we sound like a mob of show ponies. All prance and privilege.

"What I'm interested in," a voice behind her persists, "is how to describe sex now, or, more to the point — sex being sex — the buildup towards it?"

Ah, the sure and certain expectation.

"It used to feel like an intravenous injection of heavy liquor: intense, reckless, inevitable. Now it's more like very high-class green tea, steeped properly in a pot and served in celadon mugs."

"That's going a bit far, I'd say. The closed door, the warm room, the sheets, the silky bodies: all unchanged, still the same."

"Only the sheets are more expensive."

"Now we're getting somewhere. Designer sheets."

"The joy of sheets."

Bernie wonders how much longer they're going to stay. She'd love to go upstairs, do her teeth, take off her clothes, have a bath, get into bed. I'll just do my teeth, she decides. We can clean up tomorrow.

AT LAST THE STAGE IS REACHED when the group, mellowed on wine, or at least carbohydrates, is ready for a calmer time, in the mood for stories.

"How come you guys never got married?" asks one of the biologists.

"I believed it would be an exceedingly reactionary move," says Bernie. "Besides, we'd both been married once before and had made a mess of it."

"Didn't you guys have a honeymoon, anyway," someone asks, "to consummate the non-nuptials?"

They did indeed, Bernadette responds.

Patrick took her into the Vermont woods, to a clearing on a ridge, to a tarpaper shack he called a camp. He pointed out to her what he saw: red oak, beech forest, red maple that looks black. Inside the shack there was a bed on a makeshift loft, a table, a few open shelves, a wood stove for both heat and cooking. The stovepipe stuck out the side of the shack, curving. In a poster on the wall, a man's head turned into a forest.

Close to the shack, Patrick found a place in the grass where a deer had made its bed. Without any self-consciousness he knelt down, curled himself into it. Lay there, relaxed and replete.

A quarter of mile through the woods was a shallow lake that gathered the light and sent it back to the sky. Between sky and lake, a rim of dark trees. Going down to the lake, Patrick showed her the marks of bear claws on the smooth-barked beech. "Exit pursued by a bear," she said. On the red maple, nearer the water, vertical lines made by the teeth of a moose. He expected her to touch these trees, to put her hands into the grooves made by the big wild animals. (Put your fingers into my wounds, said the risen Christ, glowing in supernaturally clean robes.)

It was a year when the beech had nuts; bears had been rooting about in the leaf litter. Patrick and Bernie sat on the moss-cushioned rocks — the moss, a bright green, held the light almost the way water does. They splashed about in the lake, their bodies slippery in the long, still evening.

Back in the shack, they got a good fire going, ate vegetable stew with a French name, drank red wine from the Hunter Valley, listened to the CBC News from across the border. The sky bled orange into red. Patrick stood in the doorway, lifted his head, and breathed in through his nose to catch the smells.

"Blue jays," he pointed out. "Evening grosbeak," he murmured, hesitant to state the obvious.

The dark gathered in the woods and entered the cabin, where the sheets smelled damply of pine and, oddly, of salt.

It was not her home.

It was, without any doubt, his.

"When everything has faded from my mind," Patrick tells the party guests (he's drunk a bit too much), "when they've done their worst with tubes and probes, when they're wheeling me along a corridor on a gurney — the woods are what will remain."

He's thinking of the shape of the glacier-scarred hills, the camp in the clearing, tracks in the earth, the smell of trees. His older brother, driving down snowy back roads, taking them there.

THE PARTY THINS IN STAGES. The youth contingent — those who were not yet born at the time of the first party — have set off to Spanish Banks to light a bonfire on the beach. "At least they're capable of *something* illegal," says a friend's husband, who's rumoured to have been with the Weather Underground (best not to ask, even now).

In the kitchen, Bob is engaging a few of the biology crowd with his fungus stories. Bernie's relieved to see that they appear to be enjoying both the complex details and her brother's energetic gloom. She's watched Bob at his own openings, holding forth about the dieback to young women who'd shown up for the booze and the flirting. After a few seconds of one of Bob's riffs, they'd be keenly seeking champagne.

The party talk has piled up in Bernie's head, big white cumulus clouds. (Mother-puffers, Patrick calls them.) But she's feeling better, not so drained.

She's sitting with a small group that have their feet stuck up on the deck, which looks out towards the north shore mountains. By now everyone has a blanket, and jokes are being made about slow days at the sanatorium up some magic west coast mountain.

Patrick comes and finds a place across from her. Theirs has not been a flawless union. This group includes a few protagonists in exhausting episodes of *Sturm und Drang*. (A long time ago; hard to believe how long.) Tonight, innocent of tension, confident nobody is going to lose sleep over whatever happens to be said, they turn to Bernie and Patrick and request the story of how they fell in love.

Bernie looks over at Patrick. This crowd won't want the exalted anguish.

Patrick glances back. No they won't. So what'll we give them? The long version or the short version?

"Bernie went to Italy looking for her father but found Patrick instead," says one of the exes, who's had the inside track.

Too complicated, Bernie decides. Besides, the search for the father requires too much background, is too large a theme.

Bernie's mother, Ellen, had fallen in love with an Italian POW, who'd come to work on Ardara during the Second World War. By the time the Italian left, American bombs had killed his two sons back home. And Ellen was pregnant. Ellen turned to her daughter, Alice, and between them, a subterfuge was arranged. So Bernie grew up believing that her half-sister, Alice, was her mother, and her mother, Ellen, was her grandmother.

Way too Fifties, Bernie decides. For this time of night. "We met in Spoleto," Bernie says.

She'd been on her way home to Sydney after a year of exchange teaching in Vancouver. Not knowing, at the time, that it was only the first trip in a circle she was fated to keep on making.

BEFORE SPOLETO, BERNIE HAD VISITED the town her father came from, north of Rome. Down in the new part of town, by the railway station, she'd found a monument to those killed by the bombs the Americans had dropped. The names of her father's two boys were there. No pussyfooting around with precision bombing back then. Splat cat all round.

Bernie ran her fingers over the names. *Francesco* and *Vincenzo*.

From the instant she had known whose daughter she really was, she'd been rehearsing this day. Ancient women in black would look up, startled, at the apparition. They'd avert their eyes, then look up again, drawn by the powerful moment of acknowledgment. Bernie would be recognized, honoured, taken in.

She walked from the monument up to the old part of town, ready to make her claim. And there were the elderly people, sitting on cheap wooden kitchen chairs by their doorways on the grey, stone street.

Do you know where he is?

And they shrugged, without any trace of recognition. He is not here. He went away. Years ago. We have not heard from him.

She had imagined everything except their unknowing, their own loss, their necessary turning away.

"WE MET IN SPOLETO." She'd been waiting for the church to open after lunch and Patrick's shadow had fallen over her. "The church is famous for its annunciations. Fra Filippo Lippi at the top of his game."

"Call me Gabriel," interjects Patrick, at this familiar turning point.

They'd spent the afternoon looking at the annunciations, walking in the white square, having something to drink. He had a wife, he had a baby, they were in Italy on holiday, he was a student in Sweden but he was an American, a combat vet, a deserter from the army, a war resister.

On their first evening in Spoleto, they walked out to the edge of town to look at the Roman aqueduct. They found some bushes in a ravine; they didn't know the bushes' names.

"You made out in the shrubbery?"

"Oh, it gets worse, much worse," Bernie assured them.

As Patrick and his wife and baby Zoë moved southwards, down beyond Sorrento, Bernie followed, taking the same train, finding a place to stay not far away.

All the better to love him.

In places outdoors, with the smell of thyme, where white roads led down to the sea at night. In shuttered rooms, their bodies splayed across drenched sheets, electric with the damage they were causing.

At the end of two weeks, Bernie, in tears, stood beside Patrick and looked at the dark sea. He was going back to Sweden with his wife and child. She was continuing to Sydney. They would be as far away from each other as it is possible to be.

The wind stung her face.

IN THEIR FIRST STOLEN WEEKS, Patrick had often spoken, painfully, of his time in the army, of the moral obligation to desert, of the guilt of deserting. (This was the end of the Vietnam era; war was what people were used to talking about, incessantly, obsessively.) But Bernie, listening to Patrick, had already grown convinced that their love was the centre of everything. She believed he was really talking not about the war, but about his wife and child. She imagined the pram in the hallway, and thought she recognized the Ikea colours, bright and not particularly permanent.

When Bernie spoke to Patrick, it was about her half-brothers, how her fingers had felt moving across those names. Indentations in the polished granite, forgotten particles of air.

Apart from being "in love," one of the guests asks (give that three years, tops), apart from the "in love" bit, when did she realize she would love him, if not forever, then at least for a very long time? (Knowing that such moments are, to the outsider, arbitrary, but to those involved, irreducible.)

"I was in an op shop in Sydney," Bernie says. "What you'd call a thrift store. The op shop was next to the train station, so I passed it every day on the way to and from my teaching job. This was when I'd come home from Italy after having met Patrick.

"That day in Sydney, I stepped inside the op shop and began poking about in the clothes. The radio behind the counter started to play the song, "Galveston, oh, Galveston." You remember, he could hear the sea waves crashing while he watched the cannons flashing, pretty appalling.

"I thought of Patrick. He didn't come from Galveston, of course — he grew up on the east coast — but he was twenty-one when he went into the army. I was trying on a velvet jacket — dark green — and there was that strong, stuffy smell of second-hand clothing.

"I'm not sure which of the lines did it. It could have been, 'your sea birds flying in the sun.' Or it could have been, 'I am so afraid of dying.' What do you think, Pat?"

"I think it's one trashy song," Patrick says.

But the faces are now turned to him, for his version.

It was the second time they were together. He'd returned to Italy, leaving his wife and child behind in Sweden; Bernie had flown up from Sydney. Their visit, the result of so much convoluted plotting, the object of such hectic expectation, had been — as anyone could have predicted — uneven. They were coming to the end; the distress of parting was approaching like a tidal wave. They were walking, there were lemon trees; he couldn't remember exactly where. Bernie had just said he had shapely legs. He'd laughed at the word, "shapely." It was so, he didn't know. Unexpected. Inappropriate. Unusual. Foreign. He couldn't imagine any other woman he'd ever known using that word, of him.

Then they looked up and saw a hoopoe.

"I sensed her body go quiet because she was watching a bird. I'm not sure, but I think it was the first time she'd seen a hoopoe. Bit like a flicker, here, in some ways," he explains, remembering that not everyone in the crowd is a biologist. "But with an incredible crest. It was preening itself — probably after a dust bath — and you could see its black-and-white wings. I told her it had this wonderful name: *Upupa epops.* I said that in Teutonic myth it was associated with adultery, like the cuckoo, but that in England it favoured vicarage gardens.

"I was enjoying saying the name: *OOO puppa EE pops.* Bernie looked at me and said, in an ordinary pass-the-salt voice, 'Whatever the bird does is perfect to the bird.'"

And from that point on, Patrick had assumed the composure of someone who knows his choices have been made.

"THIS IS THE BEST PART of any party," says Patrick. He's been up for hours. So has Bob. They've been for a run, done the dishes, and are now having an early lunch of abundant leftovers.

Bernadette sits at the table, waiting for the kettle to boil for her first cup of tea of the day. "I would have brought it up for you," says Patrick, "if I'd known you were awake."

Bob is scooping up the remains of the Brie soufflé, getting his fork into bits that have stuck to the edges of the bowl. "Excellent. Tastes like bread pudding."

"Won't have to cook for days," says Patrick, patting his stomach.

"How about those house plans, Bob?" Bernadette says. "The yurt?"

The yurt, which they are building on a corner of Ardara, is to be their retirement bolthole, their one bit of bush.

"Okay," says Bob, "I'll get the stuff."

The plans have been approved. Bob's going to organize the builders.

"What we have," says Bob, spreading out a diagram, "is a computer-managed solar power system. Simple to operate, low maintenance. Far more reliable than being hooked up to the power main. It produces two kilowatts of power, ample for running your toaster and so on."

"Enough to operate the computer?" asks Patrick.

Bernadette stares at the floor plans. Kitchen, living area, two bedrooms, bathroom-laundry. Slow-combustion wood heater.

She's taught for so many years (high school, ESL, women's studies, and — rock bottom — business English for engineers); she's endured being looked at for so long: she's going to wear pants forever. "I'm never going to have my hair done," she announces. "I can't believe I used to fool around with *rollers*." Her hair, as it greys, is growing wiry. All she has to do is comb it. "No makeup. Just a bit of that anti-aging cream. Not that it makes the least bit of difference in the long run."

Patrick will still have another year of work to go. The plan is, she'll move into the yurt, and Deirdre will come up from Sydney, and together, they'll write the book.

Bob's shed, the one where he paints, will be about eight hundred metres away.

Bob still lives in the old house, although he's sold the main property, and its name has been changed. (Now it's Terrylynne, after its owners, who at the time of purchase were excited newly-weds.) Bob says there's an obscure legal term for his arrangement — the right to live in the house and do whatever he wants with the home paddock. He likes to sit on the verandah (falling about its ears) and survey his curtilage.

All they can now call Ardara is the southeast section, the wildest, the rockiest. They used to run cattle there, but Bob doesn't any more.

"How far away is eight hundred metres in real measurement?" Bernie asks.

For the first year, Patrick intends to commute, as it were. Patrick is fond of saying there should be a modest monument in the Honolulu airport to all the regulars, those whose cracked hearts are half in North America, half in the South Pacific. At the Honolulu airport, for these travellers, it is always three o'clock in the morning.

It should be an installation piece, he says: eyeshades, socks, and those silly little toothbrushes.

But everything changes. Now they go non-stop L.A. to Sydney. A pile of books, three meals, two movies, one sleeping pill, and you're there.

"What trees have we murdered for the yurt?" asks Bernie, looking at the floor plans.

"The roof, ceiling, and kitchen are casuarina," Bob says. "The floor is box. The weatherboards are cypress. Doors, windows, and trim are western cedar."

"Are we ever disgusting," says Patrick.

I wonder if I'll die in that house, Bernie thinks. Not of PPS, this stuff doesn't kill you. Or mostly not.

"There you have it," Bob says. "All the comfort and the guilt of home."

Will going back be worth it? To say that in the beginning is my end? Is that just self-indulgence? Bit of fancy footwork?

"What I want to do," she says, "is look at the hills, lucid and sharp, and know they don't give a stuff whether I exist or not."

"No worries," says Bob. "On Ardara that happens every day."

UPSTAIRS, BERNADETTE LIES on her bed and listens to the voices in the room below. Play one day, pay the next. To her ear, Bob's accent sounds good-natured no matter what's being said. She's so used to Patrick's voice that it sounds entirely free of any accent. It's just his voice.

She's always enjoyed this, lying in one room and listening to the murmur of familiar voices in another. Reminds her of being a kid.

When Ellen and Alice had finally told her the facts of her birth (the Big Revelation), when they'd identified themselves not as grandmother and mother but as mother and half-sister, the pair of them sat together in the kitchen, facing her, awaiting judgement.

Bernadette, at sixteen, had felt an immense, disorienting surge of power, followed by an even stronger sense of isolation. Nothing, she discovered, is more exclusive than prolonged, shared deceit.

Only Bob, her little brother, whom she'd taken for granted in so many ways, had not been in on the lying.

And a curious thing happened. Ellen and Alice each seemed to become about twenty years younger — they dropped a generation almost overnight. But Bob remained her brother. Bob did not change. ("Nephew" was some shabby party joke — too silly to be in any way plausible.)

She must have slept for a long time, because when she wakes Bob is saying something, Patrick is laughing, and night has fallen.

She doesn't bother switching on the light. An aching has crept into her left leg, right inside the muscle. God, the dreary recitative. Whatever could be more tedious than symptoms? When she tries to stand, both legs will tremble.

She can hear the TV. No, VCR. They're watching *The Blues Brothers* yet again. They'll spend the next few days putting on hats and sunglasses, doing "Soul Man" routines and telling one another: "We're on a mission from God!" "For Sister Stigmata!"

A bit of pale sky is still hanging above the north shore mountains — she can see it from her bed. At Ardara it's different: at one stride comes the dark. There's a lemony light on the stairs, from the lamps in the living room. Her real mother, Ellen, could remember as a child seeing the lamplighter in Sydney, doing the rounds of the street with his ladder, firing up the gaslights. Holes in the darkness. That would have been Ocean Street, where her mother grew up in a grand Victorian house. Here comes a lamplighter to light you to bed, and here comes a chopper to chop off your leg. What took you so long?

She burrows deeper under the quilt. PPS can make you feel the cold; your body temperature is in fact lower than anyone else's in the room, and you spend your days dreaming of hot sand.

What's this? The comfort-smell of dough, rising in the oven. Those lazy buggers, they're having frozen pizza, with all that food in the house.

She thinks in an idle way of something Patrick did when she came back to Vancouver after Alice's death. The day she got off the plane, she'd had to teach two classes. It was already dark before she drove to Patrick's office in the biology wing. Keeping calm, holding herself together in the public world.

On some trivial pretext, Patrick took her to the room where they keep the skins: long, thin, wooden cupboards, old-fashioned drawers made of oak. "We certainly don't do this any more," he reassured her. "These are old skins, most of them seventy, eighty years old."

"They're creepy," she said. "I don't know how you can stand to touch them."

He selected a skin and held it up for her. He knew how to start with the low-key colours, when to turn it over. At first he held it so that she saw only the head, upper parts, wings and outside tail feathers: the deceptively drab olive-brown. Then he slipped it round, brought it up slowly, so that the light caught flashes of extravagant gold opalescence. The body had long gone, but there it was: the tangible, physical memory of a golden bird.

Patrick did this with a complete lack of flirtation. A tribute from him to the dead bird, and she was its witness.

That's it. That's what she hopes to do. For her mother and her family, for their vanished lives, and the land they called Ardara.

*A*CKNOWLEDGEMENTS

The title of this collection is from a poem by A.D. Hope, "The Wandering Islands." Quoted from *Collected Poems* (Sydney: Angus and Robertson, 1972). Used with permission of the A.D. Hope estate.

The following materials assisted me with a depiction of Australian experiences during World War II: Alan Fitzgerald, *The Italian Farming Soldiers: Prisoners of War in Australia 1941-1947* (Melbourne: Melbourne University Press, 1981); Molly Keep, *Bellbirds and Blowflies* (Quirindi: Quirindi Newspaper Corp, 1990); Peter Ryan, *Fear Drive My Feet* (Sydney: Angus and Robertson, 1959); Jean Scott, *Girls with Grit: Memories of the Australian Women's Land Army* (Sydney: Allen and Unwin, 1986); Osmar White, *Green Armour*, originally published in 1945 (Sydney: Penguin Books, 1992).

Almost Touching
The descriptions of a bubonic plague epidemic owe a debt to Peter Curson and Kevin McCracken, *Plague in Sydney: The Anatomy of*

249

an Epidemic (Sydney: New South Wales University Press, 1991).

The lines, "Ah, fill the cup . . ." are from *The Rubáiyát of Omar Khayyám*, as translated by Edward Fitzgerald.

THE BRIGHT BLUE AIR

The brief allusions to a massacre (also in the final story) are fictional but owe their genesis to John Ferry, *Colonial Armidale* (Brisbane: University of Queensland Press, 1999), which describes an attack on Aboriginals at Ramornie Run in 1841, led by Commissioner Macdonald.

The lines "Tea for two . . ." are from the 1923 hit song by Irving Caesar and Vincent Youmans.

IT COMES OF ITSELF

"Mulga Bill's Bicycle" is by A.B. "Banjo" Paterson. It first appeared in *The Sydney Mail*, 25 July 1896.

The lines "He ought to be home . . ." are from Paterson's poem "Lost," which first appeared in *The Sydney Mail*, 19 March 1897.

I THOUGHT MY HEART WOULD BREAK

"The Persimmon Tree," by Marjorie Barnard, was first published in *Coast to Coast* (Sydney: Angus and Robertson, 1942).

THAT POLIO KID'S COME BACK

The references to newspaper items are based on material that appeared in *The Armidale Express* (Armidale, New South Wales) in the early 1950s.

The line "Every angel is terrible" is from the first of Rainer Maria Rilke's *Duino Elegies*, published in *Rilke*, translated by J.B. Leishman (New York: Alfred A. Knopf, Inc., 1996).

The lines, "The sun was shining on the sea . . ." are from *Through the Looking-Glass* by Lewis Carroll.

ON ANOTHER FAR SHORE

The incident of the fox terriers is taken from Douglas A. Aplin,

ACKNOWLEDGEMENTS

Rabaul 1942 (Melbourne: McCarron Bird, 1980).

The reference to lyrebirds as "shy, fabulous, dying poets," is based on "Lyrebirds" by Judith Wright (*Birds*, Angus and Robertson, 1962). The lines read: "I'll never see the lyrebirds — / the few, the shy, the fabulous / the dying poets."

The comments on marriage are from Rilke and are taken from *Selected Letters of Rainer Maria Rilke*, ed. Harry T. Moore (New York: W.H. Norton & Company, Inc., 1960).

WATCHING THEM

Words and music to "Blue Moon" are by R. Rodgers and L. Hart.

Lyrics to "Shall We Dance?" by Richard Rodgers and Oscar Hammerstein II, copyright © 1951 by Richard Rodgers and Oscar Hammerstein II. Copyright renewed, Williamson Music, owner of publication and allied rights throughout the world. International copyright secured. All rights reserved. Reprinted by permission.

OPEN WIDE

The lines "The horror of that moment . . ." are from *Through the Looking-Glass* by Lewis Carroll.

POSTSCRIPT ARDARA

The lines "I wandered around and finally found . . ." are from "It Had to Be You," lyrics by Gus Kahn, music by Isham Jones, 1924.

References are made to "Galveston," words and music by Jimmy Webb, 1969. Copyright © 1995 by EMI Music Publishing. All rights reserved. Reprinted by permission.

I am grateful to my editor, Marnie Kramarich, and my agent, Carolyn Swayze, for unwavering support; to Bob Sherrin and Eleanor Wachtel for impeccable judgement; to Evelyn Constable, for generous assistance; and to Barry Davies, for everything.